Bad Man Blues

Bad Man Blues

A Portable George Garrett

Foreword by
RICHARD BAUSCH

Introduction by
ALLEN WIER

SOUTHERN METHODIST UNIVERSITY PRESS
Dallas

Versions of some of these pieces have appeared in the following magazines and anthologies: *Black Warrior Review, Bred Any Good Rooks Lately?, Chronicles, Chattahoochee Review, English as a Discipline, or Is There a Plot in This Play?, Gone Soft, Five Points, Literary Cavalcade, The Marjorie Kinnan Rawlings Journal of Florida Literature, Micro Fiction, The Peregrine Reader, River City, The Sound of Fiction, Southern Excursions, South Carolina Review, Sports in America, Style, The Wedding Cake in the Middle of the Road, Witness.*

Requests for permission to reproduce material from this work should be sent to:
Rights and Permissions
Southern Methodist University Press
PO Box 750415
Dallas, Texas 75275-0415

Jacket art: George Bellows, *Dempsey and Firpo*, 1924. Oil on canvas, 51 x 63¼ in. (129.5 x 160.7 cm.). Collection of Whitney Museum of American Art. Purchase, with funds from Gertrude Vanderbilt Whitney. 31.95. Photograph Copyright © 1998: Whitney Museum of American Art.

Jacket and text design: Tom Dawson Graphic Design

Library of Congress Cataloging-in-Publication Data

Garrett, George P., 1929–
    Bad man blues : a portable George Garrett / foreword by Richard Bausch ;
    introduction by Allen Wier. — 1st ed.
        p.   cm.
    ISBN 0-87074-439-9 (cloth : alk. paper)
    I. Title
    PS3557.A72A6   1998
    818'.5409—dc21   98-26106

Printed in the United States of America on acid-free paper

10   9   8   7   6   5   4   3   2   1

For Susan

And in loving memory of
Alice Benedict Dunn
and
Rosalie Toomer Garrett

Contents

Foreword   *ix*
Many Voices
BY RICHARD BAUSCH

Introduction   *xiii*
Skin and Bones: George Garrett's Living Spirits
BY ALLEN WIER

Author's Preface   *xxvii*

I. SHORT STORIES

Genius Baby   *3*
To Guess a Riddle, To Stumble on the Secret Name   *17*
The Pornographers   *21*
A Letter That Will Never Be Written   *29*
The Right Thing to Do at the Time   *45*
Dixie Dreamland   *49*
The Misery and the Glory of Texas Pete   *69*
Bad Man Blues   *73*
Three Occasional Pieces   *79*

II. ACADEMIC ANECDOTES

Body and Soul in Connecticut (Wesleyan) *85*

A Great Big One (Rome) *91*

Send Me In, Coach (Rice) *95*

A Hole in My Shoe (Princeton) *99*

Come On, Baby, Light My Fire (South Carolina) *105*

Garbage and Other Collectibles (Bennington) *109*

Flying Elephants (Michigan) *115*

Snickering in Solitary (Virginia) *119*

A Perfect Stranger (Alabama) *131*

III. ESSAYS

Hanging from the Trestle While the Train Goes By:
Some Notes on Working for a Living *143*

It Hums. It Sings and Dances *149*

Locker Room Talk: Notes on the Social History of Football *161*

Heroes *169*

Going to See the Elephant: Why We Write Stories *181*

The Lost Brother: Summoning Up the Ghost
of Who I Might Have Been *189*

Many Voices

BY RICHARD BAUSCH

Let me begin with a simple statement: There is no writer on the American scene with a more versatile, more eclectic, or more restless talent than George Garrett.

There.

I've been wanting to say that in print for a long time.

The versatility and eclectic aspects of Garrett's work are evident in a glance at the list of published books. But the word *restless* requires some explanation, I think, because that word may be assumed by some to be expressing the obvious matter of energy. I am speaking more about a kind of *sensibility* than about energy. The fact is, Garrett's energy, whether in producing his own creative work or in helping other writers to produce theirs, is legendary, and is quite evident in the amount of published writing he is either directly or indirectly responsible for. But I do not wish to talk, here, about all the generosities, the continual record of kindness to other writers, the practical support for them, the nitty-gritty, down to the bone *help* he has provided countless times, in the thousand different places, over the last forty years.

No, these remarks are about Garrett the artist.

And it is quite clear to me that the most dominant trait of this—say it, *great*—artist's talent is restlessness. I mean that George Garrett's restless sensibility is not, and never has been, comfortable with the accepted or usual forms of address, whether they involve fiction, or poetry, or essay, or anything else, for that matter. This phenomenon of his work has often been hinted at, by critics of the novels and stories, as a kind of challenge to perception, or an exploration of the nature of perception. Well, all right. But I think that what is seen as an interest in the nature of perception is a by-product of a more basic matter of ability and temperament:

Garrett's talent grows irritable and itchy in the constraints of tightly controlled forms.

In so many of the stories, and certainly in the novels, the matters of fictive technique and approach are constantly being tested or questioned by every single gesture he makes. And this is largely true of the poems, and the essays, too. It is even true of a good deal of the criticism.

He is always straining against the expected, the comfortable. Indeed there are times, reading him, when one can feel him straining at the very basic assumptions about form and language that are implicit in the smallest gesture on the page. The result is that this enormously gifted writer has not only worked in every genre there is, he has often stretched the accepted boundaries of those genres.

For instance, one cannot read his monumental Elizabethan trilogy —*Death of the Fox, The Succession,* and *Entered from the Sun*—without a sense that the nature of the historical novel has been substantially challenged. The same is true for the most recent novel, *The King of Babylon Shall Not Come Against You.* There are elements of fictional time, of the sequencing of events and actions, and of characterization and irony in that novel that are entirely original to it, and do not, to my knowledge, anyway, have very clear antecedents anywhere else in the world's literature. I mean I have never come across anything quite like it, anywhere else, in a lifetime of reading novels. *King of Babylon* is somewhat like Sterne's old great book, I suppose, in its intentional discontinuity, but the bumptious Mr. Shandy is the one speaker of that early English novel, and *King of Babylon* has many voices. Faulkner's *As I Lay Dying* has many voices, but its time scheme is fairly straightforward (compared to *King of Babylon* it is positively linear). I would say that the American novel *King of Babylon* most resembles, at least in terms of the treatment of time, is another masterpiece of Faulkner's, *The Sound and the Fury,* except that, again, while both are similarly discontinuous, the earlier novel uses the *absence* of time for much of its effects, and Garrett's novel uses time, its speed and fluidity, as a wheel.

The point here is that Garrett has given us poems, stories, novels, commentary, memoir, jokes, satires, biographies, plays, cartoon strips, magic shows, and movies for more than forty years—he has even given us criticism, and of a much higher order than you, gentle reader, are treated to in this foreword—and at sixty-nine years of age, he is still growing, and changing. Still restless.

What you will find herein is a wonderful, complex, engaging, outrageous, mischievous, and deeply wise man, giving everything, as always. Giving forth a multitude of voices, each distinct and purely itself, from the baldly vernacular to the formally sophisticated. There are stories so widely divergent, one might, if this were almost any other author, suppose different people had written them. Take the monstrous and yet curiously moving confession called "Genius Baby," and set it next to a small gem like "To Guess a Riddle, To Stumble on the Secret Name," and then move from that to "A Letter That Will Never Be Written," which is set in 1626 and partakes of some of the tone and style of the Elizabethan trilogy, and you have some sense of the stretch of treatment, the range, of this unexampled imagination.

There is a little of everything here, a smorgasbord of Garrett's concerns and interests—though, of course, having read widely in his long list of books, I hasten to add that no one volume could possibly contain *everything* he is interested in. The anecdotes, especially the academic ones, are uniformly enthralling, and in several important instances, wickedly hilarious. There are poems here, serious and otherwise, and there are moving portraits of the author's father and mother, a loving homage to them, really, and, by extension and implication, to a lost time in American life. The experience of reading this book of voices, then—this newest addition to a long record of restless exploration—is of being in George Garrett's company. And, folks, there is no more charming, nor more goodly human, companion.

Broad Run, Virginia
June 1998

Skin and Bones:
George Garrett's Living Spirits

BY ALLEN WIER

I met George Garrett in the summer of 1972. As the prize for winning a fiction contest, I had my expenses paid to a summer writing conference on the campus of Eastern Washington State University, where I was to assist one of the visiting writers. The prize turned out to be greater than I had anticipated when I was assigned to George Garrett, who treated me, publicly and privately, not as a helper but as a partner. Garrett's *Death of the Fox*, the first of his trilogy of novels of the Elizabethan era, had been published the previous year and had received rave reviews and appeared on the *New York Times* bestseller list. I vividly recall the first session of the conference: I had just finished teaching a three-hour class on fiction writing with George Garrett, and I was trying to keep up with him, walking across a concrete courtyard between red-brick classroom buildings, headed back to our dormitory lodgings, where Garrett had a bottle of something and there were ice and glasses. His seersucker sport coat billowed in the gusty, warm wind, and his regimental tie (navy with orange stripes) blew back over his shoulder, fluttering like a pennant. In the crook of my right arm was a stack of manuscripts. Garrett swung the black wedge of a full briefcase. There had been a drought that summer, and the horizon was smudged with the smoke of distant fires, mysterious smoke signals. I'd been on campus for a few days before the conference began, and I'd come to think of Eastern Washington, especially on the three moonlit evenings I'd been there, as eerily lovely—a lonely, lunar landscape. I was a long way from home, from the familiar, but George Garrett had made me feel immediately comfortable. I was twenty-six; Garrett was forty-three. Portly in a compact, solid, fit-looking way, and full of animated, barely contained energy, Garrett made me think of athletes—muscular sprinters, small linemen, light heavyweight boxers.

All of which Garrett has been. (When he was fifteen and sixteen, Garrett boxed for Sewanee Military Academy and fought in the Southern Golden Gloves Championship in Chattanooga before going on to Princeton, where he was on the boxing team.) And it just so happened that, as we made our way across campus, we started talking about boxing. And that's when I first heard of the Joe Louis, Max Baer fight—which you'll soon read more about in Garrett's essay "It Sings. It Hums and Dances."

"Hemingway got it wrong about Max Baer's being yellow," Garrett said. "*Courage* is just stepping into the ring. After that, the rest of it is skill."

In the dormitory lobby, standing before the inoperable elevators, Garrett told me how his boxing coach at Princeton, Joe Brown (a former great heavyweight who never lost a match and who was also a fine sculptor), wanted to protect college fighters. The coach insisted that his boxers wear headgear and follow several safety rules.

"Joe Brown wanted to take the blood lust out of college fights," Garrett said. We headed for the stairwell and Garrett, his forehead shiny with sweat, went on, "When you're really angry, after blood, you can't focus *or* relax. But if you develop your skills enough, you can sometimes forget what you're doing and throw a knockout punch."

Other schools refused to go along with Brown's rules so Brown refused to compete with them, and Garrett and others on the Princeton team fought only one another. Garrett shook his head again, we laughed together over the irony, athletes having to go up against their teammates, and, huffing and puffing, chuckling and bumping elbows, we climbed the dormitory stairs all the way to our fifth-floor rooms.

In the twenty-six years since that afternoon in Cheney, Washington, I've tried to keep up with George Garrett walking across campuses and streets in quite a few cities. I've listened to him tell hilarious jokes and wonderful stories, and I've read nearly all of his books. The one you hold in your hands, *Bad Man Blues: A Portable George Garrett*, is his twenty-eighth and one of his most personal. Intimate glimpses into Garrett's life—his family, his boyhood in central Florida, his teaching venues, his views on subjects ranging from boxing and football to the relevancy of art in a world of profiteers—make *Bad Man Blues* a key to understanding the man behind the many books. Carefully varied selections—fictions, anecdotes, essays, even a few poems—make *Bad Man Blues* a good introduction for readers who have not yet read widely in Garrett's considerable and diverse body of work.

In an essay he was asked to write about himself—"one of the most difficult things I have ever tried to write"—Garrett tells about hosting Shelby Foote when he came to lecture and to read from his work at the University of Virginia. Garrett's students knew that Foote had been a friend of William Faulkner's, and after Foote's reading someone asked him what Faulkner was really like.

"Have you read the books?" Foote asked back.

"Yes, sir."

"Well," Foote went on, "that's it. That's all there is."

That moment, Garrett says, defined for him his own ambition that he might write books into which he, the *real* George Palmer Garrett, Jr., could disappear: "Let my whole life be only in my work and everywhere equally, whether in a long knotty novel or in the four verse-lines of a brisk epigram."

My own quarter-century friendship with and respect for both George Garrett the person and the writer, coupled with Garrett's reluctance to talk much about his artistic intentions, make this introduction to his newest book one of the most difficult things *I* have ever tried to write. I know some of the facts about Garrett and about his books, but I hope in this essay to get beyond the facts to approach the truth of the man in his work.

Bad Man Blues displays many of the moves of one of America's strongest, most talented and gutsy writers. What a fight card, what a diversity of events. But *Bad Man Blues* is not the first book through which George Garrett (ventriloquist, impersonator, conjurer) has spoken in myriad voices and used a rich variety of forms. *Whistling in the Dark* (1992) gathers "true stories and other fables" together with a selection of "academic anecdotes" similar to the ones in this newest book (though Garrett saved the best of these for *Bad Man Blues*). *My Silk Purse and Yours* (1992) is a collection of unorthodox reviews and essays in which Garrett throws his voice and takes on different guises to illuminate the publishing scene and American literary art.

Garrett's wide-ranging literary repertoire includes novels and collections of stories, poems, essays, criticism, and reviews. He's the author of several plays, including one for children, *Sir Slob and the Princess* (1962), and of several film scripts, including *Frankenstein Meets the Space Monster* (1965), winner of a Golden Turkey Award as one of the one hundred worst films of all times—an award Garrett cites with a proud grin. *The Magic Striptease* (1973) contains "a comic strip fable, a story, and a movie soundtrack." *Welcome to the Medicine Show* (1978) collects short verse he calls "postcards/flashcards/snapshots." His satirical novel *Poison Pen* (1986) is "written" by, narrated by, John Towne, a character from Garrett's unpublished novel *Life with Kim Novak Is Hell*, the title of which Garrett took from a *National Enquirer* headline. (You'll meet the chameleonlike Towne in "Genius Baby," the first story in this volume.) *Poison Pen* mixes elements of the epistolary novel (letters to Masters and Johnson, George Wallace, Brooke Shields, Timothy Leary, Linda Lovelace, Jean Shrimpton, Ronald Reagan, Hugh Hefner, Truman Capote, Bo Derek, James Farmer, and Christie Brinkley, among others); found poetry (newspaper headlines and clippings, academic course outlines and syllabi, lists of contemporary poets and their *real life* analogues: "George Garrett is the Don Rickles of American Poetry"); and other ingredients of satire—irony, topicality, indecent humor, vernacular language, dialogue, shifts in tone, and authorial intrusion—to create a meta-fictional commentary on contemporary American life and culture. One reviewer of *Poison Pen* wrote that "behind the elegant facade of the Elizabethan novelist there lurks Bad Georgie, a comic spirit waiting to be unleashed." In *Bad Man Blues* you will meet both Garrett the Elizabethan novelist and Bad Georgie.

Garrett is probably most widely known for his extraordinary trilogy of Elizabethan-era novels that redefined the possibilities for historical fiction: *Death of the Fox* (1971); *The Succession* (1983); *Entered from the Sun*

(1990). Garrett's depiction of the landscape, history, politics, art, and literature of Elizabethan and Jacobean England is utterly convincing; his characters (both historical and imagined) are brought so vividly to life that they become indistinguishable from living people. Combining the broad sweep of history with meticulous detail, these novels merge great storytelling with dazzling style.

What makes a writer raised in Florida during the Depression begin a relationship with the Elizabethans, and what sustains that relationship for three decades? Partly, Garrett says, it was poetry. After World War II, on the GI Bill, Garrett went to graduate school at Princeton, where he was reintroduced to the poetry of the Elizabethan period. Two poems by Sir Walter Ralegh, "Three Things There Be" and "The Passionate Man's Pilgrimage," seemed to speak directly to Garrett. The first of these, a poem for Ralegh's son ("my pretty knave"), delighted Garrett with its bittersweet wit and wisdom. The poem's "three things" ("the wood, the weed, and the wag") flourish apart but do harm to one another when they "meet in one place":

> The wood is that which makes the gallow tree,
> The weed is that which strings the hangman's bag,
> The wag, my pretty knave, betokeneth thee.

And the young Garrett was struck by these lines from "The Passionate Man's Pilgrimage":

> . . . Christ is the king's attorney
> Who pleads for all, without degrees,
> And he hath angels, but no fees.

which reminded him of his father, a feared and fearless lawyer who often represented needy clients for free. Inspired by the poems, Garrett read more of Ralegh's works, read more about Ralegh, discovered there hadn't been a biography in half a century, and began to think about writing one. The result, years later, was a different kind of biography, the novel *Death of the Fox*.

One of Garrett's primary interests as a writer is the relationship between the world of hard facts and the world of fiction. His Elizabethan trilogy explores that relationship with an interesting progression. The characters and events of *Death of the Fox* are factual, though Garrett relied on memory to write the novel. *Death of the Fox* is based entirely on historical research (Garrett didn't visit England until after the novel made enough money to pay for a trip). When he began writing, he put away his notes. Only the facts that he could recall would go into the book. *The Succession*, published a dozen years later—after Garrett had been to England—has more imaginary characters than the earlier novel, but the setting is more factual. Garrett says: "I had walked up and down the Great Northern Road and made notes and damned if I wasn't going to put it all in there." *Entered from the Sun* is about the mystery (facts unknown) of Christopher Marlowe's death. Historical figures appear—Marlowe, Ralegh, Shakespeare, Queen Elizabeth, Sir Francis Walsingham, The Earl of Essex, Robert Cecil, Ben Johnson, Robert Greene and others—but the major characters are fictional: Captain Barfoot, Joseph Hunnyman, the Widow Alysoun. As a medium in whose consciousness imagined minds meet, Garrett's sensibility, his aura, surrounds characters who speak through him, and he instigates a many-sided conversation between writer, reader, and a confluence of ghostly voices. As in the earlier Elizabethan novels, though more overtly, Garrett's storytelling methods are as much a part of the pleasure of *Entered from the Sun* as the tale itself.

In his most recent novel, *The King of Babylon Shall Not Come Against You* (1996), Garrett once again takes on the question of what fiction has to do with fact. The facts involve the assassination of Martin Luther King in April of 1968. Two murders, a suicide, a kidnapping, and arson also taking place in April of 1968 in central Florida are fictional. In fact, Garrett grew up in Kissimmee and, later, Orlando. The fictional setting is Paradise Springs, to which, twenty-five years later, Garrett's fictional investigative reporter journeys to try to make sense of those earlier, violent events. In the juxtaposition of past and present Garrett creates a kind of timeless bitter season.

This relationship between the present and the past is a central concern in much of Garrett's work, and the ways in which the stories, anecdotes, and essays of *Bad Man Blues* at once prefigure and echo one another also link the present to the past, revise history, and create a seamless loop, a lasso that twirls back and forth between the worlds of fiction and the world of facts, encircling both. His characters, whether they are as "factual" as Sir Walter Ralegh or as "made-up" as Ruthe-Ann Coombs (in the story "Dixie Dreamland" in *Bad Man Blues*), are so flesh and blood "real" that they continue to exist in a reader's consciousness just like other "real" characters (family members, friends, acquaintances) continue to exist when the reader is away from *them*.

Garrett himself is not immune to the spells he casts. In *Bad Man Blues*, as he does in many other books, he returns to characters from previous works. Ruthe-Ann Coombs is a minor character in *The King of Babylon Shall Not Come Against You*, and Sir Robert Carey, Earl of Monmouth (who lived on after his cousin, Queen Elizabeth), lives on after *The Succession* in references made by his young clerk, the narrator of "A Letter That Will Never Be Written." Garrett often realizes he is not through writing about a character from an earlier work because: "There's something incomplete about a character's story. The identity of a fictional character continues to shift, just as the identity of a real person may shift."

Using technical devices (such as unreliable narrators, authorial intrusions, "real" people in fictional situations, "imaginary" people in historically factual situations) and, more obviously, using characterization, Garrett's work repeatedly raises questions about what constitutes an identity. Most of Garrett's major characters have a dual nature, are fallen from grace yet contain enough good to make redemption possible. In Garrett's imagined world the only sinners who are beyond salvation are those who refuse to recognize, or at least acknowledge, their sinful ways. First we must see that the world is unspeakably evil, then we must realize that that is not all there is to the world. The voice of Garrett's poem "Rugby Road" speculates:

> How can a mind begin to wander free
> until at last the last pride of the flesh
> falls away like a sad fig leaf?

For any mind to wander free requires faith in the imagination. I know few writers whose work demonstrates such a freely wandering, "serious" imagination. "Serious" does not, of course, mean "solemn." Consider, in *Bad Man Blues*, the whimsy behind all the possible scenarios of "A Perfect Stranger (Alabama)." Consider, also, the rich ambiguity of that title and how it recalls Hebrews 13, verses 1 and 2: "Let brotherly love continue. Be not forgetful to entertain strangers: for thereby some have entertained angels unawares." Garrett had earlier used these verses as the epigraph for the Prologue to *An Evening Performance: New and Selected Stories* (1985).

Bad Man Blues is justifiably subtitled *A Portable George Garrett* because so many of the generative elements of his separate works are here gathered together. Part I consists of Short Stories in which there's biting, darkly comic satire; a compressed love story; a return to Elizabethan England; the story that reincarnates Ruthe-Ann Coombs, a character Garrett was not yet through with; and stories that return to Garrett's childhood in Florida.

Part II contains Academic Anecdotes (stories first told orally, tales based on, if not slaves to, the facts). Many people who know Garrett personally or have attended one of the many readings or lectures he gives throughout the country, know him as a highly entertaining teller of jokes and of elaborate stories. There are many (myself among them) who hang around Garrett all evening in the hopes of settling in somewhere—on the steps below the lectern, or better, at the banquet table; in a hotel lobby or, best, in the barroom, to hear Garrett tell the one about the time Leslie Fiedler came to lecture at the University of Virginia during spring break when there were no students on campus to make up an audience, or the one about the visiting professor at Bennington cajoling the novelist Bernard Malamud into divulging the name of his garbage collector, or about the semester Garrett spent in Tuscaloosa and was waked one morning by loud noises and thick smoke only to discover hundreds of barbecue grills and tipsy Crimson Tide fans who had parked their red and white motor homes all around the visiting writer's house. You, lucky reader, don't have to sit on the steps—these and other wickedly funny anecdotes are right here in *Bad Man Blues*.

By Part III, Essays, Garrett has moved from fiction through fiction-based-on-fact to fact. In these very moving personal essays he writes—directly and indirectly—about several of the sources of his literary works.

Garrett says: "It was never, never once for a minute, my ambition *to be a writer*. Rather to be, for some supremely transcendent moments, anyway, the work itself." In the ring, as in his writing, Garrett has experienced those moments of the harmony of mind and body in which the boxer, like any good athlete, becomes the moves he's making—the bob and weave, the feint and parry. Nonetheless, Garrett acknowledges that, in spite of Shelby Foote's proposition about Faulkner, no writer can ever disappear completely into his work.

Another legacy at least partly passed down from Faulkner is the expectation that a Southern writer's work have a strong sense of place. Central Florida is often the setting of Garrett's fiction and essays, though the Elizabethan novels make it clear that Garrett is not limited by region or by era. The academic anecdotes in *Bad Man Blues* are set in some of the places Garrett has lived—Florida, Connecticut, Texas, New Jersey, South Carolina, Vermont, Michigan, Alabama, Virginia, even Italy. Perhaps Garrett's mobility, a relatively modern experience that most of us share, gives him more reason to look back to *family* in order to feel rooted. More than *place* (though connected to it), *family* is an important source for Garrett's work in its many manifestations.

In this volume the story "The Right Thing to Do at the Time" and the essay "Heroes" make it vividly clear that Garrett's father, who died when his son was only seventeen, was a huge influence. To assuage his loss, Garrett keeps his father alive imaginatively. A hero not only to Garrett but also to the poor and downtrodden whom he courageously represented, *pro bono*, Garrett Sr. was a lawyer who took on and whipped formidable opponents (such as the Ku Klux Klan, which he ran out of Kissimmee, and the big railroads, which he beat again and again). Garrett tells the story of how his father, with one speech, saved a county and thus an election for Florida Senator Claude Pepper. (Garrett returned to Florida politics for the subject matter of his first novel, *The Finished Man* [1959].)

From his father, Garrett inherited independence, generosity, courage, and a combative sense of fun. In "Heroes," Garrett tells how, after his daddy had repeatedly beaten the big railroads in court, they sent representatives to persuade him never again to accept cases against them. Garrett Sr. politely rejected the fortune they offered, telling them that if he agreed not to battle them in court he'd have nothing left to do for fun. That combative sense of fun perhaps prefigured Garrett Jr. in taped hands and gloves, laughing and punching, as it prefigured his many darkly comic pieces. In "Hanging from the Trestle While the Train Goes By," Garrett's uncle was often caught walking the tracks by a freight train and forced to hang from a crosstie while the train rattled overhead. Garrett sees that as an apt image for the artist, literary or otherwise—the artist as comic and entertainer who is getting where he has to go the best way he knows how and who, regardless of the predicament in which he finds himself, is expected to laugh.

Garrett's characters both major and minor face life's difficult lessons "laughing and scratching." But Garrett's laughter is never sentimental; his wit has a keen edge. Take, for example, this "flashcard":

I MUST HAVE PEAKED TOO EARLY

"Sir, Madame, Person, Occupant,"
the National Endowment addresses me.
"There's still space available and plenty of time
to reserve some of the same for your mortal remains
at the Tomb of the Unknown American Writer."

Literary hucksters and hustlers often promote glitz over substance and readers may be slow to appreciate substance over what is slick and shiny. Growing up, Garrett had to look no further than his father or boxing for an example of substance and principle. In "It Sings. It Hums and Dances" Garrett writes a tribute to Joe Louis: "He had integrity and character, not charisma. He was only modestly colorful, never a showboat, never a showoff. In our own celebrity-ridden era, characterized by uninhibited self-promotion, it is hard to imagine that there ever were any athletes or performers who let their skills speak for themselves." In a business in which many movers and shakers take themselves more seriously than they take literature, Garrett has refused to jump on the bandwagon of any literary movement or school because "the main aim of these is to make the poet, whether as prophet or charmer, into a respected and respectable citizen." In another "flashcard" Garrett pokes fun at the literary establishment:

MY MAIN CONFESSIONAL POEM

> I confess
> I am not guilty
> of anything I'd care
> to tell you about.

Whether it's the KKK in 1940s Florida, or the American *literati*—the powers that be are always fair game for Garrett's dark comedy.

The variety in Garrett's work, the variety in *Bad Man Blues*, shows that he has steadfastly refused to become too comfortable as a writer. Even after *The Finished Man* gained him national recognition as a new Southern novelist, he was determined not to keep writing "Southern" novels, and he published an army novel set in Trieste, Italy, *Which Ones Are the Enemy?* (1961). This radical shift in material made it harder for critics to focus on him and diminished the reception of the second novel. As if to prove that he could if he wanted to, he returned to "Southern" material in *Do, Lord, Remember Me* (1965), about a tent revival preacher in a small Southern town.

A few years ago, I asked Garrett about his unwillingness to carve a comfortable literary niche for himself, and we ended up talking, again, about sports. He told me that any professional athlete knows the difference between popular reputation and the hard world of reality, and that it's an insult to be told you believe your own press clippings. He went on to say that most prize fighters are finished by the age of thirty. "So the thing used to be to say 'They're not hungry anymore, laziness has set in, they've gotten complacent.' But I don't really think that's true. I think they're just not hungering for the *same* things, and, therefore, they aren't really fit competition for the younger fighter. The older fighter—like the older writer—has other aims and hungers, new ones he didn't know existed before." What energizes Garrett is the constant new challenge: "Such skills as I have acquired are only applicable to the books I've already written. I don't know if they are applicable at all to the books I would like to write in the future."

When, from time to time, his Princeton boxing coach, Joe Brown, got the itch to go to New York to the fights, Garrett went with him. Ticket takers, guys selling programs, and punch-drunk former fighters all recognized Brown and spoke to him, and the ring announcer introduced Brown to the crowd. "The older fighters were no longer trying to prove something," Garrett says. "They had come to respect one another."

Garrett the writer has refused to concentrate on any move that comes too easily or appears to be his best, refuses, once he's completely mastered it, to repeat an uppercut over and over. Instead, he attempts some new, some *different* move. Nor has Garrett tried to write what is fashionable and easily marketable. His work has moved away from strict realism toward the anecdotal and, then, to historical fiction. He has experimented with ways of telling stories—multiple points of view, interior and exterior voices. Given Garrett's disdain for "making it" as a literary lion, it's not surprising that his stories, essays, and poems appear regularly not in big commercial magazines but in the small literary journals. His books have been published by large New York publishers, by university presses, and by small presses. As Garrett once said of the novelist Wright Morris, "many different publishers may indicate a literary troublemaker." When he says this, Garrett's tone makes it clear that "troublemaker" is high praise.

Garrett's satiric humor reveals the teeth behind the famous George Garrett grin. In "Going to See the Elephant: Why We Write Stories," contained in Part III of this book, Garrett says the storyteller makes a leap of faith into the skin and bones of an imaginary creature (stranger?) every time he speaks (and thinks and feels) for others. There is pain behind the grin because some of the skin-and-bones creatures we become will take a beating or, maybe worse, *give* a beating. Because the world of flesh is necessarily a world of evil, of having fallen from grace. Garrett's Christian vision does not allow for self-pity. Though it is a foul for a boxer to hit when breaking from a clinch, refs always warn fighters to protect themselves on the break, and if one doesn't he has only himself to blame.

During the twenty-six years since that summer in Eastern Washington I've sat in the midst of audiences large and small charmed by Garrett. I've listened to him patiently answer every question he was asked, seen him shake every hand extended in his direction, and watched him stand alone on a wide stage looking a little embarrassed by the applause and a little weary, but focused and ready for whatever came next. Despite his observation in "It Sings. It Hums and Dances" that sports analogies don't usually make good metaphors, I compare my remembered image of Garrett on that stage with his of Joe Louis fighting Lee Savold: " . . . the stink of the place and the huge crowd, the cigarette smoke in clouds and the echoing noise and yelling. And in the center of things, the brightly lit space of the ring, seeming wide as a field, and the two big middle-aged men, alone together out there, ignoring everything else except each other. They were lonesome and beautiful." That image helps me understand better the pain behind Garrett's smile, his laughter blessing whatever has been served up. For nearly half a century, George Garrett has responded to what the world has to give and to take away by teaching his readers, among many other things, how to laugh in the midst of despair.

Bad Man Blues is about pain and lamentation, but the other side of lament is celebration. Like a good fighter, George Garrett in *Bad Man Blues* turns pain into parry and shuffle, into dance, and makes us—even if the tune is loss and suffering—stomp our feet, clap and whistle.

Knoxville, Tennessee
June 1998

What I wanted to do here (and what I hope I have done) was to arrange and present a representative selection of my work over the past few years, a gathering of new and previously uncollected stories, anecdotes, and personal essays. By doing it this way, I aimed to say what I believe to be true—that these separate forms of narrative writing are close kin to each other. I can see that the way I have put together the parts of *Bad Man Blues* might possibly confuse somebody. And that is something I do not want to do.

What joins these disparate things together, in spite of their deliberate and obvious diversity of form and of voice(s), is, of course, that they were all written during roughly the same time; that no matter how much each piece may seem to differ from the others, all of them share a source of particular concerns (mine); and that all the voices, in fact, come from one voice alone (my own).

In fact . . . One of the great puzzles that interests me deeply, a puzzle not to be solved or answered here or anywhere else, is the intricate, subtle, and shifty relationship between fact and fiction. In one sense that is what this book is "about." We all try to tell our stories. Some of them are more factual than others, more closely shadowed by factual truth. But fiction can be, indeed *must be,* real and true also.

We begin here with several kinds of stories, selected and arranged precisely to show their variety of forms and tones of voice. Because I have written all my life, and professionally for about fifty years, I have learned enough over all those years to see where at least some of these stories come from and how, inevitably, they are related to my earlier and other work. Thus "Genius Baby," for example, is a kissing cousin to the narrative world of my novel *Poison Pen.* And if you stay with the sequence of things, first to last, you will discover, as I did, the presence in "Genius Baby" of a character from that novel. "A Letter That Will Never Be Written," though it stands alone (I hope and pray), would not have even occurred to me to write if I had not already spent thirty-odd years of my life writing a trilogy of Elizabethan novels. I spent a long time as an alien visitor in that age and I now feel as free to imagine it and to write about it as I do to write about the time of the Great Depression when I grew up ("The Right Thing to Do at the Time," "Bad Man Blues," "The Misery and the Glory of Texas Pete," and "Independence Day"), as I do about the groves of academe where I have labored in the vineyard ("To Guess a Riddle, To Stumble on the Secret Name" and the academic anecdotes) or the U.S. Army where I served my time (see *The Old Army Game*). I am by birth and heritage a Southerner, though I have (in fact) lived in many other places, and so it should be no surprise that some of these stories (notably "The Right Thing to Do at the Time," "Bad Man Blues," and "Dixie Dreamland") have Southern settings and speak in Southern voices. And there are connections: Willie Gary of "Bad Man Blues" is also a character in my most recent novel, *The King of Babylon Shall Not Come Against You*, and will be present in other fiction in the future; the father (mine) of "The Right Thing to Do at the Time" is the factual father of the essay "Heroes." Some of the academic anecdotes are purely and simply Southern; and, of course, all of the essays in the last section of the book are concerned with my Southern family.

What is here, then, in *Bad Man Blues*, with and without my intentions, is a kind of guided tour through my whole life, my world, and my work so far; new works which refer to the works and days of my past; old and new hopes and fears, songs and sorrows.

Live long enough as a writer (and, pushing seventy, I have been lucky, am lucky to be here), and you will sooner or later learn that even when you try hard not to repeat yourself and keep working in new directions with different forms, you will always have some things that you keep coming back to. You will always be haunted by the same ghosts. You will never be able to escape from your own history. An early reader of the manuscript of this book, a writer whom I greatly admire and trust, called the whole of it "a camouflaged autobiography." And in a real sense I reckon that there is some truth in that. I think that all the stories (fact and fiction) that we make up and tell each other add up to being the story of our own lives, disguised or naked as the case may be.

All of which, all of the above, sounds leadenly serious. Well, it's not supposed to be so. Even when its purposes are sad and serious, even tragic, a story ought to be entertaining, fun to read, a pleasure.

I sincerely hope that the reader—you whom I can only imagine and to whom I am always speaking—can have some fun and find pleasure in these pieces, in this book.

A word about and to the "real" people and the "real" events that appear and take place in some of these pieces. They are the gifts and creatures of my memory. They are remembered here as well as I can do so, without any malice and with no intent to do harm. But my memory, like yours, reader, is not without flaws and faults. Where (and if) memory has gone wrong, I apologize.

George Garrett
Charlottesville, Virginia
June 1998

Bad Man Blues

Virtue is of so little regard in these costermongers' times
that true valour is turned bear-herd, pregnancy is made a tapster,
and his quick wit wasted in giving reckonings; all of the other
gifts appertinent to the man, as the malice of this age
shapes them, are not worth a gooseberry.

SIR JOHN FALSTAFF

PART I

Short Stories

All the confusion of my life has been a reflection of myself. Life is a holiday. Let us live it together. That's all I can say to you and the others. Accept me as I am. Only then will we discover each other.

GUIDO IN FELLINI'S *8½*

Genius Baby

It is getting late now and finally the hospital is more or less quiet. I am now in the so-called lounge. Where people waiting to see patients gather during visiting hours to watch TV (soap operas and talk shows and game shows) or leaf through ancient copies of *Time* and *Newsweek, Vogue* and *Cosmo, Field and Stream* and *Guns and Ammo.* Together with some fairly recent issues of the *AMA Journal* and the *New England Journal of Medicine.* The latter two will sure enough scare the living pee out of you, quicker than the sight of a sadistic nurse coming straight towards your bed with a catheter in her hands. Not only scare you because of all the horrible diseases and conditions that you never even heard of until now, and from now on will be certain, as all the symptoms will clearly indicate, you have been suffering from all along. But also on account of the professional attitude openly displayed therein. The truth is that doctors are a whole lot worse than we ever imagined they could be or would be. The bad news that I have to report is that in spite of all the honor and respect and reward, no matter, they are just like the rest of us—ignorant, insensitive, greedy, and ruthlessly dedicated to the advancement and enhancement of old number one.

But never mind. I'm not bitter. Just wary.

During other odd hours occasional ambulatory patients (walking wounded) wander in to take a breather in the beat-up armchairs. And usually some of the orderlies and nurses, sometimes even doctors, to watch their favorite programs. Woe betide any patient in this place who has an emergency during *General Hospital!*

Now, however, it is late. And empty except for me. I'm sitting at a table with my long, lined, yellow sheets of legal pad and with a Japanese felt-tip pen. Most of the lights have been turned off and it is very quiet here. Except for the sudden and surprising (yet always expected) cries and the long groans you can count on hearing on any given night in any hallway of any staph- and staff-ridden, dirty, crummy, poorly administered and badly maintained, typical too-expensive American hospital in the general surgery section. Where I—yes—am. Oh the hair-raising and horrible stories of hospitals, and especially this hospital, that I could tell you if I had the time and a decent pair of glasses! But, then, anyone else could probably match my stories or even top them. For, according to the numbers, one out of four of us has already experienced the mundane horror of the hospital. Well, a hospital like this one does have at least one thing to recommend it. Once having been there you won't ever want to come back. If you live through it, then you will die first, if possible, before being sent back. And that is a very important factor which has already served to reduce overcrowding in American hospitals and may have a positive effect on slowing the rising costs of health care.

At the moment the only soul awake and about and nearby is the pleasingly plump night nurse sitting at her station, reading *Cream* magazine. She is a dead ringer for Shelley Winters. Her main hope, maybe her only real hope at this point, is that all of the patients under her so-called care won't dare to need a damn thing all night long. She needn't worry about it. We all really do try to live up to her best expectations of us. Most would rather die quietly than press the buzzer for her attention.

Never mind. Let me quit complaining. Here I am, on the mend, feeling better than I ought to, ready to write all night long. If they would let me. And I do owe you some apologies and explanations. I'll be the first to admit it.

Before getting going on all that, however, I would like to say a few things about my family. My former family, I guess you would have to say. I have not been completely fair to them, and I haven't given a completely fair and objective picture of them. Neither Annie nor Genius Baby was ever entirely devoid of human warmth. And, in all fairness, I have to admit that little Allyson, my favorite, was often a whiner and a troublemaker.

Having attended the best schools, Annie was not utterly without intellectual interests and abilities. And—and this cannot be emphasized and reiterated too much—she was really and truly rich. I don't mean well off or well-to-do. I mean fuckin' rich. Moreover, and no denying it, pound for pound and inch by inch, she was one of the most attractive women I have ever known intimately. And (no bragging but no kidding either) I have known more than a few both pound for pound and inch by inch. That one of them happened to be your good wife, Geraldine, and that you happened to find out about it, I deem truly regrettable. I wish it had been otherwise, Ray, I really do. But that was a long time ago, as the world turns; and I can't see any good purpose in my pretending that it was different. Even for the sake of good manners. May I say, though, without malice or hard feelings, that even though your wife was very attractive in every way and could put out like a wild mink in heat when she felt like it, she really wasn't in the same class as Annie?

Very few people seemed to realize this about Annie. And Dr. Smartheim is probably too inexperienced to fully appreciate it.

Before continuing with my family album and the subject of Annie as a sex object, please permit me to fill you in briefly on Smartheim and what happened after we all went our separate ways.

Is this a digression? So be it. Digression is the essence of my literary style. Besides which the medication they are giving me seems to make my mind wander.

Smartheim was her psychiatrist all along. You probably didn't know Annie went to a shrink and needed to. But she did. Nothing really deeply serious, as far as I know. Just the usual neurotic tics and tremors. Plus one little problem that was direct trouble for me. Annie had no special hangups when it came to sex. I mean, she would cheerfully do almost anything you can think of. But . . . the only thing that *aroused* her, the only way she could get turned on, was reading pornography. If you gave her some porn to read (it had to be half-decent porn with some mildly literary pretensions, too), she got all hot and bothered. If you didn't, she didn't. It was that simple. Problem, though, Ray, was that there wasn't all that much half-decent, mildly literary porn available in those days. At least in English. We ran through just about everything I could get hold of during the first year or so of our marriage. After that I could either wait around for the next batch of material to appear in print. Or I could do my own.

Well, we were both young and healthy and eager. So I became a creative writer, Ray. That was the one and only reason I started writing. It may not have been a noble reason, but surely you have to admit it was a compelling one. Anyway, I was hoping that maybe Dr. Smartheim could cure her of that little problem. I heard that he finally did, too; but only after the divorce. Then they got married, Annie and Smartheim. And everything was copacetic until she had a relapse and fell back into her old ways. Smartheim may be a pretty good psychiatrist. Who knows about a thing like that? But as a writer of pornography he was a dud. You know? Nothing he wrote seemed to arouse her. So, to my everlasting joy, the son-of-a-bitch had to write me to ask if I would be willing to create some more porn. For a fee, mind you. Good bucks! Better than any publisher ever offered me. It was honestly a temptation. I needed the money. And it gave me a certain sense of artistic pride to think that I had the craft and skill to keep his marriage together. And it would be kind of like seduction by proxy. Neat idea for a short story, huh? Only thing, Ray, the bastard did steal my rich wife away from me. In the end pride and morality triumphed over prudence. I told him to go find his own pornographer.

Where was I?

O, yes, Annie . . .

In several ways Annie was incredibly attractive. That she had all the necessary equipment in appropriate sizes and proportion, goes without saying. But Annie also smelled, tasted, and felt so . . . *good!* She had marvelous, utterly smooth and beautiful skin all over. Without mole or scar or blemish of any kind. She never wore any makeup because she never had to. It would have been wasted on her. Her muscle tone was equally marvelous, a perfect complement to the beauty of her skin and complexion. It is difficult to describe precisely what I mean. Do you remember a movie actress, a starlet, named Pamela Tiffin? Well, in case you don't (and why would anyone?), she was in some "B" movies and a couple of Broadway shows, and part of her talent was the adroit exposure of considerable portions of her own bare and not unremarkable flesh. A very attractive woman I know was quite startled by this. And perhaps a little jealous. "Pamela Tiffin is truly amazing," she told me. "She is like a baby's bottom only all over." I cannot comment on the aptness or accuracy of the analogy as far as Ms. Tiffin was concerned. But it suggests something. If I had to, I would describe my ex-wife Annie as like the best inside-of-thigh you ever imagined. And all over.

Okay?

But the real thing I wanted to deal with, here in this epistle, was my problems, then and now, with Genius Baby. It is true that I favored his sister in every way. And made no bones about it. But, even so, I have to admit he had some qualities, even as a little kid, that were unusual and maybe even admirable.

I remember one time I was trying to find some efficient, if not especially humane, way to discipline the little prick with ears. I had tried just about everything I could think of. Nothing seemed to work to my satisfaction. Generally, I took my leather belt off and addressed it, as hard and as crisp as possible, across not his bony buttocks but instead his long and very skinny legs. I could tell it hurt him quite a lot and that he was afraid of it. Signs of fear—yes. But, beyond that, I never got the satisfaction of the yowls and tears you would get from an ordinary normal child. He would bite his lip and just hang in there, soundless and tearless, until my arm got tired.

One time I asked him outright why he acted like that. Why did he do it when he knew damn well that all I really wanted from him was one good loud yell or some routine crying? Just to establish, briefly and once and for all, who was the actual boss around our house. He declined to answer. So, trying to be sly and a little bit subtle, I expressed admiration and amazement at his Spartan fortitude. I asked him how he did it.

To which he had a cheerful answer. One which, without undue parental pride, may I say was a pretty good yarn for a seven-year-old kid. He began by mentioning the obvious things—geological and astronomical time and how, viewed against those vast scales, all human enterprises, pleasure and pain alike, from the misty dawn of history up to and through the last wham-bam of the Apocalypse, fade into pointless insignificance.

Of course, that was the kind of answer to be expected from a kid with a scientific cast of mind. But the next thing really surprised me.

"I think a lot about the insects, Daddy."

"The . . . insects?"

"They keep multiplying and breeding and everything," he said condescendingly. "They already outnumber all other forms of life. And they are going to win. Man is done for."

"So fuckin' what, Genius Baby?"

"Well, I think about that when you're spanking me. I think how it doesn't matter anyway because the insects are winning."

By God, that son of mine has had some fine moments. I was really proud of that one. I thought of having it done up in needlepoint. Or maybe made as a flag. THE INSECTS ARE WINNING! I would gladly climb Mt. Everest in order to plant it proudly in the eternal snows. If I were a rich fat Greek with a big huge yacht and a whole boatload of great incredible girls in teeny-weeny bikinis and opera singers all covered with jewels, I would fly that message and warning on my mast in the alphabet of signal flags. If only more people would pause in their daily and miserable pursuit of happiness and simply contemplate those wise words, it would surely be a much better world for one and all, including the insects.

I'm not too proud to give Genius Baby full credit for it, even though I plan to use it as the title of my next novel.

I am also not too proud to admit—especially in this context, since this started out to be a kind of confession—that it was, in part at least, my cruel mistreatment of Genius Baby which led towards the breakup of my marriage. And, let's face it, the end of my easy meal ticket. Not the belt which was, honestly, administered only on rare and drastic occasions. Such as attempted arson on our house or attempted murder of Allyson or grand theft of my most precious possessions. And, speaking of punishment by belt, I have to say that Annie was rather proud of Genius Baby's stoicism and encouraged him. You see, Annie's family, at least on her mother's side, was pretty distinguished in the land of the broad "A," which, taken together with a style of speaking which is not so much a matter of deep drawling as it is a pretty fair imitation of the initial phases of vomiting, is the hallmark of upperclass Eastern Society. I like that just fine and dandy. And so did her self-made pappy who had nothing at all but a pisspot of money to distinguish or recommend him. He liked it even if his understanding of all the shades and nuances of said society— say, for example, in Philadelphia the complete difference, evident at first sight and first remark, between the Mainline bunch and the Chestnut Hill gang—was about on the primitive level of the Updike novel. Which is a very polite way of saying that Annie's old man had the whole thing bollixed up. But Pappy liked it that way, because of his very distinguished wife. His name was to be found in *The Social Register*. And I liked it too. I got in there, too, by the hem of Annie's half-slip, so to speak. Of course, I got dumped when we got our divorce. But, then, so did she (ha-ha) when she married that sneaky Jewish shrink Smartheim. Which must have been a bitter pill for him to swallow.

Anyway (never mind all that) Annie's mama was a direct descendant of one of George Washington's principal Indian agents; a gentleman from what is now upstate New York. Now, the whole thing is that this Agent made great friends, became a diehard, bunghole buddy of Red Jacket, the famous Mohawk chief. In fact, Old Red Jacket liked him so much that he would sneak off from time to time, from the tedious routine of being the tribal chief. And he would come visit the Agent's house. He especially liked to pay a call and stay for some length while the aforesaid Agent was way to hell and gone out in the boondocks doing his official bit with the savages. Well, the net and final result, the bottom line as they all insist on saying, is that every so often, like an Injun in the woodpile, somebody crops up in Annie's family who looks astonishingly like a Mohawk far from home. I have seen a portrait of Red Jacket in the Philadelphia Museum. And I can report that Annie's grandmother is an unquestionable dead ringer for Red Jacket. And (you guessed it) so is Genius Baby. I swear to you that Genius Baby's hair grew out in a natural scalp lock.

We had one hell of a time with Genius Baby during toilet training. In spite of all his extraordinary intellectual attainments, he was still wearing diapers when he was maybe four years old. I tried all kinds of psychology on the little ratfink. Who was thoroughly enjoying all the trouble and embarrassment he was causing. You see, he loved all the cowboys and Indians stuff they had on TV in those days. One day I just grabbed him in a grip of iron to keep him still long enough to carry on a serious conversation.

"Genius Baby," I said. "How come you won't go to the bathroom?"

"I don't know."

"Cowboys go to the bathroom."

"Sure," he replied cheerfully. "But Indians don't."

Annie loved it. She loved telling about that exchange between us. She liked the fact that he could take and bear pain like a young Mohawk brave. And there was a certain social value to the whole thing. These days we are at last far enough along so that a little chap with a dollop of Indian blood, together with a good, solid Colonial Dames background, can claim a definite social advantage.

To tell the truth, Ray, it was a bad scene when Annie found out that I had not only been diddling your wife, but also had been caught at it, too. Not all laughing and scratching over at our house. But that wasn't the real occasion or proximate cause of my final breakup with Annie. She blamed Geraldine more than she blamed me, anyway. No, it was the problem of Genius Baby that drove a stake through the heart of our relationship. (Heh-heh! Block that fuckin' metaphor!)

As I recall it was a Saturday morning. Not just any old Saturday morning, but the one after all the shit had hit the fan; and you had been fired outright; and I had been told that my services would no longer be required after the end of the current academic year. I was feeling fairly bad about getting the boot and even worse that Annie was adamant about staying on here in the community, job or no job; because we had such a nice house to live in, and it was good for the children to have some continuity, and she liked it and a lot of the people, etc., etc., etc.

"Listen," I told her, "I am perfectly willing to retire from the rat race and live off of your money. I will devote my life to literary pursuits. I will do a major research project on the subject of pure leisure, a terribly important subject now that full automation is almost upon us . . ."

"What about Milton's use of dreams and dream visions?"

That was supposed to be the topic of my, pardon the expression, dissertation, Ray.

"Bugger Milton and his dreams and visions!"

"My, you are being childish about this whole . . . contretemps."

"I would love to goof off for the rest of my life. It's what I have always wanted. But it's too humiliating."

"Humiliating?"

"This is a small town. I won't be able to go buy a pack of cigarettes without running into one of my ex-colleagues. Who, probably out of pure jealousy, will be thinking: 'There goes that no-good lazy bum, who couldn't even make it in academe and is now living off of his sweet, kind, hopelessly indulgent and misguided wife.'"

"Why should the truth humiliate you?"

"Because, in spite of everything, I still have about an ounce and a half of pride left."

"Jesus, here we go again."

"What are you talking about?"

"Jack, when are you ever going to grow up? When are you going to set yourself free from all that silly, defensive, pointless Southern pride of yours?"

"Pointless?"

"You and all those creepy Erskine Caldwell relatives of yours!"

Of course, I had no choice but to slap her face in response to that crack. But not hard. It was more a symbolic gesture than anything else.

Just then from upstairs in Genius Baby's room came the sound of the theme of *Captain Kangaroo*. Coffeeless, breakfastless, paperless, and feeling guilty as hell for belting Annie even if she was asking for it, I was also about to be deprived, once again, of the Captain. And on Saturday, the day they usually dropped the Ping-Pong balls. The only other sound, besides Annie's deep breathing as she controlled her anger with me, was little Allyson crying helplessly and hopelessly because her sadistic older brother wouldn't let her in his room so she could watch TV, too.

"Okay," I thought and maybe said out loud. "That cuts it. Enough is fuckin' enough!"

I jumped up and ran down to the basement and got the ax. When I came back up with it, I finally got some kind of a reaction from Annie. She stood in front of me and could have posed for a nineteenth-century drawing entitled "Woodsman, spare that tree."

I spoke as slowly and as distinctly as I could through gritted teeth.

"I am fixing to take this here ax upstairs and to chop the door to Genius Baby's room into a neat little pile of kindling wood so that his sister and I can watch *Captain Kangaroo* on the only TV set in this house."

"Wait a minute!" she said. "You could at least have the common decency to call him up first and ask him. He might let you look."

A word or two of explanation. Because Annie hated TV (and probably still does, except for the pinko-liberal-faggot stuff they show on PBS), the only set in our house was in Genius Baby's room. He was allowed to have one so he could keep up with the latest scientific and technical developments. Second—calling him up. As a result of Annie's continual prodding, I had purchased and rigged up an old army surplus field telephone set. That way we could at least communicate with Genius Baby even after he had locked himself into his room.

Annie's plea for preliminary negotiation seemed logical and reasonably sincere at the time; so, still holding my ax, I went to the field telephone and cranked and cranked until he finally got around to answering it.

"Laboratory," he answered. "Do you realize you are interrupting?"

"That's not all I am about to do."

"Please be quick. *Captain Kangaroo* is on."

"I am fully aware of that fact, Genius Baby. And that is the reason I am calling you. Your little sister and I are coming into your so-called laboratory to watch the Captain whether you like it or not."

"Lots of luck, Daddy," he replied. "The door is locked and bolted."

"I intend to chop the door down."

"You'll be sorry," he said. And he hung up on me.

Annie yelled at me as I ran up the stairs. Behind me the field telephone started ringing and ringing. I could picture the little shithead crouched down and cranking like crazy.

I made a brand new doorway about as quick as any fireman could have. And there he was, old Genius Baby, the coward, cringing in the corner. I might have let him go. He was just a scared little boy, after all. But when he saw me hesitate and sensed my inner mood, he had to go and push me too far.

"You're too late!" he cried, laughing in my face. "You missed the Ping-Pong balls. You already missed the Ping-Pong balls!"

So, what could I do? I smashed the TV set and then went to work on the room. When I got through with that crummy so-called laboratory of his, the only thing left in one piece was the walls. I even managed to chop up the bed.

At that point Genius Baby really surprised me. He started bawling like a baby. Which may have been the one thing he could have done that saved him from being chopped into bite-size chunks, himself.

Deeply pleased, I threw down the ax and started downstairs.

Annie (needless to say) was not deeply pleased. She soon ordered me out of her house. And she meant it. I didn't know whether to shit or go blind; so I sauntered out without another word, got into my car, and drove out to the Finlandia Sauna to sweat it all out of my system.

Well, Ray, I probably wasn't the best father in the world. But I am pleased to be able to report that Genius Baby has grown up into a half-decent-looking young man, not unlike his old man at that age. And he seems to have done very well in school. He appears to be a shoo-in for the college of his choice. Most likely Ivy League. He has also managed to display some athletic prowess and he has cultivated the guitar. He plays folk music on a Spanish guitar and, they tell me, uses an electric bass guitar as his contribution to the cacophony of a so-called singing group which is known as "The Rednecks." Like any well brought up Connecticut youth, he is very high on The Civil Rights Movement, provided it stays in its place down South and does not interfere with his neighborhood, his privileges, or his prerogatives. He was even arrested once for biting a policeman during a nonviolent street demonstration. All of which indicates he is a normal and supremely typical product of the lower New England, privileged-class environment and background. I might add that I am absolutely certain he would not permit Allyson to marry One if she ever even met One socially and the idea ever occurred to her.

All in all, I might be slightly disturbed that I have left no mark whatsoever upon the life of my only son. Except for the fact that for some time, though he was very good at his studies, he was, I gather, and believe also, a real high-class Disciplinary Problem. He was kicked out of several schools and the "broken home" was always cited as a factor in his antisocial behavior. At least I made that much impression on his life. I never worried about him. After all, Smartheim is an analyst. Like, why worry about cavities if you've got a dentist in the family? That's the way I put it to Dr. Smartheim. Who was not amused.

Monster I may be—sometimes. But never inhuman. I often miss my family, even as I realize they are probably much better off without me.

On which happy note I reckon I'm going to have to call it quits. Soon anyway. This place of the sick and the dying (and the healing, too, I hope to God) is closing down for the night. I've got MTV playing on the tube. MTV is unbelievably silly without benefit of sound. The night nurse is sitting fatly at her station now reading *People* magazine. My roommate, who has some kind of cancer, and is a goner I guess, is probably sound asleep by now. Asleep and dreaming. What do the dying dream about? Beats me. But I know it's bad enough, sufficiently depressing when you are well enough to allow yourself to imagine a future. As I do. I'll be out of here in a few days. And yet I can't stand the idea of going back in that room and going to sleep. Where bad dreams can always do damage.

Not much choice, though. Night Nurse has come, even as I write this, and blinked the lights in the lounge. She'll be back again in a few minutes to put me and this place into the dark. Better finish up quickly now . . .

Did I ever tell you about the last time I saw them, my family, in person?

It was when Allyson graduated from this swank little nursery school. Genius Baby would have been nine or ten then (I can't remember his birthday for the life of me) and Allyson was going on six. Well, I wanted to be there and tried to figure a way that I could come back and not create a big scene. I drove up and saw our minister, one of these youngish, fresh-out-of-seminary cats. He was supposed to go to the ceremony and read the invocation. I begged, pleaded, coaxed and cajoled and finally persuaded him to let me take his place. I would borrow a clerical collar and put on a pair of dark glasses. I did a fast dye job on my hair, and I must say I was pretty confident. I could have fooled me. All I was going to have to do was read a little prayer just before the Pledge of Allegiance to the flag. Then I could step aside and in my disguise and anonymity I could see my little Allyson participate in the Teapot Dance and receive her nursery school diploma. No one would ever know. And naturally they weren't expecting me.

Everything was going along just fine. I kind of blended in with the shrubbery and saw the kids getting ready, posing for pictures, etc., wearing their white suits and dresses and their red and blue capes. It was outdoors in a garden behind the house. Miss Whitman, who ran the thing (and made plenty of moola doing it), scurrying about. Parents, dressed to kill, arriving and sitting in folding chairs facing a raised level of ground, rather like a putting green, which served as a stage for the children. Old Glory, planted on a stand on the green, fluttered proudly in the fresh spring air. Spring flowers blooming all around. And then, so pretty she might have been one of those flowers herself, there was Allyson arriving, taking her place. My heart was a muffled snaredrum. I looked, safe behind my shades, and watched the others. Smartheim impeccable, but comically littered with leather camera straps, cases, carrying a couple of cameras, light meters and God knows what else. Annie exquisite, a marvel as always, in her simple, very expensive linen dress and, for some reason, a hat and gloves. Cool and lovely. Genius Baby skulking about at the edges of things looking for whatever mischief or trouble he could find, his scalp lock bristling, his fly half open, wearing mismatching sneakers, one white and one black one. For that one moment I loved them all.

I glanced down at the *Book of Common Prayer* and rehearsed my reading to myself. Then feeling a tightness in my throat and wanting not only a good clear voice, but also a controlled one which was not obviously my own, I looked around for something to drink. No fountain. No water. I saw Genius Baby over by the punch bowl (where else?), all prepared for punch and cookies afterward. Stuffing cookies and sandwiches. I strolled over.

"Care for some punch, sir?" he said politely.

"Why, thank you, sonny boy."

He actually handed me a cup and I thought: *The little Bastard is shaping up. Somebody has finally taught him some manners.*

Just then Miss Whitman was announcing that Reverend Perry was unable to be here today and that the invocation would now be given by the Reverend Birnham Woods. And would they all rise please and bow their heads? I belted down that cup of punch and hurried to take my position in front of the audience.

Two steps or three and I realized the truth with horror. No wonder Genius Baby had been so polite! Something, some diabolical and fiendish substance, was in that punch. It included a lot of alum to be sure, for my lips were already puckering and wildly out of control, as if I had just taken a belt of the essence of green persimmon. My eyes were smarting and fogging my dark glasses. My throat was burning and already my poor stomach was wincing and starting to growl. What to do?

I couldn't go back, ignoring the bowed heads of one and all, and just belt Genius Baby in the chops. Much as I wanted to—for when I looked back he was standing by the punch bowl grinning like a possum, and he fluttered his tongue at me in a silent Bronx cheer. A couple of restive heads were already bobbing up to see what was keeping me. Nothing to do but brazen it out. I opened the prayerbook and, offering a silent prayer of my own, began to read out loud:

> *O Lord Jesus Christ, who dost embrace all children with the arms of thy mercy, and dost make them living members of thy church; give them grace, we pray thee to stand fast in thy faith. . . .*

Try that one sometime with a mouth all shriveled up with alum.

That was as far as I got before Annie reached me, snatched off the glasses and gave me the look that kills.

"Son of a bitch!" she whispered. "You're drunk!"

It wasn't my place or the time to argue. I tried to twist my puckering, suffering lips into some sort of a grin. She slapped me so hard it sounded like a firecracker going off and my legs turned to rubber.

"You rotten bastard!" she was yelling now. "You always have to show up and spoil everything!"

The second blow was with her pocketbook. I protected myself as best I could, knocking her flat on the ass with the prayerbook, then fled to the nearest flowerbed where, my back to the uproar and confusion behind me, I barfed. Then, I jumped the hedge and ran off down the street as fast as I could go with various angry fathers in hot pursuit crying "Stop Thief!" Because, I suppose, there wasn't any other sensible cry to utter under the circumstances.

To Guess a Riddle, To Stumble on the Secret Name

A little past noon on a fine spring day. A man, the professor, is driving to school, tooling along the freeway.

"In his Porsche," she says.

I don't see where that's relevant. It's a detail we can do without.

"It's the most relevant thing about him," she says. "And it was half mine before the divorce."

Who's telling this story? I say.

"It's his story, but you go ahead and tell it anyway."

Okay, so the professor is driving along at a pretty good clip when all of a sudden this car passes him. A beat-up, rattly, old, gas-guzzling heap, pumping out a cloud of pollutants. With shoes and tin cans tied on the back and all the usual "Just Married" graffiti painted all over it. And then the car cuts him off. Swerves back into his lane and he damn near has to ride right up the back of it. So he leans on his horn. And then at the back window lo and behold there is the blushing bride, herself, wearing her bridal gown, a very pretty girl with wild bright eyes and a great big smile. And she is giving him the finger and calling him every name in the book.

She says: "How can he hear her?"

He's a lip reader. Everybody's reading lips these days.

She goes: "Read mine." Then: "Is that all there is to it? I mean, it's a pretty simple story for Mark. Brief and simple things just don't happen to him."

Well, what happens next is the guy in the heap, the groom I guess, cranks up and just leaves him in the dust and smoke. Must have been doing a hundred easy. Mark tries to tailgate him for a while. Notices that the muffler is hanging loose and about to fall off any minute. Then the Westside exit comes up and he has to slow down to turn off. And here, right behind him, comes a whole convoy of cars, all of them blowing their horns like crazy and chasing after the bride and groom.

He's already pulling into the college parking lot before he wonders what in the world the bride was doing in the back seat.

She says: "Everybody's got to be somewhere. Even a bride."

So, anyway, he teaches his classes and then has a couple of appointments at his office.

And she says—"Cute little flat-tummied coeds who all call him Mark and tell him how much they love learning about all these different things like minimalism and postmodern metafiction and stuff like that."

Don't be bitter.

She says: "Why not?"

So I shrug and go on: He picks up his mail and heads for home.

When he gets back to the freeway, on pure impulse, he decides to go in the other way to follow the direction the wedding party had been going. He doesn't know why, he just wants to. And that's how he happens to find it.

"Find what?" She asks.

A wedding cake. Notice that I did *not* say *the* wedding cake. Because there is nothing whatsoever to connect this particular wedding cake with that particular bride who gave him the finger some hours ago, just the resonance and synchronicity of things. But there it is, anyway, in the big middle of the grass median. Just sitting there—a perfect three-tiered wedding cake, undamaged, more like it was just *put there* than dropped or lost.

She says: "Purposefully abandoned, you might say."

Mark parks in the breakdown lane. And when there is a little space in the traffic he sprints across to the median. Chases away a couple of hungry crows. Then kneels down to get a good look at it. This cake has something weird about it. At first he can only *feel* the weirdness, but then he finally sees what it is. On top there is the usual candy bride, but there are also *two* little candy grooms. Two little candy grooms just standing there side by side.

"Maybe she was marrying Siamese twins," she says. Then: "I don't believe a word of it."

Mark didn't think anybody would. So he ran back to the car and got his Polaroid and took pictures. Here. Proof. See for yourself.

"I don't have to," she says, shaking her lovely head and sounding almost happy, smiling now as if she had suddenly guessed a riddle or stumbled on the secret name—Rumpelstiltskin!

She says: "It's the kind of thing that always happens to him. Mark's nasty little world is full of misery and mischief, and he likes to share it with other people."

Give the guy a break.

"I did already," she says, "one time too many."

Then with an abrupt vehemence, something close to fury, she says, "Don't you see? He wants to make trouble for us. The whole thing is a message to me. And the beauty of it is that he got you to deliver the message for him.

"And what's the message? Simple enough. That, divorce or no divorce, wedding cake or not, he'll never let me go."

You really hate him, don't you? I say, hoping that it's true, hoping I won't have to hear the answer that, in fact, I do.

"No," she is saying. "I don't hate him. I never did and I guess I never will."

The Pornographers

Listen to this, will you? Here I am talking to the Sheriff of Quincy County, a lean, good-looking guy name of Dale Lewis, curly, pepper-and-salt hair, carefully cut, a neat khaki uniform and wearing designer glasses. (There goes your old stereotype. He's New South all the way. Uses the word *nuance* as if he owned it.) Here, believe it or not, verbatim from my tape machine, is what he is telling me:

"There is no escaping the moral climate of the modern world. It comes here, too, of all places, in all of its twisted fury and madness. Maybe there was a time, a long time ago, long before my time, when you and I could just sit here at a great distance from the throbbing heart of things and thank the good Lord for all our blessings and the difference. Let those big Yankee cities go ahead and drown in their own cesspools. We could sit right here in safety and virtuously point and say 'I told you so.' But not anymore. We have our very own cesspool cities now—Atlanta, Miami, Birmingham, Jacksonville, Houston, New Orleans (though New Orleans was always a place of corruption, from the earliest Spanish and French days; New Orleans was Third World before that was either a term or a concept). And all of the plagues and diseases of the times have been visited upon us. . . ."

Joey Singletree is the name and True Crime is my game. You know what I mean. I hover in thin air like a lazy buzzard waiting for a meal. World that we live in, sooner rather than later somebody will shoot up a school yard or an abortion clinic. Someone will torture and murder a couple of kids or some old lady living alone. Sooner rather than later there will be another abduction and rape. Something maybe to raise the eyebrows a little. Something that may turn out to be good material and I can get at least an article, maybe even a book out of it.

It's a living.

Downside is that they don't pay a whole lot for this kind of stuff unless it involves celebrities or bona fide public figures or a novel gimmick. And the talk shows are killing the market. How can the printed word compete? Beats me.

Anyhow, I was tired of the hustle. Up to here with all the usual urban sex and violence. And I joined together an idea and a yearning: the yearning being to get back home to Florida and soak up a little sunshine and get paid for it; the idea to see how crime is playing out in the boonies, the heartland. Is it better or worse out there? Either way I've got a little story.

So I put together a half-ass proposal, part of which follows:

"These days the world comes galloping at them whether the people in the heartland like it or not. How do they deal with all that? How do they live with it?

"To be sure, this is all small potatoes when measured against the slaughterhouse of this dying century or against the life and times of crime-ridden urban America. Where, other than vigorously protecting a few of the rich and the famous, the police are mostly reduced to keeping more or less accurate statistics on the crimes being committed all around them and hoping to stay healthy and to live long enough to collect their ample pensions. When I was living in Brooklyn, my crummy and expensive little apartment was repeatedly burglarized, picked clean of everything but the cockroaches. A cop finally came around to look. His best offer was to sell me a little printed copy of a prayer to St. Christopher.

"It has been open warfare out there in urban America for half a century; and the people, like combat veterans in all the wars, have become accustomed to it. Atrocities, acts of terrorism and extraordinary violence are shrugged off, are viewed as part of the basic price for contemporary civilization.

"The numbers show that provincial America is not immune anymore. Not safe from atrocious crimes, not from drugs, not from AIDS, not from any of the habitual sorrows of Fat City.

"I have an idea that this news cheers up, warms the hearts of the folks who are stuck in urban America. It lifts their spirits to hear stories of sick stuff in the deep boonies.

"Maybe there is a story there. Maybe there is an audience for it."

My editor, a bright young hustler (originally from Nashville, Tennessee, though you would never guess it now) and self-promoter known as "Sparky" (chip off the block of "Old Sparky") to his few friends and many enemies in the publishing world, responded to my proposal with a Fax to my agent: "Frankly, I think this is a heavy-breathing, bull-shit proposal. But it has some faint possibilities—provincial sex and violence and racism and plenty of corny local color. All kinds of the right stuff. I can't see how even our boy Joey could screw it up too much. So, as long as you people are not even thinking about serious money, I can't see any real harm in going ahead with it. Let's have lunch at Daniel's (your treat) and work out the sordid details."

Deborah, my agent, wisely urged me to take what I could get. "Don't piss it away," she suggested. "You are not likely to get anything better right now. But don't make a lifetime labor of love out of it. Just get down there, have a little look around, ask a few questions, then sit down and write it. Sparky is not looking for art. Art is for kids. And they are not looking for truth and beauty, either—at least not from somebody like you, Joey. The most they are hoping for is a little fun and games. Maybe a chuckle or two, a tear in one eye if you get lucky.

"What I am counseling is—don't fuck up this time. *Capisce?*"

All of which is by way of introduction to the story of the Little Princess of Paradise Springs, Florida; though, strictly speaking she is from Quincy County since she and her family lived well outside the city limits in a mobile home.

And here is the Sheriff, Dale Lewis, telling it to me in his own words:

The Little Princess, blond and blue-eyed, with skin like fresh cream, looked like a movie star. Like she could easily grow up and be one. Like she already was one. A truly beautiful little girl, maybe twelve years old. She attended Quincy County Elementary School. Which is where this story begins. Because it was there that she kept falling asleep, dead, deep asleep in the classroom. Her teacher and the school nurse finally decided it was something more serious than a bad habit and took her over to the emergency room of the hospital. Where the doctor examined her and concluded that she was exhausted and also that she had probably been sexually abused by someone.

The Little Princess said nothing. No complaint. No cooperation. Wouldn't answer any questions.

Following procedure, then, the County sent a social worker out to where she lived to evaluate the situation. Social worker didn't come up with a whole lot. Seems that the Princess had a whole family— menagerie would be more like it—living out there in that glorified trailer. Brothers and sisters, cousins of various kinds, an aged grandfather, various and sundry "uncles" who came and went, and her mother who may or may not (no good evidence) have been turning tricks with the "uncles."

County looked into it a little more closely and came to the tentative conclusion that the real means of support for this whole family network was the Little Princess. That what she was doing was starring in some pornographic movies that somebody was making, probably over in Gainesville.

That was the best educated guess of the County.

Wasn't a whole hell of a lot we could do about it. I won't bore you with the complexities of evidentiary details except to point out that we would have had a terrible time, almost impossible, of convicting anyone in the absence of a statement or admission from the Princess. Unless and until we could actually catch some real people in the act of making one of these movies. Sounds easy, but it's not so easy if the criminals are moderately careful and about half smart.

Not so easy, either, if you have a plate full of local duties and obligations and limited resources.

Well, we finally came up with a guy (one of the "uncles") that we were fairly certain was running the whole operation. But, my friend, it has been a long time and a lot of Supreme Court decisions since "fairly certain" has been enough to bring anybody to trial, let alone to convict. That may have changed just a little bit, time will tell, since the professional feminoids have discovered the evils and dangers of pornography. We'll see about that.

Meanwhile some months went by. Every so often the Princess would be taken to the emergency room and then admitted to the hospital for a little rest and recuperation. Then, as far as we could tell, back on the job. All at night, of course. Among other things, the Princess wasn't getting enough sleep.

What was happening was that the Princess would get worn out and strung out and then check into the county hospital, like a health spa, to recover her youthful bloom. Under the circumstances, the hospital should have been getting a piece of the action. Points on the gross of the movies she was making.

Anyway, the hospital finally got tired of the whole thing. The hospital administrator and a couple of the doctors called me to come and talk about it. They wanted something done. I patiently explained the legal problems to them.

Isn't there anything at all you can do? they asked.

Sure enough, I said. I can do a number of things. But none of them are legal.

Like what?

You don't want to know. You don't need to know. And I don't want to hear one word from you all about it, even at second or third hand, even hearsay. You are ready to have this stopped? I will stop it for you.

You aren't going to kill anybody, are you, Sheriff?

Probably not. Not unless I have to.

About a week later they (and everybody else) could read in the paper the curious story of the man who was found dozing and dead drunk, sitting at the wheel of a stolen car in a rest area out on the interstate. He had enough alcohol in his system, together with serious traces of cocaine, to be embalmed. He was carrying a concealed weapon and he had a bunch of highly illegal weapons—sawed-off shotguns and submachine guns—in the trunk, together with enough drugs to open his own pharmacy and enough stolen goods and valuables to start a jewelry store. He had no logical or coherent explanation for any of it. He got a fair and speedy trial. And then the son-of-a-bitch was sent off to Raiford for forever and a day, thus ending the film career of the Little Princess, but improving her general health and well-being.

What happened to the Little Princess?

I was afraid you would ask that, the Sheriff says. The correct answer is—God only knows. It is more or less of a free country, and those folks packed up and moved on. Moved out to the West Coast, I heard. Where she probably has resumed her movie career and is hoping to be discovered some fine day and to become the next Kim Basinger or Michelle Pfeiffer. And who knows? Maybe she will.

After my interview I jot down the following observation about the Sheriff in my notebook: "He looks a little bit like Kevin Costner, if Costner had harder angles and edges. The etched lines around his pale blue eyes seem to come from a squinting but unblinking vision of terrible things.

"What about him? Is he tried and true, a force for moral order? Not quite. Not hardly. I know for a fact that he is on the take. Nothing big time. Just a little of this and a little of that. Waiting for the big one, the drug deal, to come along. I know, too, that Dale Lewis has a terrible temper and has been known to vent it on the flesh and bones of rogues and rascals who fall into his hands for care and keeping. Who dares to blame him? There are scumbags everywhere these days. He prefers to encourage them (especially those of the colored persuasion) to keep on moving, far beyond the boundaries of Quincy County. Keeping the peace. As they say."

Reader, you may be wondering how come you never read my piece about child porn in the provinces. What happened was I got a Fax from Deborah. It went like this:

"Joey, here is good news and bad news. Sit down in a nice, comfortable chair. Then read and digest what I have to say here. And then—*and only then*—give me a call so we can discuss the details.

"Let me get the bad news out of the way first. It could be worse, though you may not see it that way at the moment. First things first. Stop whatever you are doing with the piece about the Little Princess. Fact is you do not have a magazine anymore to publish it. They have just been purchased by a multinational European communications company. The story will be in tomorrow's *Times*. If you still read the *Times* and haven't gone native on us. . . . First thing these rich Eurotrash are going to do is to cancel all the ongoing contracts. They are dropping everything including your little masterpiece.

"Joey, the best I can do for you is maybe to fix it so you will get your full fee, not just the kill fee, for this one. The deal is you quit the project right now. They will 'own' the project, for whatever that may be worth. Not much. Anyway, you send them something, anything you've got—notes and draft pages, if any. Just something they can stick in their files. Where they will be buried and forgotten. Send them the stuff and I will get you your check. And that will be that.

"Now the good news. Sparky? Funny you should ask. This sudden corporate development caught our boy completely by surprise and unprepared. Pants down around his ankles. He is out of the business, at least for the time being. Tells me he has an old friend (you can believe that, a friend, if you want to), former college roommate who owns a little gourmet restaurant up in Portland, Maine. Our Sparky will soon be working there as a waiter while he tries to get his act together. A lot of people in the business will probably be making the trip up to Portland in the summer season. For all the pleasures of Maine and the special pleasure of being waited on by Sparky.

"Truth is, if you have enough enemies in this business you can always survive. People in publishing need somebody to hate, somebody who is (probably) a worse person than they are. Sparky will find a new niche for himself all in due time. I'm betting everyone that he'll be back at the Hamptons by the following summer. Back again and more obnoxious than ever."

I pack my bag and head for the airport. Back to Brooklyn. Hear my prayer, St. Christopher.

And you, little blond girl with blue eyes, Princess of downhome Porn, I wish you luck in all your adventures. One way or another we are all in the same line of work. The least we can do is admit it, from time to time, and hope for something better.

A Letter That Will Never Be Written

Spring of the year 1626. The place is London. The person here, the young man, is employed for the time being as a kind of clerk, secretary and companion to Robert Carey, newly made (by the new King) Earl of Monmouth. Carey is now an old man, a cousin to the late Queen Elizabeth who in his day was a courtier, a soldier, an inveterate gambler. His young clerk is only just down from Oxford. Where he has developed certain Puritan inclinations, not enough so that his spirit is possessed and afire with zeal, but, rather, enough so that he is somewhat uneasy with the Earl, with the City, and, of course, with himself.

Ah, Priscilla . . . she of skyblue eyes and white straight teeth and of the softly, lightly pouting lips . . . lips looking to be as fresh and sweet to taste as finest ripe fruit candied with Barbary sugar and sprinkled with wine . . . she of smooth unblemished skin the color of good ivory, of Devon cream . . . her dark hair clean and well brushed . . . she always dressed in the new plain and neat and sober styles, in gray or black accented with snowy splashes of starched white collar and cuffs . . . she always without any foolish jewelry or geegaws . . . she the roses of whose cheeks are painted there by nature, not by art . . .

How much now he would offer up anything (everything) he has or has hopes for to be the wildly lucky one who will unbutton and untie and unlace, who will peel and set free (O whitely shining!) the essential and mysterious her from those so proper layers of clothing!

She for whom, and for the sake of whose undoubted pleasures (so whitely smoothly cool and graceful) he would be glad and be blithe to dress himself, also, in shades of black and white . . . and be like any other common solemn Puritan fellow . . . if that be what's required, then so be it . . . if only he could have and hold, could feast (lawfully) famished eyes upon the wondrous banquet of her . . . all that whiteness . . . all those secret places . . .

Except for the clenching of fists by his sides, he lies still. As if he were stark dead. Unmoving, though his spirit is restless as new-caught flame in kindling wood, though his innards are wincing and seething and murmuring from much abuse. Lies atop the bed in a chamber lit only by the dying moon. Trying to fall asleep. Has heard the Bellman pass by on his rounds softly calling the hours. Can count the strokes of every bell from here to the farthest corner of London Wall. A little while ago he heard voices, a man and a woman, then the two of them laughing out loud (is that what has raised and wakened the memory of Priscilla?), then running feet in the dark. Dogs at the Earl's gate barked. He has not slept a wink yet.

Only this morning the Earl had private business to attend to and so set him free, gave him leave to spend the day as he pleased. Oh, why did he not go and join the Godly people, the Puritans, who gather daily in and around Curriers' Hall? From which, and in that good company, he might have gone to bring some succor, some food and drink, to the prisoners at Newgate. Or perhaps to the sick at the Hospital of St. Bartholomew in Smithfield. Or, as far out as the north road beyond Bishopgate to Bedlam. Where they keep mad folk. These Puritan people bring food and drink and medicines and clothing (together with prayers and psalms) to any and all whose need is great. They will even go and stand at the edge of the gallows. And will pull the legs and break the necks of some poor hanging, strangling wretch, for the sake of a quick death, if he has neither friends nor family to perform those offices. When Plague comes calling in the City in summertime, they will not flee away from it as others do. They will remain here, whole in faith and careless in charity, to do what can be done to help the living and the dead.

Well, if not works of humble love and charity, he could at least have gone forth to improve and instruct himself. Maybe—it being not yet Ascension Sunday and therefore the Easter Term of the law courts being still in busy session—he could have gone to Westminster Hall to observe them. Which at the least would have pleased his father and his brother who have been urging him to take up the study of Law at the Inns of Court.

Well (he could tell them) *I have in fact spent this day in the company of certain scholars of the Law, though we went to no courts and spent no time or energy upon points of Law.*

Trying to forget what he has left undone that he ought to have done, to still his shame and contempt, to ease himself into sleep, he composes a letter to Priscilla. She whom he sometimes believes (especially after a time of shameful waste and debauchery, such as last night) he loves with all his heart and soul. Never mind that her dowry would scarcely buy him a new pair of boots. He would marry her and cherish her for love alone, if he could. Then she would take him into her cool, smooth arms. And soon he would be clean and whole again.

Believe me, it can be done, he imagines writing to her. Even at this late day and age of the world. After all, the old Earl admits that he married for love and not for gain and ambition. It cost him dearly at the time. But now he says that he has never had any good reason to regret it.

No, that is not entirely the case. At first he had good cause to rue his action. For Queen Elizabeth (he says) was in a fury with him. Never mind troubles and affairs of state, she was never too busy not to watch over the lives (like a mother hen with the chicks, he says) of her Court. And when any of them, and most especially those who, like the Earl, were her kinfolk, would marry without her consultation and permission, why she fell into a terrible rage. And, says the Earl, the Queen would never, never have given him her permission to marry out of love and affection rather than for advantage.

"Why would that be?" I asked him.

Because she considered a disadvantageous marriage by one of her kin to be unworthy. And so insulting to her. Because the Queen always cultivated a most strictly practical kind of wisdom in these matters. If he did not marry for gain of advantage, then where would his necessary resources come from? Sooner or later, directly or indirectly, it would fall upon her to support him. If she did not, then when he fell on bad time, as he certainly would without money or land for cushions, he would blame her and become, instead of a cousin who could be trusted, yet another discontented subject. From her view, it seemed clear that one way or another it would be at her expense if he chose to marry for love and affection.

"Besides which," said the Earl, "since it was not ever possible for her to marry for love, or indeed, never really possible for her to marry at all, she was injured as well as insulted by it."

Better that Robert Carey should have married wisely (meaning richly). Allowing for affection to grow and bloom with time. And no matter if it didn't. For husband and wife and family would soon be too busy in service to Queen and country to concern themselves with such trivial matters.

There came a time, not long after his marriage, when there was an encounter between them. Which, as he tells me, was altogether stormy.

Robert Carey had been asked by the King of the Scots to bring a private message to the Queen. This was in '93 in December. He had news. Rode down hard and fast on those wintery days from the fortress at Berwick. Arriving and finding the Court at Hampton Court on the day after Christmas, St. Stephen's Day.

"Tired and dirty as I was," he told me, "I ran into the Presence Chamber. Found the lords and ladies dancing. But the Queen was not there. My father, Lord Chamberlain in those days, went directly to the Queen to tell her I was there with my message from the King. She willed him, then, to bring my message and any letters to her.

"This was a bad sign for my case. Indeed I had no case at all unless and until I could meet with the Queen.

"So I lied to my own father, saying King James had especially ordered that no one else, under any circumstances whatever, should deliver these messages to the Queen. Or to be present until they had been delivered.

" 'Ah, son, I pity you, then,' my father said. 'For the Queen is in her worst rage at the news of your marriage.'

"Dirty and bedraggled, I went at once to her chamber. Knelt at her feet and presented her the letters. She held them, yet did not trouble to break the seals. Instead she stood up and paced back and forth, cursing myself and my wife and the day we were born. Heaping imprecations upon my head like so many hot coals.

"No one there except her guards. Who were standing, struggling to be waxwork figures and to seem to hear not a word. Which was exactly as I had wanted it, hoped for. For she would never have exploded in the presence of the Court. No, she would simply have spurned and ignored me.

And probably have been more inwardly furious than ever at the sight of my face. But by seeing her all alone I gave her apt occasion to vomit up her rage at me. And so, perhaps, if I acted wisely enough, to dispose of it.

"I continued to kneel, humble on both knees, before the throne, until spent and breathless, she returned to sit herself down there. She was tearing at the seals of the letters when I first spoke.

" 'Ma'am, you are yourself the fault of my marriage,' I told her.

"Well, now. That made her pause. She had had her pleasure and had spent her wrath and her breath. I immediately added that if she had only shown me any form of favor, then I would never have had any cause to leave her and the Court. Added that since she was clearly the chief cause of my unfortunate marriage, I would not rise up off my knees and leave, not now or ever, until I had obtained a pardon from her and had kissed her hand.

"After a moment, while she squinted her eyes and frowned at me and I sweated drops the size of beans, she suddenly laughed out loud and offered me her hand to kiss. And it was all over and done with. I was back in her favor and good grace. And I remained at Court for all of the Christmas until Shrovetide came and put an end to pleasure and festivity. The Court's no place to be in Lent. When the competition among courtiers is all to do with fasting and self-denial.

"Of course my wife could never come to Court while the Queen lived. And, indeed, her name was not to be mentioned there. But we lived happily and well enough on the Borders and never regretted what we had done.

"And the paradox of it, lad, is this. In the end my marriage has proved to be the most fortunate and advantageous thing in my life. For in the reign of King James, and in this new reign as well, it has been no advantage at all to have been among the kinfolk of the late Queen. But since the little Prince Charles was well and lovingly cared for by my wife (when no other lady in England wished to take on that burden, fearing he would die in his youth) and the Prince came to love her like one of his own kin, why my profit has been considerable. Thus I owe all such offices and honors as I have held to a woman I married out of love.

"Still," he told me, "I thank God that my encounter with the Queen went well. For I often think that if I had failed or slipped on that one occasion, it may well be that I would never, never have seen the Queen's face, or known her good favor, again. Never!"

Forgive me, my dearest Priscilla, for retailing these old stories of old people. Such things are my daily bread now. The Earl talks to me and I must listen.

Often I only seem to be listening. I set my face and nod and smile. And find myself thinking of home. And always when my mind wanders and I remember home, I think of you.

Does that trouble you—to know that I often think of you? I hope not. For what should I do, what would I be and become without the thought of you? Always the memory and picture of you calms and restores my foolish spirit.

Do you sometimes think of me?

When I think of life at home, so plain and simple and yet inimitable and irreplaceable, I grow weary of this busy, noisy city with all its restless newfangledness, with all its irremediable follies and vices.

Most especially weary of it all tonight. After a day devoted to the pursuit of folly. Which day began with gray wet air, with a dense, lazy fog over the river and half of the town. Day which began early when he gathered together a bundle of things—some of his best books, a good clean gown from his college days, a small jeweled dagger which had been in his family from better days and times—and hurried away to deal and bargain with the pawnbrokers of Fetter Lane. To convert these things into money for his hungry, gaping purse.

Certainly, he continues, there are very many pious, Godly believers, brothers and sisters, here in the City. And as often as I am able to, I try to spend my free time in their good company. I have been to the Dutch and the Huguenot churches for their services and sermons. Which churches, being for foreigners, are not so strictly required to follow the latest papistical practices which are everywhere more and more infecting and corrupting our English church—by which I refer to the vanities of vestments and candles and organ music and prayers recited by the book and all suchlike signs. Why, Priscilla, I tell you that many of the churches here these days, and especially in Westminster, close by the Court, need only to say their offices in Latin to be precisely the same as the Romans.

And everyone knows how the new young Queen is permitted to have her French priests say the Mass in St. James Palace.

It is said by some elders that the terrible Plague this past year was the punishment of God on us all for permitting such superstitious excrescences to continue.

I am compelled to attend devotions in our parish church with the Earl. I lack the courage to say no and to take the consequences. Though I fear he would never understand and would attribute my attitude to bad digestion—which is the Earl's explanation for most knotty spiritual and theological problems. But, whenever I can, I have slipped away to the haven of Curriers' Hall, to attend the meetings there.

How can you lie to the woman?

Closest and nearest you have yet come to the doorway to Curriers' Hall has been a jolly place called the Sun Tavern. Which is no more than a bowshot from the Hall, on Little Wood Street. And you did not meet a single pious, Godly Brother or Sister at the Sun Tavern.

Tell the truth. That though in intellection and disputation you have often (safely enough) favored the arguments of these purest of the Protestants—if partly because full acceptance of their premises does put an end to intellection and debate, still you have never much relished their styles and fashions. The company of these people is all too often as tedious and dreary as it is solemn. Admit that although the idle repetition of rituals and ceremonies seems to have little or nothing to do with the truth of death and resurrection, with the good news that our salvation (when we are all unworthy) has been earned for us by the precious suffering of God's only Son, even so you do delight in the music and beauty and orderly service of the Church of England. You cannot believe that it is harmful to your own soul, especially since you are undeceived as to any merit in it.

And it can hardly work much mischief on the Earl's soul; for he is as armored as a turtle in its shell or a snail in its castle by his ignorance and indifference.

"Well," he has told you when you dared to speak up about these things, "I cannot speak of such deep things as the efficacy of our forms of worship as measured against those of the papists and Puritans and so forth and so on. I attend services because it will cost me money if I do not. And because it is an occasion to see how my old friends are faring. Where else would I see most of them these days?

"I sometimes wonder if God ever feels as old as I do. If He does, I can assure you, He yawns and shrugs away most of these theological problems."

Why not tell the woman you love the truth?

As, for instance: Priscilla, truly I had every intention of trying to live wisely and well whilst I was in London. I knew the dangers and temptations which awaited me. And, after all, I have enjoyed the privilege of reading and studying the great philosophers of all the ages of man.

Nevertheless, in spite of my education and best intentions, I have dedicated myself chiefly to eating and drinking, to gaming and whoring. And the only checks upon my immoderate appetites have proved to be not philosophical at all, but rather the limits of my body and the emptiness of my purse.

If my purse were not as empty as my stomach at this moment (for I confess that I was forced to kneel and to vomit in the gutter before I reached home tonight), I would most likely even now be found in the ample arms of a large, handsome young woman who's called Kate of Turnbull Street. A member of a well-known sisterhood in this City, the Maids of Lambeth Marsh.

I suppose I should be grateful and consider it good fortune that I had spent all my money before I encountered Sweet Kate. Else I should have to pay for my pleasure with the itch of the crabs and the pain of the French Pox.

Yet perhaps it would have been a worthwhile bargain. For my poor, tormented, roused and untested groin does ache with a pain as if I had been kicked by a horse. If my member could speak for itself, it would groan and howl. It would argue in French that surely the French Pox could not hurt worse than this.

This Sweet Kate promised me that if I would lie with her for the rest of tonight, I would never forget or regret it.

She stated to me that I would experience such shiverings and flutterings, such indescribably delightful and inspiring sensations that I would imagine that a wild bird had been startled and flushed from deep within me and had flown away to freedom out of my puckering arsehole.

Pardon me, dear Priscilla, but these are the exact words and persuasions Sweet Kate of Turnbull Street used in the presentation of her argument. Proving, to be sure, that she has never studied the great philosophers of all the ages of man. Yet proving also, as I reckon it, that she can endure and thrive in this world very well without them.

Ah, Priscilla, dearest Priscilla, I do here and now confess that I am no more than a beast and a fool. An ape disguised in a scholar's gown. Except that I pawned my best gown this morning to pay for my vices.

Priscilla, if you would only marry me, I am certain I could be saved from myself. With you as my wife and helpmate and bedfellow, I could take heart again and be renewed and reformed by your goodness.

And your beauty . . .

Now, I imagine you will most sweetly and modestly deny that you have beauty. You will remind me that youth and beauty fade sooner than summer flowers and, anyway, that the attractions of beauty are a snare and a delusion.

And I will have to agree with you. I will agree.

Priscilla, I will gladly agree with anything you think or say. If only you will agree to marry me.

If only you could . . . now . . . come to me as lawful wedded wife in this dark chamber. . . . Shuck and shed those layers of dark, plain, sober, decent, black and white clothing . . . be naked as a trout in my bed . . . all shining with sweaty lust like a wild nymph . . . oh never mind what that is and who they were . . . it's enough for you to know that they were very lively young women of ancient times . . .

Anyway we could wrestle in love's immemorial embraces insatiate until this bed collapses into kindling wood and pillows and mattresses burst open to make a storm of feathers (like a hundred startled pheasants) in this room!

No. Best not to write any of that. Or even to think it.

Tell her how the trouble today was this. That you were to meet some friends you had known at Oriel who are now at Middle Temple. So, out of vanity and without sufficient fear of the Devil in your heart, you rose and washed yourself, then dressed yourself in your best clothes. Including a very expensive new pair of shoes. One of which, I deeply regret to report, ran away from me and its mate and is even now out there lost in the dark somewhere. Shoes of the newest style with red cork heels and with elaborate rosettes and silver buckles. At home the children would throw stones at me on account of those shoes alone.

Then you went to Fetter Lane to pawn your stuff and to fill your purse.

At which precise time, as if in a sign from Nature, herself, the wind shifted, the fog lifted, the sky cleared. And it was a glorious sunny morning in the City.

And off you went to find your friends and to spend the day with them. Each and all of you like any other fine young gentlemen of City or Court without so much as a single doubt or cloud of worry trapped in your cheerful skull.

You must understand, Priscilla, that it was not in any way such an unusual day for such a fellow as I.

First thing, while others were busy with their arts and crafts, or buying or selling, or learning their trades, we occupied ourselves with bowling. And I am pleased to be able to say that I won wagers against all of the others. Which (I'm sorry to say) proved to be my last net income of the day.

Afterwards we went to a pleasant tavern to refresh ourselves with some adequate cream cakes and ale. And then and there to try our skill at some common games of chance. And either my luck deserted me for a more worthy player or one of my friends (who shall remain nameless) had himself a fine pair of Fulham dice. No matter. In either case I lost and lost somewhat more than I had gained at bowls.

By then it was nearly dinner time. And nothing would do but that we, a crew of gallants if ever there was one, must take ourselves to the celebrated Horn on the Hoop. Which is the most excellent tavern on Fleet Street. Where you will find many of the most excellent rogues and knaves of City and Court gathered to dine well and to drink deep and puff upon their silver tobacco pipes.

The weather having turned so bright and balmy, we paid something more than is usual to be served our dinner in the garden under a rich canopy of leaves. Ate our dinner, then smoked a pipe or two while we strolled back and forth and argued among ourselves what could be the best way to waste the afternoon.

Time on our hands. For we all agreed that the next important event of the day, not counting supper, would be when we came to the New Exchange between five and six o'clock, before the shops close there. To see what ladies in coaches (fresh from the China Houses, no doubt) were there. For these ladies, it is said, and we were willing to believe it, are only one story higher and better than whores. And come to the New Exchange for a different sort of marketing than was ever intended for that place.

Well, someone wanted to go next to see a stage play at the Fortune—which lies beyond the wall, outside Cripplegate, between Whitecross Street and Golding Lane. Another argued that the Hope, across the river, would be the better choice. I spoke up then for the Globe, but was hooted down. Because they did not wish to see any play that might be so well-spoken and well-acted that they might be seriously tempted to listen to it.

Out came the Fulham dice again to settle it. And so we hired wherries and crossed the river. Our disputes about drama had been a waste of time; for it was the day for the bears at the Hope.

The bears were old, but nevertheless had the bloody best of the dogs. Who were a mangy lot and deserved what became of them.

Now, Priscilla, I must tell you that these places—playhouses, bear gardens, bowling alleys, cockpits, etc.—are every bit as wicked as the pious authors claim them to be. They attract a great crowd of wicked people. And the only thing to close them down and scatter the crowds is the Plague. Which was very busy here last summer, carrying crowds of wicked souls swiftly out of this world. And not merely the wicked either. It fell as hard upon the just as on the unjust. Perhaps the harder—for the just are always fewer in number.

Indeed, I have to tell you my best judgment is that, Plague or no Plague, there is an inexhaustible supply of wicked folk in London. Quick as they are rooted up they spring back again. Like weeds. And flourish like weeds. London is the right place, which proves there's no answer to King David's question—"Why do the ways of the wicked prosper?"

The wicked will be here and will continue to prosper until Judgment Day.

I suppose I must count myself among them. Perhaps that means I may prosper yet.

After we wearied of watching lazy bears disposing of cowardly dogs, we left the Hope to hold another council. And determined that we needed some drink to restore our equilibrium. Which commodity (I mean strong drink of every kind) is never in short supply over there on the south bank of the Thames.

Now he recalls that, before it became too inwardly foggy and embarrassing to remember much, they found themselves seated at a large table in The Cardinal's Hat. An excellent and commodious place not far from the Bridge and close by the Bishop of Winchester's Palace and the prison named the Clink. A place full of travelers (for it serves as an inn as well as a tavern) as well as a flock of every kind of odd Southwark bird. A place most popular with the very best sluts and drabs of that neighborhood—the kind who dress themselves as well or better than any Court ladies. And who can look as pure and haughty as the wives of Bishops.

Soon we were as cheerful and content as can be, trading the stalest of quips and jests. As if these things were the fruits of deep study, as if they were shards of golden wisdom. And all of which were no more than the worn-out lewd and merry tales of such jesters as Solomon's Marcoflus, of Howleglas, of Skelton and Tarleton and Armin.

Priscilla, here is a jest that I told. It was one I had read in an old jest book, but it delighted them no end, as if I had invented it on the spot.

There were three gentlemen drinking in a tavern. And at this tavern the tapster was a fair young woman. And the more they drank, the fairer and younger she became.

Well, she said she would let each of them kiss her once. And then they discussed what might be done about it. "I cannot see," one says, "how this good woman can give pastime and pleasure to all three of us unless we are to divide and share her in three parts."

"Well," says another, "if we could do that, I would claim her head and fair face so that I might always kiss her."

"Ha!" says the second. "I'll take her sweet breasts and her heart. For there lies pleasure, and also the place of her love and affection."

"God's wounds, fellows," says the third, "you have left me nothing but her buttocks and her nether parts. But I shall not complain. I am content, believe me, truly content."

So when they later rose to leave the tavern and go home, this third and last fellow suddenly seized the tapster and kissed her full upon her lips. "Why, what on earth are you doing, man?" cries the first man. "You have just kissed the part that belongs to me!" "O pardon, a hundred pardons, please," says the third in reply. "In all fairness and justice you are now welcome to kiss my part of her, yourself."

Such laughter from one and all you would have thought I was the direct and lineal descendant of the famous Will Somers. Who was Great King Harry's favorite fool.

O Priscilla, I would gladly be your fool and even wear motley and a cap and bells to prove it, if only I could kiss any least part of you!

Pastime and good company.

But not for long.

One young scholar, the first to desert, departed with a fair-haired young Southwark slut. To take a chamber in the inn, as if they were man and wife, for the rest of the night.

As he left us, he raised his hand in benediction.

"Not good night," he called, "but rather, God send us a joyful Resurrection!"

"Amen."

"What does he mean to say?" I asked.

"Ah, country mouse," said one to me, "you have been spared the sad knowledge of it so far. For that was the most common form of farewell last summer, in the worst of the Plague. When you were never sure to see each other again."

"A kind of a jest, then?"

"Less so than you might think. I have it on good authority that there have been a number of deaths by the Plague and spotted fever already this year."

"And the worst, as usual, is here in Southwark," another added.

"Well, then," says the first. "We must drink deeply to ward off the infection of it. Never mind this beer and ale, these small wines and hot wines. Not even sack or canary will do. No, sir, it is cordials and spirits that will laugh Plague and pestilence to scorn."

And so, Priscilla, they elected to introduce me to the incomparable experience of a certain drink made part of malmsey and in equal part of burning waters which have been three times distilled and flavored with wormwood leaves and anise seeds. It is called absinthe. And when you drink it you are in real hazard that you may stun your conscience to silence and even forget your own Christian name.

So we soon lost yet another of our brave company. A most promising young scholar of the Law. Who will likely be a judge someday. But who for now was dead asleep at the table and would not wake up when it came time to leave. So, after appropriating his purse to spare him the shame of being robbed by strangers, we used the contents of it to hire ourselves a mercenary coach to cross the Bridge and come into London again. Leaving him quietly snoring there at The Cardinal's Hat.

And then the afternoon, and the evening until full dark, begins flashing in bright disorderly pieces in his memory (seeming to be memory even as it was happening) like a shower of playing cards shuffled and scattered on a tabletop.

Maybe there were cards. Real cards played. For his purse seemed to be so much lighter than it had been.

Fists on table . . . loud voices singing . . . blackjack leather tankards and flaring of rush lights in another and much plainer place . . .

Voices loud in anger and then outside in the dark alley and himself laughing and pissing against the wall while there were fists and daggers and cudgels all around him.

"Run!" one shouts.

And he runs and staggers leaving yells and someone groaning behind him in the dark.

And now there are only two of them left. Himself and another whose face he cannot now recall. In part because it is a bloody face and partly covered by a cloth. His own bloody also, nose bleeding freely. But laughing and laughing and not (yet) a pinch of pain . . .

Turning a corner they see the Watch coming. Run for safety, ignoring the shouts and footsteps behind them. Running, for it is far past curfew now.

And then alone in some poor place . . . it would surely be in or about Turnbull Street. Weeping like a child for sake of a lost shoe. While a round-faced handsome woman called Kate cleans the dried blood from his face with a soothing wet cloth.

"There, there," she says, "that's a fine young gentleman if ever I saw one. And all will be well. All will be well."

Then next penniless and yet somehow, like a dog, finding his way in darkness to Blackfriars and to home. Stopping to kneel and puke in the gutter. Managing to waken the Porter (who is not much surprised) and to walk straight enough through the gate. But crawling on all fours up the dark stairway and *(quietly, quietly, for God's sake quietly, please!)* into his chamber.

To lie atop the bed and not to sleep.

To wish that a certain Priscilla from his own home village in Devon would come here now and rest one smooth cool palm on his sweaty forehead. And forgive him and absolve him.

Until this night, Priscilla, I never understood the madness of people in the time of the Plague. Could not comprehend how so many, infected and healthy alike, could give themselves over to drunkenness and dissipation and lechery. Or how the infected rejoiced to carry their sores and breath out among the healthy so that all could be infected together and would die together.

The City's a fearsome, terrible-like place in this sweet season with summer and the black Plague coming soon.

Priscilla, London is old, old, old. And weary as all old things are weary. There is much building of tenements and of great houses for great men and of shops and places for businesses and commerce. But the only new public building here for years and years is the Banquet House, so well-proportioned, which was made for King James at Whitehall.

A banquet house is all.

Churches are old and rot and fall into decay. St. Paul's is crumbling. And still, with all the wealth in this City, no man has paid to have the steeple rebuilt. The steeple which burned in the year my master, the old Earl, was born.

London is old. England is old and weary. There is no health or hope here.

Let us then make a new beginning. Let us leave and go to the New World. Which has not yet been corrupted by the generations of sinful men.

Marry me and let us go to find new lives and new hope. We can never do any good or be contented here.

Pictures a fine stout ship in a fair breeze. Himself on board. Richly yet soberly dressed. Standing beside him, holding his hand, beautiful though clad in plainest black and white, blue eyes shining, there stands his new young wife. Behind them the coastline of England falls below the horizon and out of sight forever. As they sail south, then southwestward, smoothly, smoothly carried by a steady breeze.

He is asleep at last.

He must be and must be dreaming, too. For a pounding on the door of his chamber wakes him up with a start. He sits up. And next the lad called Geoffrey, a groom or turnspit, someone in the household of no importance at all except (occasionally) to run with messages, the lad enters grinning broadly.

How many times have I tried to teach that young fool that you do not, not ever, pound and knock on the doors of your betters? The correct thing to do is to scratch with your fingernails until you are heard and acknowledged.

It is full daylight already now and noisy with birds outside the windows.

"Sir," says Geoffrey in a voice loud enough to shatter a man's head into pieces of pain. "The Earl, he's in the garden and waiting for you to come there promptly. And sir . . ."

Here produces from behind his back a single, somewhat battered, expensive shoe, a shoe with a red cork heel, a rosette and a silver buckle.

"And sir," he goes on, "a woman has left this for you at the gate. Woman said she is known to you, sir, as Sweet Kate of Turnbull Street."

Winks!

The boy dares to wink at him!

Sweet suffering Jesus, forgive me and love me. For I do truly hate myself.

The Right Thing to Do at the Time

This is a true story about my father. A true story with the shape of a piece of fiction. Well, why not? Where do you suppose all the shapes and forms of fiction came from in the first place? And what's the purpose of fiction, anyway, whether it's carved out of the knotty hardwood of personal experience or spun out of the slick thin air like soap bubbles? "What's the purpose of the bayonet?" they used to yell when I was a soldier years ago. The correct answer was: *"to kill, To Kill, TO KILL!"*

The purpose of fiction is to tell the truth.

My father was a small-town Southern lawyer, not a writer; but he was a truth-teller. And he would tell the truth, come what may, hell or high water. And since he loved the truth and would gladly risk his life (and ours, the whole family's!) for the sake of it, he would fight without stint, withholding nothing, offering no pity or quarter against what he took to be wrong—that is, against untruth. He would go to any length he had to. And that is what this story is all about—how far one man would go to fight for the truth and against what was and is wrong.

We were living in the cowtown of Kissimmee, Florida, during the early years of the Great Depression. Disney World is near there now, and it looks pretty much like every place else in America. But it was a hard, tough place then, a place where life was hard for many common, decent people, black and white. And it was a place where some not-so-decent people had managed to seize power and to hold power and were extremely unlikely to be dislodged from power. Among the people in power in those days were the Ku Klux Klan, not a sad little bunch of ignorant racists in bedsheets, but a real clan, a native-grown kind of organized crime family.

My father and his law partner were fighting against the Klan in court and in public with the promise that they would (as they, in fact, did) represent free of charge any person at all who chose to resist the Klan and wanted a lawyer.

This exposed position led to a whole lot of trouble, believe me. And in the end it led to the demise of the Klan as a power of any kind in central Florida. But all the big trouble came later. This happened early on as the lines were still being drawn and the fight was just getting under way.

Sometimes in the early evening we would go together, my mother and father and the other children, into town for an ice cream cone. A great treat in those days. One evening we piled into our old car and drove into the center of town and parked in front of the drugstore. Went inside and sat on tall swivel chairs at the counter eating our ice cream cones. We were all sitting there in a row when a young policeman walked in. Try as I will, I can't remember his name anymore. Just that he was very young and that my mother, who was a teacher then, had taught him in high school. He greeted her politely and first. He seemed a little awkward and embarrassed.

"Mr. Garrett," he said to my father, "I'm afraid I'm going to have to give you a red ticket."

"Oh, really?" my father said, still licking his ice cream cone. "What for?"

"Well, sir, your taillights don't work."

"They did when I came down here."

"Well, sir, they sure don't now."

"Let's us have a look."

So we all trooped outside and looked at the taillights. They didn't work, all right, because they were broken and there was shattered red glass all over the street right behind the back bumper.

"I wonder who would do a thing like that," my father said, giving the young cop a hard look.

"Well, I wouldn't know, sir," he said. "I just work for the city and I do what I'm told. And I have to write you a ticket."

"Fine," my father said. "I understand that."

Then he surprised the cop and us too by asking if he could pay for the ticket right then and there. And the cop said yes, that was his legal right; and he said it would cost five dollars.

Now that was considerable money in those days when grown men with some skills were earning eight or ten dollars a week. Nobody had any money in those days, nobody we knew or knew of. Most of my father's clients, those who could pay at all, paid him in produce and fresh eggs, things like that.

My father peeled off five one-dollar bills. The cop wrote him a receipt. Then my father told my mother to drive us on home when we had finished our ice cream. He had to go somewhere right away.

He whistled loudly and waved his arm for a taxi. One came right over from the Atlantic Coast Line depot directly across the way. He kissed my mother on the cheek and said he would be back just as soon as he could. Gave her the keys to our car and hopped into the cab.

None of us heard what he told the driver: "Let's go to Tallahassee."

Tallahassee was and is the state capital, a good three hundred or so miles away by bad, narrow roads in those days.

Much later we learned what happened. They arrived very late. Slept in the cab. First thing in the morning he got himself a shave in the barbershop. Then went to the legislature. Where, exercising a constitutional right to speak on this kind of matter, he quickly established that the town charter for Kissimmee, Florida, was completely illegal and unconstitutional. In a technical, legal sense that town did not exist and never had. It would require a special action of the state legislature to give the town a new charter and a legal existence. Having made his point, he thanked the legislators kindly and left the capitol. Woke the snoring taxi driver and said: "Let's go home."

It probably cost him a hundred dollars for that ride. Maybe more. He never told us, and nobody, not even my mother, ever dared to ask him.

By the time he arrived home there was a delegation waiting to see him at our house—the mayor, the chief of police, the judge, pretty much the whole gang. Legislators had been on the phone all day to them, and they were deeply worried. Because, you see, everything they had ever done, in the absence of a valid town charter, including collecting taxes, had been completely illegal. You can imagine what that could mean if people got it in mind to be litigious about things.

Everybody came into our living room, and the whole family, too; because, my father said, we saw the beginning of it and deserved to see the end.

Before the mayor or any of them said a word, he explained to them exactly what he had done. And he told them that, under the state constitution, establishing a town was a very tricky legal business. He said that the chances were a hundred to one that they would mess it up again. He wished them good luck, promising that if they ever bothered him or us any more, he would go to Tallahassee again and close them down for keeps.

There was a lot of silence. Finally the mayor spoke.

"What do you want from us, Garrett?"

"Ah," said my father. "I knew it would come down to that. And I'm glad it did, because there is something I do want from you all."

They were all looking and waiting. I reckon they were ready to do or pay most anything.

"Damn it!" he said. "I want my five dollars back from that phony traffic ticket."

Long pause.

"That's all?"

"That's all. You give me my five dollars back and I'll give you back your receipt."

So they paid him the five dollars and he tore the receipt in two and they filed out of our house.

"You beat them, Daddy," I said. "You won!"

"That's right, boy," he told me. "And I taught them a very important lesson."

"What's that?" my mother asked, nervously.

"If they want to stop me now," he said, "they're going to have to kill me. And I don't think they've got the guts for it."

Then he laughed out loud. And so did I, not because it was funny, but because it seemed like the right thing to do at the time.

Dixie Dreamland

In all fairness and in the interests of a (pardon) well-rounded picture of my way of life, I owe it to you to give a picture of, indeed to celebrate, Ruthe-Ann. Ruthe-Ann Coombs late of High Pines, North Carolina and, more recently, a waitress at The Hitching Post Cafe. She who during the long winter months and up to the edge of spring, before I undertook to cultivate the celibacy which appears to have undone me, she who was a solace and joy to me for so many reasons. Not just or only or solely because of the bed (in this case the bunk of a small house trailer in the field behind The Hitching Post), though fairness and justice require that I at least should mention the fact that she took to the oldest dance as naturally as a duck to water and with a healthy, hearty, laughing and scratching vigor it would be difficult to imagine the exact equivalent of; asking in return neither favor nor recompense, though invariably appreciative of the symbolic, if not significant, value of any small gifts or favors I might offer; asking nothing really except that I too should ask for nothing above and beyond what she offered freely; not wholly guileless (for what woman could be and still be called a woman?), but at least, as far as I was concerned, without either plans or demands involving my future. More than that though. In truth it was her company that was my solace each night after The Hitching Post closed and before the roosters began to crow. While the Smartmobile still ran smartly on the road and during the winter months when, off and on, the TV set was on the blink or else had lost its savor, she was always there.

I could try to describe her, but would not do her justice. To picture her best would be to let her clothe herself in the raiment of her very own words, coat of many country colors. Which I intend to do here, by ear and memory, not needing a tape recorder or any of the other aids to veracity; for in a deep sense she speaks a language I have known almost since birth, though one must allow for the differences in dialect and for the particularity of her own personal idiom.

Ruthe-Ann had come over the mountains from High Pines for reasons that are not altogether clear. She left her home, her county and her job to come here where a cousin had a business—a lot of mobile homes and trailers, new and used, by the side of the road. She found herself a job at The Hitching Post and moved, courtesy of the cousin, a battered old trailer into the vacant field behind it. To which we did oft repair. And it is there that you can imagine this monologue as taking place. The two of us lying there comfortable and relaxed, draped in sheets of the bunk more for comfort and warmth than any kind of modesty. Sipping beer from a shared can, smoking a joint, maybe. In darkness, though; having seen in the light when we entered the neat and shipshape space of the trailer, its little Formica table brightened by a single unfading artificial rose, the walls decorated with carefully cut and taped photographs of Elvis Presley, Michael Jackson, and Cary Grant. Neat even now, except for the rumpled bed and two figures clutching at bits and swathes of sheet like bandages. Neat to the extent that our clothing was hung in the closet (undressing was no longer a tease) and our shoes, paired and side by side beneath the bunk.

Not the housewife's neurotic or obsessive neatness, however. Merely a function of living in a space probably smaller than a ship's cabin.

"Lord have mercy, Professor!" she said the first time when I dropped my clothes in casual puddles on the floor. "I like to live loose as much as the next one, but if I ever let go in this little old trailer, it'll be a mare's nest. I mean, if it was a mo-tel or something, that would be different. That's the best thing about a mo-tel. You can just throw everything every which way and the hell with it. Unless maybe you got to be ready to cut out in a hurry . . ."

I interrupt her on the subject of mo-tels at this point to move on to something else. Did I mention yet how she loved to talk and could talk too, as the early Church Fathers could pray, without ceasing. Regardless of the distraction . . . ?

Speaking of church, here is a typical monologue of hers; all of it evoked and aroused by a single simple question I asked her. This particular evening there were people about half a mile away from us, singing and shouting at a tent revival meeting. The loud sounds from the revival (they are all high tech and electronic these days) made an unusual background music for our lovemaking. When we were just resting and relaxing, I asked her if she had ever been saved at a revival meeting.

Frankly, I never did find out the answer to that specific question. But answer me she surely did (to the best of my recollection) in the following fashion:

I tell you the God's own merciful truth, honey, I haven't been to one of those tent revival things in years and years. Usually speaking, I wouldn't walk acrost the street to attend one. I mean there's always so many other interesting things to do. Like drinking a few beers and dancing. I do dearly love to get up and dance and I'm not ashamed to admit it, either. I always did. I started dancing, for all the company that come around, about the same time I stopped crawling. I love to go out dancing, anytime. And then maybe slipping out to the parking lot for a breath of fresh air and maybe a little smooching out there underneath the stars. Or in the back seat of a car. I like it better, what I mean is it's safer, don't you know, standing up and doing it outside in the open. Somebody will always come along in the nick of time. And even if they don't you can always take off running. One thing I can do pretty good, I don't mind telling you, is run. When I've got a good enough reason, I can pick up and stretch out and truly haul ass. I was raised in the mountains. You get good strong leg muscles if you was raised up there. And if you happen to be a girl you get nothing but a plenty of practice from about twelve years old onward.

Anyhow I have always felt and firmly maintained that the back seat of a automobile is kind of, well . . . special. I mean a girl should try her best to save that place for a special fella. Specially a good-looking one. It stands to reason. Cause once you get in there with all the doors shut you can't very well just sit and twiddle your thumbs. Truth is you're just liable to be flat on your back before somebody can say Rumpelstiltskin. He probably gets to feeling around a little . . . I'll be honest with you, there's a few places you can touch me (I'm not telling you exactly where), even accidentally and not on purpose, and I just go wild it feels so good. Most of the time you've got to be occupied yourself because most fellas are so shy or clumsy or downright ignorant, or a combination of all three put together, that they couldn't unbutton, unzip or unsnap nothing without you was to give them some right considerable help. Men are so dumb most of the time! What do they think the back seat of a car was designed for? Of course now, every once in a great while you run into one that is different from the average. You know, one that is kind of smooth and who knows what he is doing. And that is a horse of an altogether different color. Then you got both hands free to do a little pioneering and exploring on your own. I guess that is the best there is. Talk about feeling wild! If somebody was to come along and ask me what's my name along about that time, I wouldn't even know probably. And I'll tell you another thing. I wouldn't care either.

Hey, you want to hear something funny?

First time I ever got married I was so shy. I mean it! I didn't hardly know what to do with myself. There we both was, me and old Lucas, in this mo-tel room and I was shy as a deer. Kind of worried too. I mean it just didn't seem right, you know, to be there alone in a mo-tel room with a man even if he was your legal husband.

To make it really funny you would have to know Lucas. He was the meanest, no-account, worthless, rotten son-of-a-bitch in the whole world. Only I didn't know it then because I was in love with him at the time. Lucas was plain good-looking. I guess he had about the longest sideburns I had ever seen on a man, and it took him longer to get his pompadour and ducktail right than it did me to set my hair in curlers. Well, sir, we fell in love—*blap!*—right at first sight. It was out to The Wild Turkey. Which, in case you don't know, let me tell you is a real high-class kind of honky-tonk. I mean, it is practically a nightclub compared to a place like The Hitching Post. Anyway that night I had a date with Buddy Crenshaw. Buddy, he's cute, kind of, but definitely not the back seat kind. More for laughs and a good time. And Lucas, he was out with Cora Morgan. Cora, she has always had a good figure and she still does, only she was pretty in the face too then. That was before they proceeded to wrap Tommy Jackson's new Ford Mustang around a telephone pole and old Cora went flying out through the windshield.

Funny how things work out. After her face got all cut up and kind of stove in and lopsided like that, she took a job with the phone company working as an operator where she could get to talk to a whole lots of people without them having to look at her. She's got a good voice too, kind of husky and sexy. Jim Lee Baker, he's truly a joker, a real wild card if there ever was one, he swears upon a stack of Bibles that it gives him a hard-on every time he puts in a long-distance call. Which is perfectly okay within the privacy of your own home. But he says he frankly don't like it worth a damn when he's calling from a pay phone in a public phone booth. Anyhow, that was before the accident and Cora still had the impression she was pretty hot stuff. Maybe she had her sights set and had drawn a bead on Lucas. Maybe that was her trouble. Because Cora had this theory, see, that when you are fixing to marry a guy, don't give him none at all. Even if he begs you politely. Sure, let him fool around a little if he wants to, but everytime he starts to do anything real, really serious, you just rear back and holler *whoa!* and *down boy!* She claimed how it would give a much higher value to it and make him think he appreciated it a whole lot more when he finally did get some.

Personally, I am what you would call a more democratic kind of a person. I believe in equal opportunity. I can honestly say in all seriousness and sincerity that I have always tried to treat everybody fair and equal. It didn't cut no ice with me just because they wanted to marry me. And I would never hold it against a man either.

Say, I'll tell you another joke on old Cora and the way that everything turned out. Cora was always kind of uppity and superior in our crowd. Like what she had to offer was definitely special. But, boy, just as soon as her face got messed up, didn't she change her tune as fast as you could snap your fingers? Why, she started to put out on a practically mass production basis. I guess she was hoping that sooner or later she would catch one that liked it so much he couldn't plan to do without it. Or else she would get pregnant and somebody would have to marry her, face or no face. About the pregnant part, that turns out to be a joke too. She got all kind of banged up and rearranged inside too in that car accident, but it wasn't for the longest time that she finally came to find out she couldn't have a baby anyway. Which is a shame I reckon. But, like they say, we all have our cross of trial and tribulation to bear, don't we?

What I'm getting around to, though, is Men. They may be dumb all right about some things as a general rule. The only real trouble is just when you start to figure they are too dumb to worry about, they sneak up and proceed to get smart. Take Cora. Being a woman she thought it was her pretty face they were all interested in. I mean, being a woman she figured that when you get right down to it, naturally, the basic equipment is all pretty much the same in the dark and it's your face that really matters. So when she bashed up her face she thought that was that. Trouble was she didn't know how men are inclined to think. I can tell you a man's interest in a woman starts about the level of the shoulders and ends up about on a line with her knees.

Men think strange. My second husband never even knew what color my eyes were and he couldn't have cared less. I'll bet that no-good son-of-a-bitch don't even remember the color of the hair on my head. I had it a real nice shiny bleach blond then. I'll tell you something else I found out about men. The hard way, so to speak, if you'll pardon the expression. A whole lot of it is completely in their heads. Most of them are more interested in that stuff than in the genuine merchandise. Which can be pretty rude sometimes if you ask me. I mean you lay back and raise up your knees and it may not turn out to be the outright end of the living world, but it's the best you can do at the time. He ought to at least have the common decency and ordinary good manners to pretend it is you he is enjoying. But men are crazy as hell and they never do grow up. The older they get the crazier they get.

You know what that Lee Baker told me one time? I know with Lee you can't never tell if he's kidding or not and I don't think he knows either. But I'm pretty sure he was serious that time. There we were over at his place, kind of resting and taking it easy between times, and had turned on the TV. And there was that old Ann Margret in some movie. Old Lee he started to perk up and take notice. He was glued to the TV set and he wouldn't come back to the bed until the movie was all over. Finally we jumped back into the sack, but we hadn't even got started good before he wanted to engage me in a conversation about how beautiful and wonderful Ann Margret was and all that.

—That movie was made a long time ago, Lee. She is old enough to be your mama now.

—I don't care, he says.

Then all of a sudden he just stops everything and looks me dead in the eyes.

—Tell me something, Ruthe-Ann, he says.

—Hurry up before I fall asleep.

—Aw, I'm trying to be serious. Can't you ever be serious?

—All right, I said to him. Gimme a cigarette. I mean I might as well smoke if I'm just going to have to lay here and be serious.

And you know what? He lit me a cigarette. He didn't even see the joke or take the hint intended. I mean, Lee was still on top of me. I was smoking a cigarette and he wanted to discuss Ann Margret. Can you beat that?

—What if, Lee asks, what if I was to meet up with her? And then, you know, one thing was to lead to another and I ended up getting myself a little?

—That would certainly be interesting, I reply. You planning to give it a try? If you are, you better hurry up. Grab your britches and zip up your fly and take off running like a big-ass bird, because she may be dead of old age before you can get there.

—I am trying to discuss this thing seriously.

—Oh, excuse me, I say. I didn't realize.

—The question I am asking myself is this. If I made out, what would I really and truly be getting? Would it be the same person that we just saw on the TV? Or, would it be like, you know, a completely different person?

—I already told you. It would be like doing it with your own mama.

—The trouble with you, he says, is you've got a dirty mind.

—I beg your pardon.

—I know the answer anyway, says he. All I would have to do is switch off the lights and close my eyes and she would be all young and beautiful again like on *The Late Show*.

—That's real sweet and nice, I say. It's nice for you and even nicer for her. Now, you listen here, Jim Lee Baker, I am about to freeze my ass off just laying here and you aren't exactly as light as a feather pillow. So I tell you what. You close your eyes and pretend like I am Bo Derek . . .

—How dumb can you get? It was Ann Margret!

—Never mind, I say. You close your eyes and make like I am whoever it is.

—It won't work.

—If you can take the hard mileage of twenty years off a woman just by closing your eyes, you can do anything, Buster.

—It just won't work.

—Why not?

—Ruthe-Ann, he says kind of sadly, I know you too well. It would have to be with a stranger.

See what I mean about men?

So anyway, there is old Cora giving it away for free for nothing, because as far as she is concerned it's worthless now. And there are all these men. As far as they are concerned, it is the old Cora they are getting into because all they have to do is close their eyes and she has got her pretty face back again. Too bad she can't do the same thing. I bet if somebody was to tell her how it really is, she would be embarrassed. I know I would. For all the airs she used to have, she has now been screwed, blued, and tattooed by almost every white man in the county from the ages of fourteen to sixty-five. I wouldn't say she would stop with only the white men either, but I don't have any definite proof on that.

Anyway, there we all were out to The Wild Turkey, drinking our cans of Miller's High Life. Which was my favorite in those days because they call it "the champagne of bottled beer." Buddy Crenshaw had a pint of Four Roses whiskey hid under the table in a brown paper bag between his knees and every once in a while we would sneak a swallow just to give the beer a little boost. The only trouble was, with the whiskey between his knees, he couldn't get up and dance. And, as you know, I do dearly love to dance. Even more than I like to get high. A slow tune came on the jukebox and Cora and Lucas came back to our table.

—Lucas, she said. Why don't you ask Ruthe-Ann to dance? She has not danced a dance all evening.

—I'm tired, he says.

—You can take it easy. It's a nice slow tune.

—I don't like that creepy kind of music. It bugs me.

—Come on, Lucas, I said, standing up and grabbing his hand. It's Frank Sinatra.

—I don't like him either, Lucas said. He's a Wop.

—I don't care if he's a Eskimo, I said. Come on.

Old Lucas didn't like it. He didn't have but three expressions on his face ever. One was a pout and the other two were different kinds of a scowl. Which I thought was sexier than all get out in those days. And I was feeling no pain from all the Miller's High Life and the Four Roses.

And I was kind of mad with Cora and wanted to play a trick on her. The reason why she didn't like to do slow dances with Lucas was because it was so intimate. She was bound she wasn't going to let him know she even had a pussy for sure until after a preacher had pronounced them man and wife. He might even have to marry her out of pure curiosity— just to find out if she did have one or not.

Well, when we got out on the floor dancing, I snuggled up real close to Lucas. He wasn't too tall so I just shoved my hips and got it right up against him and then kind of wiggled and rubbed around a little so he would notice. It happened to be a real hot summer night and I didn't have any panties on underneath. Old Lucas's jaw fell down and his eyes bugged out like somebody got their thumbs in behind them and pushed real hard. I thought they might pop right out of his head. Oh, I forgot about that. That was Lucas's other expression. I want to give him full credit for all four. Then he commenced to sweat. Then, kind of testing, he pushed forward and did a little rubbing and wiggling of his own. And, from that moment on, it was love at first sight between us. Before you could say Jackie Robinson we were outside in the parking lot and had done it twice in ten minutes. Lucas was never much for long distances. He was more like a hundred yard dash man. But his biggest asset was his amazing power of quick recovery. You have to say that for him. We did it once in the back seat of his car and once in the back seat of Buddy's. Just for a laugh.

Well, after that we went steady awhile before we finally decided the best thing to do would be to get married. We pretty near wore out the back seat of his car reaching that decision too.

So there we were in the mo-tel room, legally and officially husband and wife. We hadn't even shut the door behind us good before Lucas, who was never famous for good manners, had shucked off all his clothes and thrown them all over the room. He was standing on top of the bed, jumping up and down to test the springs, and looking at himself in the mirror, flexing his muscles and yelling at me to get the lead out of my ass, to hurry up and get undressed.

I felt so shy and so bad about the way our honeymoon was beginning that there wasn't anything left to do but sit down and cry. Old Lucas, that boy never even stopped bouncing on the bed.

—Jesus Christ on a pair of crutches! he exclaimed. What in the hell are you crying about?

—I can't, I said. I just can't, that's all.

That stopped the bouncing. You better believe it. He walked over to the edge of the bed near to where I was sitting in the middle of the floor.

—*What can't you do?* he inquired.

—Not *here,* I said.

—It don't matter. One place is just as good as the next one. I even did it in a phone booth one time.

—You stop bragging!

—I don't ever brag, he said. I am merely stating a fact.

Then I started crying worse and louder than ever. That got him mad. So he went and turned on the TV set and turned up the volume as loud as it would go so he could drown me out and wouldn't have to listen to me bawling. It was already well past midnight so the people next door started to banging on the wall. Lucas banged back and yelled a few choice remarks at them. Then a man in there began to yell back. They carried on for a while, yelling back and forth through the wall at each other. Finally they agreed that nothing would do or settle it except a fight, and so Lucas put on his britches and went out. I kept on sitting in the middle of the floor and crying and I was still doing that when Lucas came back in holding a bloody handkerchief to his nose. That stopped me. I hate it when somebody I happen to be in love with at the time gets a bloody nose or something like that.

—Oh, Jesus! he said. The freaking TV set is still going. Turn it off quick!

So I got up and did.

—He broke it, Lucas said, looking at himself in the mirror real sad. That big bully broke my nose. I ought to go back out there and whip his ass for that.

—I have stopped crying now, I said.

—What in the hell was the matter, anyway? It is all your fault and for two cents I'd break your nose too.

—All I wanted . . . Listen, Lucas, can't we just spend our first night together in the back seat of the car?

—I reckon we got to, Lucas said. The manager has already called the police and we better haul ass out of here if we don't want to spend our wedding night in jail.

—Together?

—This here is a respectable county, Lucas said. They don't allow no women in the men's part of the jailhouse. You have got a dirty mind, Ruthe-Ann. I believe you would even do it in church if you could.

—Nobody ever asked me to, I replied.

And that—*church*—gets me right back where I started. With the tent meeting and all that happened and how come I had to leave High Pines. Don't mind me. I know it must seem sometimes like I just chatter along like a old jaybird in a tree. I take after my daddy, I guess. He says telling a story is like chewing tobacco. If you are any good at it at all you keep the plug in your mouth until the very last little drop of the suption is gone. I don't chew myself. Of course, I have tried it any number of times. Well, let's leave that subject for another time. It ain't no use making a big deal out of it. I can get to the point as quick as anybody and I will do it if I have to find a bathroom or yell *Help!, Murder!, Police!, Rape!,* or something. But as long as there isn't an emergency, then what's the big rush all about? Where is the fire? I admit I do dearly love to talk. I guess I would just fall down dead if they upped and passed a law against gossip. But they haven't done so yet.

Why worry about laws they haven't even passed yet? That's my philosophy . . .

"Mine, too," I tell her, reaching out in the darkness to embrace all her youth and energy, hoping to warm myself (as once did old King David in the Holy Scripture) by the white fire of her indefatigable flesh. Thinking: I could preach a sermon on this subject if I were a revival preacher with a tent of my very own. Ruthe-Ann continues, following the too-brief interruption:

Remember Cora who was so pretty in the face before she got all bashed and smashed in that automobile accident? Well, I had a dream about her the other night. A bunch of us had been partying Saturday night. I woke up in my own apartment on top of the bed with all my clothes on. Don't know how I got there. Couldn't remember a blessed thing from the time we left The Wild Turkey when they closed it at two A.M. in the morning and threw us all out into the parking lot. I sort of remember climbing in the back seat of Ray Joynes's car with a couple of other people. But that's all. Anything could have happened. But I seriously doubt that anything did. When you wake up all alone and fully dressed on top of your own bed there's no use to go stark raving paranoid crazy wondering what might or might not have happened to you.

The main thing that happened to me that night, the one thing I could clearly remember, was that dream with Cora in it. It was more of a kind of a nightmare in a way.

Here's how it happened:

We were all kids again. I guess it was supposed to be in summertime because we were all down at the Municipal Swimming Pool in Burns Park. All of us girls were over on the girls' side of the bathhouse putting on our bathing suits and giggling and playing grabass the way girls will. Then Cora walked in. She was the only one of us that was a grown-up. She had on a blue lifeguard's bathing suit with a red cross on it. And she had a whistle. She blew the whistle. And then she told me to go and look at myself in the mirror.

You know how in a dream sometimes you will know ahead of time exactly what is fixing to happen next. Well, that's just how it was. I was scared to death because I knew for sure I was going to get a terrible shock the minute I looked in the mirror. I went expecting to see something really horrible or sickening. I closed my eyes and wouldn't look, but then Cora made me by pinching me or pulling my hair or something. So I looked. And I didn't see a thing. Nothing. It was an empty mirror! And my breath caught in my throat and I felt like I was melting all over like hot wax. Then we were standing out by the edge of the swimming pool. Cora's whistle had turned into a little gold cross. She took it off and dropped it into the pool and it sank straight to the bottom. Then we were going to try and get it back because she said whoever got it first could have a reward. We all climbed up to the top of the diving tower and the high diving board. I was scared because I have always been afraid of high places.

—Come on. Don't be a sissy, Cora said.

And she dove right off the board. Only the pool wasn't water anymore. It was a huge piece of clear plate glass. I tried to yell at her to look out but I couldn't make a sound. She hit that glass and it made a terrible noise and crashed and splintered and broke to pieces and she went on through it. Then it came all back together again like it hadn't been broken at all. I looked down and I could see Cora through it way down there swimming deep under the glass. Like Cora was a fish in a bowl. Then it was not just Cora, but everybody I knew was swimming around down there like a school of fish and they didn't even have to come up and breathe. The water was so clear and bright it wasn't water at all. It was more like just sunlight. Like they were all swimming in the sunlight. Like they were bathing and splashing and floating on sunbeams. They all looked so happy and carefree. Cora looked up and saw me and smiled. Then they all did, smiling and waving for me to come on in too. I wanted to. I really did. But first I would have to dive through that glass. And I knew what that would be like. I would get bashed and sliced and cut up in chunks and pieces, like cut bait, and there was always a chance I would never be able to find all the pieces of me and put them back together again. Or maybe I would hit the glass and not get through to them at all. I would just go *splat!* and then be spread all over the glass like a mosquito when you slap it.

But they wouldn't stop waving and smiling and calling and I knew that I had to go. So I closed my eyes and held my nose and jumped. I fell and fell and kept on falling like one of those skydivers. I never hit. I kept falling and falling until I screamed and woke up on top of my bed at home.

Aren't dreams just the weirdest things? Most of the times my dreams are very real, though. I don't pull any punches when I'm dreaming. I'm pretty much the same person awake or asleep, I'm proud to say. No, I'm not going to tell you anything about my dreams. That's a secret. I'll tell you a story about somebody else's dream I was involved in once, though.

There was this boy named Carver Smith. He is the one that ran off and joined the navy. Which is funny, I guess, because he had never seen the ocean in his whole life and couldn't swim a stroke. It must be pretty scary to be way out in the big middle of an ocean on a boat and you don't even know how to swim. What would you do if the boat was to take a notion to sink?

I know what I'd do. First I would pull off all of my clothes like it says to in the *Red Cross First Aid Manual.* If you are ever fixing to drown, it says, don't forget to pull off all your clothes first. It helps you to float better. Especially women, if they are normal and not too flat chested. What if you didn't drown and they saved you? They would drag you up on the beach and give you the artificial respiration. Mouth to mouth looks like it could be fun. I reckon it would be, too, if the lifeguard turned out to be Paul Newman or somebody like that. Or if I was floating around in the ocean I would keep hollering *help!* and hope that some sailor boys might come along and save me. It's for darn sure there are always sailor boys hanging around when you don't need them. Maybe they should pay more attention to the ocean.

So, anyhow, I hardly even knew Carver Smith. I had seen him around here and there in different places and he was a nice-looking boy, but kind of a lone wolf. He never even owned a motorcycle. Sure I had seen him around, but I couldn't have possibly ever done any more than maybe smile back and exchange a couple of words. Carver Smith was about the farthest thing in my mind, you know.

Well, one day he came in the store. He walked right up to my counter, grinning and winking like we were a couple of old friends. That kind of took me back. I didn't know what the rest of the girls in the store might think. I mean, there I was supposed to be going steady at the time with Jay Ray Finn—the one everybody called Mickey. I hadn't even so much as mentioned the name of Carver Smith to anybody. And here he comes, strutting into the store like he owned it, hollering *hey there, Ruthe-Ann!* from clear across the floor so everybody would have to notice and then making a bee-line straight for my counter.

Frankly, I did not know what to do. I didn't want to be rude or impolite to the boy. I always make it a rule to be nice and polite to any of them that are at least half-decent. But I did not want the other girls to think that I had been holding out any secrets on them either. Of course everybody has got some serious secrets. They are supposed to be really secret. The whole thing is, you have to keep your reputation for being honest and straightforward by sharing a few of your secrets, the kind that don't really matter much, with the rest of the girls. Besides being good for keeping friendships and killing time, it can be a help in other ways too. Once everybody gets used to it they take it for granted. Now, sometime you may have a secret you really don't want to get around. All you have to do is tell it flat out and you are as safe as if you had written it down on a piece of paper and put the paper in a safety deposit box at the bank. Nobody will ever take it serious once you have got them trained. That is a kind of nice insurance to know about in case the day comes along, as it is bound to, when you really have something to hide.

Carver came right up to my counter where I was working and leaned on it, still smiling and winking at me like he had a nervous tic or something, and shoving his face real close to mine.

—Hello, honeybunch, he said.

—I believe you are sitting in the wrong pew, I replied.

—What's that supposed to mean, beautiful?

—I can't sell you anything, I said. We probably don't have anything to fit you, and even if we did, I wouldn't sell it to you.

That got a laugh out of him because I was working in the ladies' lingerie section at that time.

—How about if I was to buy something for a girl?

—Who?

—Never mind who.

—What size?

—Oh, he said, about your size. What size are you?

—None of your beeswax, I said. Anyway it's *sizes*. Different things on a girl have different sizes.

—Tell you what, he said. You pick out an item, anything you got in the store that you really like, and I'll buy it for you.

—Carver Smith, what has come over you? Have you gone and lost your mind?

Then he actually pulled out his wallet and laid it on the counter for all to see. I could tell the other girls were watching. I could feel their eyes and I was burning.

—Don't you want anything? he said. Maybe you don't wear no underwear.

—I will slap your big fresh face.

—I read where Marilyn Monroe don't.

That was back when she still was alive. Wasn't that a crying shame, though, how that pretty girl took all those pills and then drowned in a swimming pool with no clothes on? I heard a rumor that she couldn't swim a lick either. People that can't swim ought to avoid swimming pools.

—Well, just pardon me, I answered. I am not Marilyn Monroe and that is her own sack of rocks.

—You're pretty nice anyway, he said. You'll do until she comes along.

—Thanks a bunch of bananas!

—I'm serious. I really mean it.

I could not think of another thing to say. Nothing! Carver just stood there looking at me sincerely right in the eyes. And he certainly had beautiful long eyelashes for a boy. I guess I could have walked away. I could always have gone to the Ladies Room and sat on the pot and hid or something. Or maybe I could have turned my back on him. I could have folded some things or have fooled around with paper work. It would have been my slickest move, definitely the smart thing to do. But you know me. I will just be damn if I am going to let any man look me in the eyes and try to stare me down. So I kept looking right back and waiting to see what he would think of to say next.

—Lots of ladies don't, he said.

—Don't what?

—I read in a book where a whole lot of ladies, more than anyone knows, don't wear any underwear.

—Panties, I said. Panties is what they don't wear.

—Do you wear panties?

I should have slapped him good that time, too, but I didn't. The only excuse for not doing it that I've got now is I had never had a conversation like that with a stranger. I was curious. By that time it was too late to worry about the other girls in the store anyway.

Well, I thought to myself, *I might just as well keep it going long enough to get them good and curious too.*

—You ought to be ashamed of yourself, Carver Smith, I said. Here I don't hardly know you from Adam, except to say *hello there* to you. And yet you walk in here and barge right up to the counter and ask me do I have any panties on which is none of your business. I can only assume that you have been drinking or else you have flipped your wig and are headed for the boobyhatch.

He kind of blinked and made a face like I had hurt his feelings.

—I'm sorry. I forgot, he said. I know you so well that I forgot you don't know me the same way.

—You do? Where from?

That remark of his gave me the goosebumps. If you try to enjoy a really active social life, like I do, you sometimes can forget things. I really raked my brain in a hurry, trying to figure out if maybe somehow there had been a time and a place. The only particular time I could think of was that time when I passed out cold in the middle of the YMCA Picnic. Only I doubted it. I don't think Carver Smith was even at the picnic. I know who was involved in that shameful episode and I could name names right now if I felt like it would do any good. About the only thing I could think of was that some smart-aleck with a big mouth and an even looser tongue, which is another cross all us women have to bear, some loudmouth smartass had been talking out of turn.

—We were married, Carver said.

—Now I know you're crazy as a woodpecker flying backwards, I exclaimed. If we had ever been married I would damn sure remember it.

—In my dream, he said. Last night I had a dream where you and me were married.

—Well! Why didn't you say so?

When Carver told me about his dream I began to cry. I cried right there in the store in front of everybody and he ended up having to buy me a brand new Irish linen handkerchief so I could blow my nose. Which is very unusual for me. Usually I would prefer to blow my nose on most anything except a clean handkerchief. Especially a brand new one that cost too much in the first place.

In his dream he said I was a bride all dressed in white. He said I was a beautiful bride. We got married in a great big huge stone church somewhere with pipe organ music that was not just a record playing and lots of flowers and crowds of nice-looking people all dressed up fit to kill. It was like we were both Episcopalians in his dream. Then in the next part we were at the wedding reception. There were green fields all around and the party was under a big striped awning. There was all the food you could ever want to eat and champagne to drink and good music to dance to. Not jivey stuff or rock-and-roll either. It was beautiful classical music like on the *Lawrence Welk Show*. And we both knew how to do the waltz. We danced around and around and drank champagne and people took our picture with flashbulbs. It was just like something in *Vogue* magazine or *Harper's Bazaar* that you read at the beauty parlor while waiting to get your hair done. Carver said we danced round and round doing the waltz and how I was the most beautiful bride he had ever seen. Radiant . . .

He said I was radiant.

Then the next part of the dream is where he took me to a Hilton Hotel somewhere. It was really a great place. We got a room overlooking the ocean. There were palm trees by the beach and little boats out on the water just parked around with their lights winking. There was a nice full moon over the water and more music playing in the background. And more champagne. I drank a little too much of it. That's how true to life his dream was! I mean, it was spooky and weird. I got real sleepy and fell out across the bed to rest my eyes a little. I still had my bride costume on, so he tried to help me get out of it. He said I mumbled at him and told him to be really easy and gentle because I was still a virgin. He said I wasn't kidding either. In his dream I really was one. He undressed me all the way. He said I had the most beautiful shining white body he ever saw. He said he would never forget it. I was right curious about that. I wanted him to describe me to me to see how accurate it was, but that would have been going a little too far right there in public in the store. He said he reached out and touched me very gently, not feeling or groping around or anything but just to see and be sure I was real. Maybe I was a statue. The minute he touched me I opened both eyes and I smiled at him.

And then we started screwing and we screwed all night long. And we were still at it when all the roosters crowed and they rang the bell for breakfast.

—You were the finest piece of ass I ever had, he said. The absolute finest, bar none.

He said he had never had better and he never hoped to. He told me he didn't care if I never spoke to him again or gave him the time of day.

Because everything that happened in the dream was real to him. He said if he died tomorrow, and never got laid again, that would still be enough to last him for a lifetime. He said it had been his privilege in a dream to have the ultimate piece of ass and all he wanted was to say thank you, ma'am.

You know me. I have always been a fool for romance and flattery. And, well, that bride business got to me too. Because I have never been officially married in a church. The only times I got married the guy was always in a hurry so we ended up at the Justice of the Peace. I couldn't think of anything to say for once in my life and so I busted out bawling and cried and cried and ended up actually blowing my nose in one of our brand new top quality Irish linen handkerchiefs. Which may have been extravagant and silly, but it seemed like the right thing to do at the time.

The more I thought about Carver Smith's dream the realer it got to me. It was realer than if it had been my own dream. It seemed like it had really happened that way, and I will always have a warm memory and a soft place in my heart for Carver Smith on account of it. Nothing can ever change that or spoil it for me. Not even when I let my curiosity get the best of me and gave old Mickey Finn his walking papers and then really tried it out with Carver in mo-tels for four counties around High Pines. We worked hard to make the dream come true, but it didn't work out too good. For one thing there isn't anything that even resembles a real Hilton Hotel in that part of the country. The closest you can come is a Holiday Inn, but I am very literal minded. And then Carver, poor boy, he always got so excited before we even got started good. . . . I don't blame him and I don't hold that against him for a minute. He couldn't help it. Poor boy, he tried everything from ice water to Linger Ointment. Some joker suggested Med-i-quick, the pain killer, to him. And that like to have driven him straight up the wall, it burned so bad. He was yelling and fanning himself with the evening paper and dancing around the room like a Indian on the warpath. I couldn't help laughing because it was so funny. But my laughing didn't help much either. I have learned that it is usually a mistake to laugh at a man when he is having an intimate sexual problem. Romance will just fade, fade, fade away if you do.

Anyhow, I will always be grateful to Carver Smith and his beautiful dream. And I will not be jealous if he has a girl in every port. If the gossip is true, though, girls don't have to worry about sailors anymore. They are too busy elsewhere, if you get what I mean. I don't doubt it. If you coop up a whole lot of men on a ship way out in the ocean it's bound to happen. And nowdays they put some girls on every ship. I might even volunteer if I was young enough. I'll tell you one thing for sure, though. Until they figure out something to do about sex at sea, even if it is just to put up a whole lot of saltpeter in the food, no son of mine is ever going to join the navy!

The Misery and the Glory of Texas Pete

And then there are those stories that become a kind of common property. That, in the absence of anything more than myth and memory, we can freely choose to believe or doubt.

Here's one of those, a story I first heard in the Downtown Barber Shop when I was maybe ten years old and have heard ever since, most recently when I went back home for a visit after many years and was taken to be a stranger in my own hometown.

Way back in the bitter days of the Great Depression our town couldn't afford to maintain a real police force. They kept cutting budgets and pretty soon they got down to a single constable. Then they tried to make do with what they called in those days a "day marshal," a guy who was on duty (and on salary) only during daylight hours. After sunset it was anything goes.

Pretty soon they couldn't even afford to pay for a day marshal.

What to do?

There were some—jokers to be sure, but not completely kidding— who thought maybe there might be a future for our town as a sort of sanctuary for criminals, common and otherwise. A free city, kind of like some of those pirate communities in the Caribbean way back in the days of big-time piracy. But, as the more sober citizens were quick to point out, what moderately successful, self-respecting criminal would want to come and live here?

Well, in the end they decided to keep the position of day marshal, but to ratchet down the credentials and requirements as well as the pecuniary rewards and fringe benefits.

They advertised, as widely and cheaply as they could, for a low-rent day marshal. The only application they got came from an eighty-five-year-old gentleman, a retired sheriff from Wild West days. He was mainly interested in the climate here because he thought it might help his arthritis—his "misery," as he called it.

So the old fellow (everybody called him Texas Pete, but not to his face) tottered around town during daylight hours, wearing a nice, clean khaki uniform with a big, shiny five-pointed star badge pinned on his shirt pocket. And he strapped on an antique single-action black powder pistol, a big old .44 hog that looked to be too heavy for him to lift out of his holster, let alone to shoot somebody or something with.

Everybody in town liked the old gent. They really did. Everybody was on their best behavior. We were almost crime free. People behaved themselves so as not to cause him any trouble or aggravation. The town elders were absolutely convinced that they would never be able to hire a living lawman as cheaply as that.

Well, then, one fine day, it being the high season for such things in the U.S. of A., a gang of bank robbers came driving into town in a souped-up four-door Ford that would outrun anything in town or the county either, assuming anybody would be foolhardy enough to chase after them. They parked right in front of the old Sunshine Bank and Trust Company, the only bank left in town in those days. One sat at the wheel with the motor running while the other three went in to rob the bank.

So there they are right in the middle of robbing the Sunshine Bank when here comes our day marshal, old Texas Pete, stumbling and tottering along the sidewalk, headed in the general direction of the bank, aiming, apparently, to deposit his pitiful monthly check. He's about fifty yards away from everything when all of a sudden the outside alarm goes off—*Clang! Clang! Clang!*

He stops walking and puts on his thick old glasses and peers from under the shade of his wide-brim hat and sees, sure enough, the three bad guys, guns and loot in hand, come out of the bank. He raises his left hand in admonition and starts tugging at his pistol with his right. "Halt in the name of the Law!" he says in a thin, quivery but nonetheless audible voice. Almost matter-of-fact. Like it is something he has said before in dim days beyond recall. And, quivery or not, it has some ghostly authority to it.

Now the bad guys can't believe this whole scene. They think it is funny as a whoopee cushion. And they start laughing loud and shooting at him as fast as they can. Bullets are zinging and ricocheting all around him while he keeps tugging at that old pistol of his. He finally pulls it free of the holster, cocks it (you have to cock those single-action jobs for each and every shot), takes it in both hands, points it, aims very carefully, and pulls the trigger.

WHAMO!

There is this tremendous explosion and then a cloud of smoke all around him. And one of the bad guys is down and dead as can be with a shot directly between the eyes.

By the time this dawns on the other perpetrators, he has already managed somehow to cock the pistol and shoot and kill another one. With one shot right between the eyes. Hands up and we surrender, from the last two, the driver and the other guy. They can't quit quick enough.

Some thoughtful person calls the undertaker to come and pick up the stiffs, and the day marshal deputizes a few men on the spot. And they march them off to the pokey. Which hasn't been used in so long that they have to get the lights and water turned on.

Never mind. The word goes out and spreads like wildfire in the criminal community: *You better stay away from that place, I'm telling you. They have got some kind of a Hoot Gibson policeman there who can blow your head off with one shot at fifty yards. And he will sure enough do it, too. I mean to tell you, this fella is some kind of a cold-blooded killing machine. You want to do yourself in? You want to die quick and young? Just go on down there and try to knock over the Sunshine Bank.*

Now, you know and I know that criminals tend to exaggerate, especially when they are describing the power and the glory of the lawmen who have managed to collar them and send them away to the cooler. You have to believe that the man (or woman nowadays) who took you down was not much shy of being Superman. And locally the myth is just the opposite—how this helpless old-timer somehow pulled it all together long enough to stop the only bank robbery we ever had. Because that was, in fact, the beauty of it all—that there has never been another bank robbery in our town. Throughout the rest of the Depression banks all over the South were being held up and robbed so often they barely had time to conduct normal banking business. Bonnie and Clyde, John Dillinger, Machine Gun Kelly and Pretty Boy Floyd, all of them and many more. But not here. Not as long as the old guy was still alive. Not as long as the story outlived him.

The man who tells it to me, taking me for a stranger, is, like many another American of our end-of-the-century era, more than a little disillusioned with how things have turned and are turning out.

"From Wild West to sensitivity training," he says. "From pioneers to pansies in one generation."

Then he says: "Poor old Texas Pete, he put in for the price of the two bullets, and they turned him down flat, arguing that they didn't authorize the use of the pistol for anything but decoration, anyway."

"Is that a fact?" I say.

"Take my word for it."

Bad Man Blues

"Do you want to hear about the last lynching we had here in Quincy County?"

I can assure you that none of us is eager to hear that story, whatever it was and wherever it might lead. I mean, we're just a bunch of young yuppie lawyers sitting at one of the big round oak tables in the air-conditioned bar of the old Osceola Hotel across the street and halfway down the block from the county courthouse where we have spent a long and tedious day, and here we are knocking down a few beers in tall frosty steins and swapping a few jokes and stories.

None of us is eager to listen to Willie tell us about the last lynching in the county or, for that matter, about any lynching at all, early or late, first or last. All that ancient history has nothing to do with any of us. Not really. Think of us as being like young yuppie lawyers anywhere in America. Might just as well be in Connecticut or Iowa. None of us would even dream of bringing up something like that, you know?

Problem is, that's Willie Gary talking. And when he talks (which isn't all that often, really) we usually listen. Young as he is, and Willie is my age, he may well be the best and the brightest among us. He didn't go to Gainesville or Stetson. No, sir, Willie went to Harvard. Best and brightest (as they say), he is already a partner in his firm.

And then there is the undeniable fact that Willie is a black man. There is still that difference. If I were to bring up something like that, here and now in the Osceola Hotel, the guys would hoot and jeer and tell me to forget it. But, let's face it, Willie's equality is so new that nobody dares to treat him like an equal. Know what I mean? That is still a ways away. Maybe a whole generation or two. Maybe never.

So. There are no groans or anything. Everybody at least feigns interest. I expect some of the others, like myself, wonder why on earth he wants to tell us a lynching story. But never mind. Willie has the floor.

The last lynching in Quincy County. Last one so far, anyway. Now, I don't honestly know how many they may have had in the old times. Some, I am sure, but probably not many. Had to be some, though, because this whole area, this whole part of the state was a hard, tough place full of hard, tough men having a hard time making a living.

If you listen to the Negroes—and who else did I have to listen to while I was growing up?—and the tall tales they tell, you would think it was a fairly commonplace event. I think they exaggerated. I think they liked to make the old days sound a lot worse than they ever were, or could have been, just for the sake of the story. It's an ethnic habit. All the more so since the lynching had stopped right after the events I'm going to tell you about. Stopped long before I was born, in fact.

Now this took place during the first big Florida boom in the 1920s when everybody, even including some lucky Negroes, was getting rich or richer and there looked to be no end to the sweetness of it.

Now then. Buster Ford, who stands at the center of this story, was without any questions or doubts a badass nigger. He was nothing but bad. Baddest man to come out of Quincy County in living memory. Born that way and lived that way. Doing bad things all the time.

This particular thing was pretty bad. A brutal rape-murder involving some white woman. That was what usually upset the white folks more than anything else. If it had been a black woman, he would have been in trouble, too. But not serious, life-threatening trouble.

Of course now, maybe he didn't do it. Bad as he was, he may have been innocent. But he was suspected and that was enough. The main idea of a lynching in a case like that was to prevent a trial from taking place. To preserve the public reputation, even posthumously, of the victim. Somebody had done it to her all right. And somebody was going to have to pay the bill. It didn't matter exactly who that somebody happened to be. Buster had a terrible reputation and record anyway. Nobody would miss him very much.

You see, the idea behind lynching wasn't only to preserve the privacy and repute of the victim. It was also a deterrent and, on the whole, a fairly effective one. You can't be alive in this century and not understand the terror of random, indifferent punishment. Stalin knew how it works. Did okay for him, didn't it? Killed millions and then died of natural causes in a comfortable bed.

There was a little twist to this one, though. Buster was so bad, such a bad human being, that the black community was perfectly willing for him to pay the price for the crime. Nobody knew who really did it. Hell, he probably did do it. And even if he didn't, he would have if he could have.

Buster was in deep. And he knew it, too. He may have been bad, but he sure wasn't dumb. Black and white all agreed he was smart and slick.

So there he is locked up tight in the county jail. And there is a mob gathering and working itself up. They have to do that, you know? Most people just can't bring themselves to kill somebody else in cold blood. That's what civilization does to you. That's the edge a guy like Buster has. It don't bother him even a little bit to kill a perfect stranger in cold blood, black or white, and regardless of religion, country of national origin, or sexual preference.

Buster's in the jail and the mob is coming together. And all the help and the other inmates are scared shitless. Then the Sheriff comes calling on Buster. They sit down side by side on the narrow cot in Buster's cell. Both of them smoking the Sheriff's Lucky Strike cigarettes (in a nice green pack in those days).

Sheriff says, "Buster, I figure they will be coming for you very soon, ten or fifteen minutes maybe."

"Most likely, Sheriff," Buster says.

"Now here's the thing, Buster. If you were an innocent man—and I mean innocent of *any* serious crime, not just this one—why, then I would feel compelled to save your life for the sake of the Law, come what may. I think I would kill to save your life if I had to."

"Yes, sir, Sheriff, I believe that. But how about a case like mine, you know, one that's a little bit more complicated?"

"You got me there, Buster. You put it aptly. It's a complicated case. But the long and the short of it is that I am not fixing to defend you to the death. That would be a waste. You know and I know that you are not worth that."

"Of course, I understand your argument, Sheriff. You got a point, though it don't quite persuade me."

"How do you mean?"

"Well, sir, it's more involved than just me and them. Here I am on the topmost floor of county property. Now, if those folks come to get me, you're going to have a big crowd of hotheaded, out-of-control peckerwoods, all kinds of white trash, along with the good and decent people, of course, tracking up your jail. Doing damage. They can't hardly help from doing considerable damage to county property. Besides that you got a goodly number of other inmates locked up in here. What's going to happen to them? They are helpless once that mob gets inside, intent on blind vengeance, why they might do most anything. What I'm saying, Sheriff, is you got more niggers to look after than just me."

"Point well taken, Buster. And I have to admit to you that I thought of it already. But then I asked myself what would happen if they never got inside the main door."

"How would that happen, Sheriff? Wait a minute. You are not thinking what I think you are thinking, are you? You are not planning just to hand me over to them at the front door?"

"Got a better idea?"

"Well, yes, I do. It isn't perfect. But it's a way we can both agree on."

"And what would that be, Buster?"

"Let me go. Now. *Before* they get here. Give me a chance at least to make a run for it. I can run like the wind, Sheriff. I can run like Jesse Owens and maybe faster than that with a lynch mob on my tail. How about it?"

"Well . . . I don't know."

"What do you got to lose, Sheriff? I mean, chances are they will catch me quick enough, anyway. Where can I go? Where can I hide? But at least I will have a chance. And whatever happens and comes to pass, you won't be to blame."

"All right, Buster. Let's go right now. Because I think I hear them coming."

So they ran down four flights of steps and the Sheriff gave him a big push out of the main door and then slammed it to and locked it behind him.

Buster looks left and then looks right. From the right a couple of blocks away, here comes the mob yelling and milling its merry way. One look and Buster is gone. Gone like the wind, if not with it, in the other direction.

Behind him he hears a sudden shouting, an uproar and then the patter of feet on pavement like a hard rain. He won't waste precious time and energy by looking back.

After running a few blocks down Main Street (now called Orange Avenue), he crosses the Atlantic Coast Line railroad tracks and is getting close to home, in the edges of what was then actually and officially named Black Bottom. Turns off on a side street. First thing he sees is a black man coming along towards him.

"Hey!" Buster yells at him (he would say Hey, Brother nowdays, but then that Brother and Sister stuff wasn't in common currency around here except in the church). "Hey! You better turn around and haul ass. Because a mob is right behind me. Run! Run!"

That poor nigger didn't even pause to take a breath. He took off running as fast as he could go.

Buster, meanwhile, turns around and heads back towards Main Street. Strolling, man, I mean *strolling,* and whistling a tune. The mob comes around the corner.

"You! Boy!" they say. "Did you see a nigger running away?"

"Yassuh," Buster says. "I surely did. And there he goes now."

Points at the vanishing brother. Mob takes off in high gear. Some of them maybe (I would like to think so) even say thank you to Buster for his help.

Buster goes off, still strolling and whistling along, having successfully bet his life on the proposition that, give or take a little familiarity, all black men look alike to white people.

What happens.

Buster, of course, escapes. The other fellow is not so lucky. They catch up with him and promptly hang him from an oak tree. Only later, the next day, do they discover that they got the wrong guy.

Now then.

Embarrassment, as we all know, is a great source of social ameliora-
tion. And the folks around here are very embarrassed. *Not,* though you
might think so, about hanging an innocent man. Guilt and innocence are
irrelevant in this matter. Somebody paid for the crime and that's good
enough. No, sir. They don't waste even a raised eyebrow over the unfortunate Negro they just disposed of. The true source of their shame is that
Buster outwitted them. *Outwitted!* Walked right through and past them
and escaped. The idea that Buster fooled them is unbearable. And that
shame, and nothing else, is the reason, the main one, anyway, there hasn't
been a single lynching in Quincy County since then.

Nobody says anything at first. What is there to say? Mighty quiet. You
can hear the vacuum cleaner humming in the lobby or the dining room.

Willie holds up his empty beer glass for the waitress.

"Tell me something, Willie," Joel says.

"What?"

"Whatever happened to this Buster . . . ?"

"Ford. Buster Ford."

"Yeah. Whatever became of him?"

"God knows. I don't. God knows and won't tell. And you know why?"

"Beats me."

"Because God doesn't care what happened to Buster Ford. Buster
knew that. It was what gave him his edge, his advantage."

"I think you are turning into a cynic, Willie."

"You do, huh? You do?"

"Sometimes."

"Well . . . ," he laughs and gestures for refills all around. "Sometimes
I feel like one. Maybe that's what gives me my edge."

Three Occasional Pieces

Everybody knows about the style and substance of the occasional *poem,* that poem written on demand for one or another particular occasion— the five hundredth anniversary of Columbus's voyage to the New World; Billy Joel's birthday; Valentine's Day at our house. W. H. Auden was a modern master of the form and content of the occasional poem. So, also, are Fred Chappell, R. H. W. Dillard, and David Slavitt, among others.

The occasional work of short fiction is not so widely practiced or well-known. Sometimes an editor will write to a writer to ask if he or she happens to have anything available that might possibly fit in with an actual or a thematic occasion. Once, more or less by accident, I put together an anthology called *The Girl in the Black Raincoat,* full of stories and poems about girls in black raincoats. Ever since then, I have been doing my best to come up with something or other when asked or challenged to contribute an occasional piece of fiction. I always give it my best shot.

Now, it is certainly true, no question about it, that an occasional fiction, like occasional poems, tends to be slighter and lighter, in form if not in substance, than a writer's other work. And there are usually all kinds of limitations. But not everything has to be heavy or heavy-handed, does it? And, anyway, isn't it true, don't you see it in the work of the writers you know best and admire and enjoy, that a good writer always does his or her best come what may in every enterprise large or small? If your purpose is to tell the truth (mainly), you aim to do it every time. It would be cheating, then, not to stand by your occasional work. And, besides, it's a change of tone and pace, which can have some value in a collection.

Here, then, are some occasional pieces from the past few years.

James Charlton was putting together a little book whose title says it all—*Bred Any Good Rooks Lately?* "Lupe Has the Last Word" was my response and contribution to the challenge for fun and games. Why not? I don't know of any art form, high or low, that doesn't allow for some place reserved for the purely and simply silly.

"Hurray for Hollywood" was written in answer to a challenge of the late Jerome Stern to come up with a short-short story of less than three hundred words. He collected the results in *Micro Fiction: An Anthology of Really Short Stories*.

Finally, *Style* magazine of Richmond, Virginia, wanted something of roughly the same length (one typewritten page), this one to be devoted to a summer memory. For which I recollected "Independence Day."

1. Lupe Has the Last Word

"Hey!" Hector's wife Lupe always used to say, back in the early days when he was playing in the minors and couldn't get shoes big enough to fit him. *"If you can't stand the feet, get out of the pitching!"* Sure, you remember Hector Espanola, the Tex-Mex with the blazing fastball and plenty of junk, too, in his repertoire. Five times a twenty-game winner; pitched a shutout in the Series; nine consecutive strikeouts in a Red Sox game; Hall of Fame just a few years ago.

But, like everybody else, you probably don't know that he never got shoes until he went up to the Yankees. He would complain about it all the time and Lupe would nag at him for being such a whiner. "Nag, nag, nag," he said (who had never heard of Sam Goldwyn). "Criticism rolls off my back like a duck."

People have forgotten, too, all the trouble he had with those Urdu brothers, the rowdy Finnish twins who played in the outfield for Waco. Somehow they could hit everything he had, and they damn near kept him in the minors forever with them. Hector had no alternative but to dust them off and knock them down every time they stepped up to the plate. They had no honorable choice but to go after him, aiming for the big head or the bare feet with their bats. Plenty of bad feelings all around.

When he was called up to the majors, they hooted and jeered and made bad Bronx cheers in the newspapers. But years later, when he made the Hall of Fame, they swallowed their anger and pride and sent him their warm and hearty congratulations. "Well, we've passed a lot of water under the bridge since then," Hector opined, showing Lupe their telegram.

"Hey," she cried (who never heard of Leo Durocher). *"Finnish guys nice at last!"*

2. Hurray for Hollywood

"Couple of minutes is all, Sammy. Please?"

You call him Sammy, like everybody else, carefully. He looks at a wristwatch you will never be able to afford.

"Here's the thing. Big bank and a couple of Fortune 500 companies get together to create a magic credit card, ultimate card, the Aladdin card, absolutely unlimited, billions in credit. Just the one. To be awarded by a computer to one person only. So the fix is in. Card is supposed to go to a particular charismatic guy who's in on the gag. Only the computer goofs. Card goes to this nerd, a librarian in some heartland place like New Hampshire.

"Now the nerd doesn't believe in credit or credit cards. Won't use it. Act One is they got to make him use it. They ruin his life and he disappears. Turns into an outlaw. They hire his dopey local fiancee to go after him. Meantime, Act Two, everybody else wants the card and is after our boy—the Mafia, the FBI, the IRA, the CIA, the Democratic National Committee, I mean everybody. Cut to the chase. He's in all kinds of disguises. Ties in with a basic blond bimbo and they crisscross the country, fuckin' their brains out. Sharon Stone could do the bimbo. Or Kim Basinger. So, anyway, Act Three is how he goes bananas. Starts buying everything in sight including the whole state of Idaho. Now everybody wants to kill him. Even the bimbo. But just in time the dopey fiancee catches up with him. He sees the light. Shreds the card. Marries the broad. Goes back to his library where he checks out books to little old ladies and horny teenagers. Lives happily ever after with memories. For the nerd I see Tom Hanks . . . maybe Tom Cruise . . . Tom Robbins?"

"It's Tim."

"Whatever . . . Wait a minute, Sammy . . . How about Kate Moss and Johnny Depp together at last for the very first time? . . . Good talking to you, Sammy, sir . . . See you around . . ."

Nice watch you got there, asshole.

3. INDEPENDENCE DAY

Time: Early in the days of the Great Depression. Place: Florida east coast, just south of the still-undeveloped, still-unspoiled Daytona Beach; a cottage in the dunes facing the sunstruck, breezy Atlantic. Persons: Ourselves, kith and kin, mostly cousins and children, camped there for a whole month. Also, from the only other cottage nearby, a group of pale young men, Yankees by their accent, but nice and quiet and neighborly, though having some odd habits like going to and from the beach in their bathrobes.

Then came the Fourth of July. We waited for dark with our sparklers and Roman candles. Grown-ups, uncles and such, set off rockets over the ocean. A fine time until, all of a sudden, out on the front porch of their cottage the young men appeared, stood in a row and amid blooms of flame and earth-shaking, ear-shattering noise fired off fully automatic tommyguns. Shooting at the sky in happy celebration.

Couple of days later our neighbors were gone. Lucky for them, because soon after here came the police and the FBI in many cars.

"You boys are too late," my father told them, laughing.

They told us that the pale young men were the one and only John Dillinger gang. They said we were lucky to be alive.

"Well, one thing for sure," Father said. "They are all patriots."

"And they had very good manners," my mother added, "even if they were Yankees."

PART II

Academic Anecdotes

We all know, that as the human body can be nourished
on any food, though it were boiled grass and the broth of shoes,
so the human mind can be fed by any knowledge.

RALPH WALDO EMERSON

I wrote my first sequence of academic anecdotes, "Tigers in Red Weather,"
for my book *Whistling in the Dark* (1992). That awakened my memory
and interest, and I realized I still had a few more things to say.

One day, years and years ago, when the chance came along (the GI
Bill and a fellowship that nobody else wanted) to go to graduate school,
I took that chance. What could possibly be the harm of a brief exposure
to the academic life? It was certainly going to be brief, because I had
already decided to be a writer, preferably a rich and famous one, and I had
no plans whatsoever to take on the professorial yoke for a lifetime. Off I
went, then, to graduate school at Princeton. How well my casual life plan
has worked out is witnessed by the fact that, somehow or other, I am now
in my fortieth year of full-time teaching, though still optimistic that one
of these days something will lift me out of my past and present and into
the respectable life of a "professional" writer.

Meanwhile I have this string of anecdotes, more like worry beads
than a rosary, a group of true stories, none of which carries more weight
or significance than a *fabliau,* but all of them at least exemplary.

"Exemplary of what?" you ask, as you are entitled to.

Exemplary of an academic life and of the academic profession in our times.

And if that is too grand and too vague a claim, then look at it this way: each anecdote/*exemplum*/parable offered here has, in fact, a plain and simple moral, as much so as any fable by Aesop or Avianus, here for the taking. *(And he said unto them, He that hath ears to hear, let him hear.)* And there is likewise a subtext for each and every part, even this prologue. Which, as you will have noticed, asserts that though our lives have greatly changed and are greatly changing, still the subtle, complex, fragmented, always local American class system, as fiercely rigid as razor wire, seems not to have changed much in a century or more.

(And he said unto them, Know ye not this parable? And how then will ye know all parables?)

Body and Soul in Connecticut

At Wesleyan, my first teaching job, they were suddenly discovering the life of the body. Professional types, who had, so far in their sedentary lives, broken less sweat than wind, were suddenly trotting around the track in brand-new sweat suits and shiny white sneakers. This was well before the fashions of jogging and real running shoes. I remember standing in the shade of the old nineteenth-century gymnasium with some of the coaches (one of which I was, on a part-time basis, thanks to the wasted jock time of my youth) watching this new development with uniform bafflement. I was relieved that they didn't choose to hoot and jeer at my academic colleagues. I would have been on crutches, having broken a leg—I forget which one—trying to run back punts against the varsity football team. Served me right. Coaches aren't supposed to do that kind of thing. When it came to exercise, coaches in general followed the customs of the army: Never run if you can walk; never walk if you can ride.

"What's going on?" the old head coach of football asked me. "Beats me," I replied. What else could I say? How could I stand there and tell him, this nice old man, what was going on in academic offices and classrooms?

These academics, who as recently as the 1948 election had, most of them, supported and a few had even run for state offices in the Progressive Party, trying at the least to topple a man they seriously considered an enemy of the people, Harry S. Truman—these guys had recently turned their failed (and mostly imaginary) revolution inward, where it was less costly and less embarrassing. All of a sudden there was a lot of talk in the usual places about discovering and cultivating the free, impulsive animal life of the body and, beneath the skin, the dark and Dionysiac gods of the blood and a lot of other stuff that should have been discredited with the rise and fall of the Third Reich.

Imagine trying to explain to the coaching staff the deep meanings involved in the actions of a few out-of-shape faculty members trotting and skipping around the track.

My friend and colleague Ihab Hassan put on the gloves with Norman Mailer and earned a black eye, some swelling and a few minor bruises as the price for an interview. There was a certain amount of arm wrestling going on at the lunch table and some instances of necking with other people's wives in dark parking lots. A thrilling time to be in the profession. Other colleagues began to go around singing the praises of the newly revealed Beats, some of whom I knew from here and there and almost all of whom had been to good graduate schools. Many held more advanced degrees than I did. The whole Beat thing, even though a lot of it was the smoke and mirrors of publicity, was a part of the same self-styled revolution.

One of the leading local figures, indeed soon to be a guru and an ideological monitor for the larger movement, was . . . let us call him Corydon, to spare the guilty and myself. Who transformed himself before our very eyes (and without benefit of phone booth) from a straight, mild-mannered classics professor into a supermensch, babbling not of green fields but of blood and guts, enough so as to be named in due time the General Patton of the counterculture. I liked old Corydon and I enjoyed hearing him hold forth, though I didn't and still don't claim to understand what he was talking about. I figured that maybe he and the rest of them were on to something and that maybe some day I would have the time to find out what it was all about. Meantime a heavy load of classroom teaching was eating up my waking and working hours.

Since I was the newest and lowest-ranking member of the English Department (except for my office mate, who was coming off four or five years as a Pinkerton detective and very soon would wisely decide to return to that line of work), my office, *our* office, was the least desirable space in the old house which served the department. To get there I had to go through the office of Robert Lucid and enter his closet and go up a flight of stairs that began there. What I climbed up to was a converted pigeon loft. A lot of pigeons did not believe or accept the fact that it was now an office. They came and went. There were a couple of high, small, dirty windows that you could look through if you stood on a chair. The view was across the rooftops of town, over the Connecticut River and of a cluster of large ugly brick buildings on the other side. These were part of the state mental hospital. I would climb up on a chair and look. Down below, out of sight in the backyard of the house next door (still lived in), a chained dog moaned and barked and howled most of the time.

A student of mine, enrolled in an evening class in remedial reading and writing, worked at the hospital as an orderly for the senile and geriatric wards. He told and wrote some truly horrendous stories about what went on at this workplace. The one I always remember had to do with the tricks, the japes and pasquils, the day shift played on the night shift and vice versa. Like giving the incontinent old people a heavy dose of laxative just before going off duty.

You want to celebrate the life of the body? I'll give you the life of the body . . .

I wrote a poem based on all that. I guess now that it was really all about depression.

SOLITAIRE

The days shuffle together.
Cards again? No, No, I mean
little convicts in lockstep,
like the patients on the senile ward
I saw once, gray and feeble,
blank-eyed creatures in cheap cotton,
brimful of tranquilizers.
("It's the only efficient way to handle
this situation," an attendant told me.)
So lethargic they could hardly pick up their feet.

The gray days shuffle together.
The trees are picked and plucked,
sad tough fowl not fit for stewing.
The round world is as shaved and hairless
as the man in the moon. Screams!

But I can't hear it.
Next door a dog howls and I can.
Break out a brand-new deck for God's sake!
Bright kings and queens and one-eyed jacks.
Free prisoners. Let the old men go home.

One break I had in the routine was every Wednesday night I took a two-hour train ride on the decaying New Haven Railroad, from nearby Meriden to New York City, where I was enrolled in an evening course. This was followed by a two-hour return on the last train back. My journey began at a bus stop near the campus in Middletown. Every time, half a mile or so beyond Wesleyan, Corydon would board the bus, too. This seemed vaguely odd because it was such a good way from school and was not anywhere near where he lived. He seemed slightly furtive as he entered the bus, took a seat by himself up front, and quickly hid behind a newspaper. He seemed even more furtive when he got off the bus, a couple of blocks before the railroad station, and after a quick look around (as if to determine whether he was being observed), ducked down an alley, a dark alley, as it happened, that time of year, and disappeared.

Week after week the same thing happened until my curiosity was as itchy as athlete's foot. What could Corydon, apostle of the dark secrets of the body and the immemorial music of the blood, be up to in a dark alley in downtown Meriden, Connecticut? Finally, my itch to know was so bad that I knew I had to follow him and find out. Even at the risk of missing the train to New York.

I was almost certain that he never noticed me on the bus, and I was glad that I had never greeted him. So I took my usual seat in the back of the bus and waited. At his usual place he signaled and boarded the bus. Furtively. Took a front seat and opened up a newspaper. At the usual place he pulled the cord and the bus stopped. He got off, looked left and right and all around, then vanished into the alley. At the last possible second—the driver had already shifted gears—I pulled the cord myself and leapt off the back exit. I then tiptoed down the alley. Up ahead of me a light went on, on the second floor of a dark building. I kept close to the wall beneath, outside of the pool of light. Then in a moment I heard music, Latin music, and a very slightly accented woman's voice saying over and over again: "One, two, three, cha-cha-cha! One, two, three, cha-cha-cha!"

I stepped briefly into the light so I could look in the window. And there was Corydon with a partner, an instructor, actually (a sign on the window announced the place to be an Arthur Murray Dance Studio) learning to do the *cha-cha-cha*.

I turned away and ran and just made the train as it was pulling out of the station.

Feeling better about things. Feeling better about Corydon, and Dionysius and the pains and pleasures of the academic life. Like Sartre and Camus, Ginsberg and Corso, they were only about half kidding. Just messing around, as we would have put it down home. And all that it added up to, in the real world of kisses and bruises, was some private lessons at Arthur Murray's.

A Great Big One

In Rome that year a pope died and a new pope was elected by the college of cardinals. Fellini was making the movie *La Dolce Vita* (only it was then titled *La Vita Dolce,* which is not only different grammatically but also underlines the homage/allusion to Dante and *La Vita Nuova*). A group of us were busy putting together and bringing out the first two issues of the new and improved *Transatlantic Review*. A copy of the first issue is seen (less than a blink or a wink) on a coffee table in *La Dolce Vita*. But mostly I was holed up in the American Academy using this rare gift of free time to write a novel.

In Rome, at the American Academy, I learned many things, not the least of which was the difference between the critic and the artist. I might not have learned that crucial distinction from the literary world. It was easier to see in the company and by the examples of the other kinds of artists who lived and worked at the American Academy—composers and musicians, architects and painters and sculptors.

One of the sculptors was my friend, good buddy, in those days. Allen Harris was a large, powerful man with a commensurate enthusiasm for his work with clay and stone and bronze and for the good things of life in Rome. One of the things he did (and we all had a lot of fun doing "research" for it) was to write a little book, called *Tables on the Tiber,* about the really good and really cheap eating places in the city. It was a wonderful little book with maps and menus and anecdotes. Allen and I had the army in common. Our wars and experience were different, but it was a bond, something we could talk about or take for granted. He had had some extraordinary times, serving as a rifleman (just seventeen years old) in an infantry assault company in Patton's army. Less than a dozen of the original company that landed in France were still alive at the end of the war.

Allen's kind of sculpture—mostly figurative and based on modeling—was not exactly fashionable at that time. In America he had earned his keep, between sales and commissions for sculpture, as a bronze caster for other artists and anybody else who wanted something cast in bronze. He was really good at that work, a master; and so he soon made contact with the bronze casters of Rome. Sometimes he would knock off work in his studio at the Academy and take me along to see the Romans working with bronze. We visited a busy little group in a run-down farm at the edge of the city who made fake Etruscan bronzes. They were very well made, and, after they had been soaked in a barrel of urine (and other things) to acquire a good patina and buried in mud for a while, they looked authentic enough to be successfully sold to Americans and others who wanted Etruscan artifacts. Once, in another place, we were watching them pour a casting for some local sculptor when Allen suddenly grabbed me by the elbow and said, "Let's get out of here right now." We didn't run, but walked quickly out of the shed and into the fabulous Roman sunlight, hearing behind us a lot of voices yelling all at once. He explained that they were working on a shoestring, that the only way they could possibly make a profit was not to waste anything. While we were watching them carefully pouring the cast, he had realized there wasn't enough bronze to do the job. It was going to be a complete disaster, not only for the casters but for the sculptor who was pacing nervously in the shadowy background.

"Didn't you want to see the shit hit the fan?" I asked.

"Oh no," he said. "That would be *brutta figura.*"

Meaning a bad scene, the worst kind of bad manners to bear witness to somebody else's misfortune.

Another time we were at a more elegant foundry watching them cast works for a Middle Eastern sculptor who did large public statues of leaders all over the Third World. These figures were all pretty much the same except for a few details and, of course, different heads. He was working on a big one that had already been cast while the new casting was going on. When he found out that Allen was a sculptor, too, he apologized for his work, especially the casual, even sloppy care of details.

"You have to understand," he said. "I make the statues of the leaders of these countries. They pay me very well for this. But it is heartbreaking.

None of them can last, can stay in power for very long. The statues go up in the parks and squares. Then after a while comes a revolution. And what is the first thing the new regime does? They topple and destroy the statues and order new ones. It's a good living for me, but it's discouraging. You can understand why I am indifferent to the little details."

At the American Academy there were conventional academics, too. A lot of classicists, who impressed me more than any other academics I have ever known before or since, at least in the so-called humanities, because they had to know so much as a matter of course—languages, archaeology, anthropology, and so on. They seemed real in ways that other academics did not. There were various other critics and scholars as well. And we all got to know each other during the long leisurely lunch hour and in the evenings at cocktails and dinner. One man I met and enjoyed talking to was an art historian who was doing a book on Bernini's public sculptures. I liked to hear him talk about what he was doing. He was excited and enthusiastic and I could go get on a bus and in fifteen minutes see for myself what he was talking about.

Once he asked me if any of the sculptors at the Academy were working on anything that might be considered public sculpture. He knew about Milton Hebald and the zodiac he was making for the Pan American building at La Guardia. That was a big operation and he had been to see it. But how about anybody else?

Happened that Allen had just won a contest for a big piece to be made in honor of a dead basketball player in Kansas City. It had been kind of a feat because the people in Kansas City wanted something big but cheap. Allen had figured out a brilliant way to do it, flashy and inexpensive. He had a scale model in his studio.

Did I think I could arrange for the art critic to visit Allen in his studio?

Maybe. Probably. All the artists were more than a little edgy about letting people come to their studios unless it was definitely a potential buyer. Even then they might be or seem reluctant, because the buyers generally liked the idea of acquiring a work of art from a real and maybe "difficult" artist.

I asked Allen and he said okay. A date and time were set, and when the time came I took the art historian to the studio. Allen showed him around first, looking at a lot of different things, large and small, Allen was working on in various stages. I could tell the art historian's enthusiasm was fueled by what he was seeing. He understood what Allen was up to and he didn't care if it was fashionable or not. Finally they came to the scale model of the Kansas City piece. It was really something—neat, efficient, beautiful—and the art historian got very excited looking at it, talking about it. For maybe five minutes he talked rapid fire in a multisyllabic jargon that might as well have been another language but which certainly was intended to be praise. He talked and Allen listened, nodding, poker-faced. He talked until he ran out of breath, then smiling looked directly at Allen as if waiting for a reply. Always good mannered, never wanting to make a *brutta figura,* Allen cleared his throat and spoke softly.

"Well . . . yes . . . I guess you're right. It's a great big motherfucker, ain't it?"

Outside I walked across the gravel courtyard with the art historian. He seemed spent and depressed. I didn't have to ask him why. He told me.

"All my life," he began. "All my adult life I have dreamed of what it would be like to have some time, maybe five minutes, with Bernini. We could meet outside of time and space and I could ask him about, oh, the colonnade and the obelisk at the Vatican or maybe the four rivers statue in the Piazza Navona. I would ask him and he would tell me. Now I know exactly what he would tell me."

The art historian was a true gentleman. The punch line, emphatic, raucous, insistent as a train whistle, echoed in the empty air.

Send Me In, Coach

Rice University, which until very recently had been called Rice Institute, had approximately six hundred students, all of whom attended free of charge. It was, of course, impossibly competitive to be admitted for a free education. Rice was a very wealthy school with oil wells, land investments (they even owned the land that Yankee Stadium stood on) and a football team which was always a serious contender in the Southwest Conference and, thus, also a national power. That was no mean feat for a little school with very high academic standards. Actually, in those days (to the best of my fading recollection) all the football players came from the same department, the Commerce Department, a mysterious brick building located off by itself and close to the shadow of the huge stadium. The Commerce Department, as I understood things, took care of all of the courses and requirements of its own undergraduate students for the whole four years. In fact, students from that department were strongly discouraged from taking any courses outside of their department. All of the students in the Commerce Department were athletes. The chairman of Commerce was Jess Neely, who did double duty as the football coach.

All in all it seemed to be a pretty sensible system. The "real" students at Rice hated football players in general and with good reason. These brilliant students had suffered all through high school at the hands of the athletes and their active supporters, the overwhelming and mediocre majority. Now, though only about six hundred, the serious students were the majority. They wouldn't even walk across the campus to the stadium to watch a football game. The stadium was usually filled, but not with Rice students.

Over coffee the young and ambitious instructors and assistant professors in the Department of English, taking their cue from their own students, muttered mutiny and rebellion. It was a sure enough shame (on you and on me, on them, on everyone), they said, that a potentially top-flight university, filled with first-rate students and paying better-than-average salaries, should go on blandly permitting something like the blatantly bogus Commerce Department not only to exist, but also to thrive. They agreed to (pardon the expression) tackle the problem head on at the first big faculty meeting.

Even though I was only a lowly lecturer and anyway thought of myself, as ever, as just passing through this place, I figured the upcoming meeting might be more than mildly entertaining. Not to be missed. I could see all kinds of possibilities.

I am here to tell you, however, that what really happened took me completely by surprise.

Here is how it went. Purely and simply by accident, I ended up walking across the campus to the meeting with the chairman of English. We made some pointless small talk as we walked across the well-kept sunstruck sward towards the air-conditioned auditorium where the meeting was scheduled. When we entered the lobby of the building, there, lo and behold and looking altogether fine and dandy in an expensive and perfectly tailored suit, was himself, the chairman of Commerce, Coach Neely. Smiling, he stepped up to our chairman, greeted him warmly and then openly handed him an envelope.

And he said (in words to this effect, as I recall): "We had a much better year with the stadium concessions than I had anticipated. So I feel it's only fair to share our windfall profits with you and the other chairmen. Buy yourself some books or something."

Our chairman accepted the envelope, put it in his inside coat pocket, thanked the coach kindly, and then we went inside and took seats. Untroubled, the chairman ripped open the envelope and exposed for my easy inspection a check made out to our department for eighty thousand dollars.

Soon the meeting got under way. The young Turks were up on their feet savagely attacking the Commerce Department, attacking Coach Neely, making motions to change everything for the better once and for all.

I wondered what the famous coach would find to say in his own defense. As it happened, not one word. He could just as well have been snoozing for all I knew and all he cared. Then what we witnessed was truly wonderful, as, one by one in turn, each department chairman rose and eloquently and seriously described the Commerce Department as an outstanding, indeed essential part of the Rice academic family. Neely was a true scholar and a gentleman, and his students brought credit and distinction to this institution.

Hey, it never even came to a vote.

Later Coach Neely went to Vanderbilt, his old school, to be athletic director. Vanderbilt, that fine university, has a boulevard named after him.

A Hole in My Shoe

Princeton (again, a couple of times), and we were usually and relatively poor. Tough town to have no money in. Still young, then, and strong and healthy enough, we didn't worry about it too much.

First hitch there as a visiting teacher in the early 1960s taught me a thing or two. Our children were little then and went to the public elementary school at 185 Nassau Street, directly next to (and now part of) the university. It was a mostly black school. Most of the faculty children went to private schools. Individually these faculty people were the most uniformly liberal group I had met so far, even passionately so, outspoken in meetings and at cocktail parties. But their children went to private schools. I became a kind of pest by politely (always politely) asking them why. Down home, in the Southern schools, the faculty mostly sent their children to the public schools. For all the usual good reasons. Here they invented even more reasons for us, and others elsewhere, to do so. But they flatly refused.

"Are you kidding or something?" they would answer my polite question. "These are my kids. They are bright kids and they are going to get the best education that's available. I cannot in honesty sacrifice the future of my children for my own social principles."

The next step was to segue from sacrifice to the high cost of tuition at the local private schools. They had come to see this as a kind of sacrifice to principle.

"Hey, I pay taxes for the public schools," they would say, "whether my kids go there or not."

By the second time around, in the 1970s, the Nassau Street Elementary School had been bought by the university with federal funds and was being used to house the arts, including the creative writing program.

Nothing inside had changed much. The fountains and urinals were low, made for little kids. The odor of sweat and chalk was by now permanent. There was even a little room, I discovered, which could set off loud bells all over the building. Once in a while I did that, too, causing always a brief loud flurry of excitement. It was fun to make the poets and painters jump.

Princeton was always a great party town. A lot of drinking and merry-making. So much so that some people got jaded and had to come up with new and different themes for frivolity. One of these was when Paul and Betty Fussell had a "Come as You Were in World War II" party. Most of the women came as little girls. It wasn't my war but I came in army costume, anyway. Still able to fit in my old uniforms in those days. I was one of the two who were dressed as enlisted men. All the other guys came as high-ranking officers of the various services; and maybe they really were officers. Or maybe they had stayed on in the reserves or something. I didn't know whether to salute or what. So I got thoroughly drunk instead. And here my memory is a little cloudy. I remember trying to join in with three women who were lip-synching with Andrews Sisters' tunes. And then my people, friends and family, were taking me home. I remember looking in a coat closet near the front door and discovering a row of high-ranking hats, well-kept, with gold "scrambled eggs" on the shiny visors. I put one on and it fit. I refused to remove it. Took it home with me.

Next morning, with a trembling hangover, I had to return it. Turned out the hat belonged to a prominent Princeton psychiatrist who wanted to discuss the meaning of the whole event with me. Try that sometime while sweating out a terrible hangover.

Later, at my desk, I revised the experience and wrote this poem about it. Sent it to the shrink. Meaning? I'll give you meaning:

LITTLE TRANSFORMATIONS

Leaving the cocktail party
I steal the Admiral's hat
At home I try it on
See how much it changes me

Now I am purely different
I am handsome I am jaunty
I have pride and power on my head

Let him be sad and ashamed
Let him curse himself and whoever took it
Let him feel hopeless and lost without it
Let his wife laugh in his naked face

Listen Admiral it fits me fine
It looks just right on my closet shelf
My family will preserve it in my memory
My future history will be worthy of it

Sir I thank you kindly for it
And I solemnly promise never to stand
downcast and shifty in front of anyone
with your hat humble in my hands

But I started out talking poor, always a relative thing. Call it a limited cash flow. My wife had gone back to school in New York to earn a degree from Baruch College and Mount Sinai Medical School in health care administration. Soon enough, it turned out, she would be in charge of a community hospital in Maine. My wife was in school and one of my sons was expensively and desperately in the hospital. His brother and sister were well enough but were soon going to be off to college themselves. And how would that be? We didn't have enough money to make ends meet or pay our basic bills.

Now if I make the claim that I was much troubled by all this at the time I will be lying. I felt lucky a lot of the time. I was sure that everything was bound to turn out all right sooner or later.

Meantime, though, a few self-imposed economies might be in order. I quit smoking, cold turkey. (I was a three-pack-a-day man.) I quit buying anything new. And I was always looking for a way to save a buck. About that time I found a large hole in the sole of one shoe. The other shoe looked fine and dandy, but one had a hole you could wiggle your finger through.

It was a student who pointed it out to me. We were having a manuscript conference in my office at 185 Nassau Street and my feet were (rudely) up on the desk. I had just been running a number on her, urging her to try to write poems about ordinary mundane things. She had real talent, but was inhibited by her own self-imposed demand that she write about highly serious things, rich with meaning, resonance, implication. All the students at Princeton seemed to be very well-trained as critics. They went after symbols like greyhounds chasing a mechanical rabbit. Sometimes it made them too tight to write and respect their own things.

"You can write a poem about anything," I told her. "Be it ever so humble."

"Oh, yeah? You really believe that?"

"Yes. I do."

"Well, then," she said, tapping a shoe sole, the one with the hole in it. "Why don't you write a poem about that?"

I really liked this talented young woman and did not hold it against her that she was rich. In fact, in my present state it fascinated me. So did she, ever since she had left a note on my office door: "Mr. Garrett, I regret that I shall be unable to keep my appointment this afternoon; but, you see, my analyst has just died." People who knew about psychoanalysis told me that, true or false, it wasn't funny at all. It was the worst possible scenario.

"I don't know . . ."

"Put your money where your mouth is," she said. "See you next week."

So I had to write a poem about a hole in my shoe.

Directly across Nassau Street there was a shoe repair shop. I went and talked to the guy about my problem. I wanted to know if I would save anything by just having one shoe, the bad one, resoled. Sure, he told me, but the only trouble is you will be out of sync. The way it will work out is that one shoe or the other will always have a hole in it. Better get them both resoled. I did that. But I wrote the poem for her, imagining that I did not get both shoes repaired. You can see that a lot of poems are not true, strictly speaking. It was a slight poem, only an exercise. But now, looking back on it after a good many years, it's clear to me that I put a lot of true things into it, everything that I have already told you and then some, some things I wouldn't, then or now, have had the pure nerve to tell myself.

The last laugh is this. The speaker in the poem (myself, once upon a time) manages to disprove his own theory and thus is as much a hypocrite as anybody else.

LUCK'S SHINING CHILD

Because I am broke again
I have the soles of my shoes repaired
one at a time.

From now on one will always be
fat and slick with new leather
while his sad twin,

lean and thin as a fallen leaf,
will hug a large hole like a wound.
When it rains

one sock and one foot get wet.
When I cross the gravel parking lot
one foot winces

and I have to hop along on the other.
My students believe I am trying
to prove something.

They think I'm being a symbol of
dichotomy, duality, double-dealing,
yin and yang.

I am hopping because it hurts.
Because there is a hole in my shoe.
Because I feel poor for keeps.

What I am trying not to do
is imagine how it will be in my coffin,
heels down, soles up,

all rouged and grinning above my polished shoes,
one or the other a respectable brother
and one or the other

that wild prodigal whom I love
as much or more than his sleek companion,
luck's shining child.

SOUTH CAROLINA

Come On, Baby, Light My Fire

One of the things that happened at South Carolina, one of the good things, was the local premiere of *Deliverance*. Jim Dickey generously invited my wife and me to ride with him and his family in the huge stretch limousine to the theater. It was a black-tie affair and a large crowd, maybe everybody in Columbia who could rent, beg, borrow or steal a tuxedo, showed up. The theater was packed. Once the lights went down and the movie started, Jim jumped up and patrolled the aisles. He was giving a running commentary on the action ("Look at that! Look at the expression on Burt Reynolds's face!") and sometimes preparing the audience for what was to come and how they should react ("You're gonna love this next scene. Watch what happens to Jon Voight when he falls out of the canoe."). When the sheriff, played by Dickey himself, appeared near the end of the movie, Jim received a standing ovation as he spoke the sheriff's lines, loud and clear, in perfect sync with his image on the screen.

It was reliably reported that, from time to time, afternoon or evening, Jim would show up at the theater and, to the surprise of the paying customers, would give the same restless commentary and favorable critique of the movie.

Later, in another context, I learned that in Japan they did not use subtitles or dubbing until very recently. From the days of silent film on into the postwar period, theaters had a live narrator, commentator and critic at the movies. This man was called a *benshi*.

It seems like an interesting idea. It seems even better to have the author of the book and the screenplay selling his product in person during the showing of the film, a wonderful combination of hands-on and high tech.

At South Carolina, during the bad years, we had campus riots just like everybody else. On one occasion, the worst, maybe, they were planning to burn down the university president's house with the president in it. All this took place at the place called the Horseshoe, roughly shaped like one and marked by the oldest buildings, one of which was the president's house.

At one part of the Horseshoe, perhaps fifty yards away from the target, there was a portable speaker's stand, some microphones and loudspeakers, torches and enough gasoline in cans to burn down a lot of the city of Columbia. Speakers were whipping up the mob of students. A couple of cops stood casually by, seeming kind of indifferent and smirky. What they knew (and I guessed on the basis of my riot-control experiences in the army overseas) was that a small brigade of policemen, discreetly out of sight behind the president's house and in his basement, was standing by ready and willing, able and eager to break heads and to shoot to kill if need be. And because arson is (or, anyway, it still was then) a felony, a very serious crime, a capital crime in many states, any amount of force they used would have been lawful. And ever since Sherman burned a lot of Columbia to the ground, people there have been especially sensitive to the use of arson as a political gesture.

My guess was that the cops couldn't wait to take on the students and that the organizers in the SDS couldn't wait, either. They could already see the headlines and imagine the sound bytes. My best judgment was that things were going to get bloody and bloody awful soon. So, first things first, I went and found myself a safe berth, next to an old oak tree, with an easy egress to personal safety, and settled in to watch whatever came to pass.

What came to pass was nothing that I or apparently anybody else expected. The mob had the torches and the gasoline, and the leaders had them chanting threats and slogans. I could picture the president up there pacing in his bedroom with a fine view of the mob. He was a nice cheerful guy, a drinker with whom I had lifted and belted a few. And I knew he would be scared shitless, not just for himself but for everything and everybody. Bad things were just about to happen any minute.

Suddenly one of the SDS leaders grabbed the microphone and yelled ("Wait a minute! Wait a minute! Listen here! Listen to me!") and got their attention.

He looked at his wristwatch, then announced in a loud clear voice: "*Star Trek* begins in five minutes."

The Horseshoe was empty of students in a minute and a half as they tossed aside their torches and dropped their gas cans and ran off in every which direction towards the nearest television sets.

Maybe they planned to come back after *Star Trek* and start all over. If so, they forgot about it. The attention span of the 1960s revolutionaries was famously brief. Only the leaders and provocateurs were single-minded and relentless.

It was widely believed that the kid who remembered *Star Trek* at the last minute was working for the CIA.

Garbage and Other Collectibles

Bennington—that progressive, free-wheeling, free-spirited, and very expensive place—is the first and only institution to censor my reading list for a class. I always liked Bennington, what I knew about it; and a couple of my cousins were interesting graduates of that interesting place. I worked for them for ten summers on the staff of the writers' workshop. And, boy-oh-boy, I could tell you a story about some of those summers. But this is about the regular academic year at Bennington, where I worked only once.

It was the censorship that made me do what I did. I was probably overreacting. But, you see, I was such an innocent. Nobody, not any state university or cow college, not even VMI, where I taught for a semester, ever told me I could not teach some text in my class in their school. I had read and heard of such things, but never encountered anything like it until I was on the faculty at Bennington. Until, as was the custom, I turned in a list of the books I was going to be teaching in a course the following semester. This was supposed to be for printing purposes, so the students could see in advance what the course requirements would be.

I submitted my list to the chairman's office, as asked, and went about my business. Couple of days later I was called to report to the chairman's office. Old soldier, good soldier, I went at once.

"I am not going to allow you to teach two books on your course list."

"Really?"

Thinking: this guy is kidding me. It is a test or something. They want to know where I stand on things like, you know, censorship and all that. The chairman (who has lately figured, faintly disguised, in a number of novels) was reputed to be a complex and subtle character.

"Yes," he said. "Really."

"What books are you not going to allow?"

"*A Streetcar Named Desire* and also *In Orbit,* by Wright Morris."

Now, friends, I was really and truly baffled. I could not imagine what in either of these works could be conceived of as dangerous or offensive.

"Do you mind telling me why, sir?"

A long sigh, indicating that I should have known, would have known if I were not unbearably obtuse.

"*Streetcar* is a play by Tennessee Williams."

"Yes, sir. That is correct."

"I knew Tennessee Williams. Knew him rather well, if you want to know. I didn't like him. And long ago I made a solemn vow not to allow anything by Tom, as we called him . . ."

"I hear his nickname was 'Monster.'"

He ignored me.

"I took a solemn vow not to allow Tennessee Williams to be taught in this school. Or any place else where I might have any authority."

"Do you know Wright Morris rather well, also?"

"Nothing personal about Morris," he said. "It's just that Wright Morris is not a novelist. He's a photographer."

"*In Orbit* is a novel, one of a good many novels he has written."

"Wright Morris was here at Bennington a year or so ago. The Photography Department hired him. He taught photography. As far as we are concerned, he is a photographer and only a photographer."

"That's it?"

"What do you mean?"

"Do I get an appeal or anything?"

"No."

"You are really telling me that I cannot teach those works in my course next semester?"

"That is correct."

"And final."

"Final."

"In that case, sir, I here and now bid you and this place farewell."

And I meant it and quit on the spot.

But that is not the anecdote I want to tell you about my days at Bennington. My Bennington story (and you can link it to the other one on the metaphorical level if your mind works that way) is all about garbage. Besides the fact that most of the students were stoned most of the time those days, and even the dogs and cats seemed to be on Quaaludes, the biggest problem at Bennington was garbage collection. Oh, there were other pressing problems for the college, to be sure. The budget situation was desperate. No endowment, you see, and a gracious plenty of debt service to be paid off with everything else. Mostly everything was paid for by the highest tuition in the world. Even so, to try to make ends meet and to balance the budget called for fiscal magic (smoke and mirrors). The unenvied president had done away with all forms of maintenance of any kind, buildings and grounds, for at least a year. Grass and weeds grew tall and taller. Windows, here and there, were boarded up. Doors hung loosely on broken hinges. Toilets and light fixtures went unattended. Half the time the heat didn't work. During the wintertime in Vermont that can be, was, a problem. Most frills were dispensed with. For example, the library sold off most of its books. For campus security the rent-a-cops were replaced by stoned and long-haired kids looking like victims of a bad rock concert. Once they disappeared, en masse and for several days, when the word went out (a joke, as it happened) that an Upper New England chapter of Hell's Angels was on the way to Bennington for purposes of loot and pillage, planning to rape all the available girls and generally trash the place.

Let trash be my segue.

Garbage collection was private and collectors in the area were few and far between. Among the faculty, almost all of them living in faculty housing of one kind and another, it proved to be easier to get the names and numbers of their favorite baby-sitters or to divest them of their cleaning ladies than to find out how to plug in to a garbage pickup service. It was made quickly and abundantly clear to newcomers that it was a local tribal taboo, an unacceptable breach of etiquette, to ask anybody directly how one could make contact with their garbage collectors. (The few collectors listed in the Yellow Pages were not taking on any new customers.) The longtime faculty people seemed to have different collectors. And these collectors formed some kind of hierarchical status—good, better, and best. None was accessible or available to strangers and newcomers except by means of some kind of personal introduction.

At first it seemed funny, even as week by week big green plastic bags piled up in my garage. Pretty soon, though, the garbage was ripe and stinking. I broke the rules, then, asking friends and strangers, anyone, for advice and comfort. In all other matters they were warm and wonderful people. But in the case of garbage disposal, they were blankly indifferent.

I don't know what might have happened if I had not scouted and scoped out the location of every Dempsey Dumpster in Bennington and North Bennington. By the dark of the moon, headlights off, I would cruise behind the shopping mall or maybe McDonald's and furtively dump my green bags. Sometimes, on a weekend, I would bring a carload of garbage bags all the way home to Maine.

One evening at a dinner party in the apartment of the poet Stephen Sandy, a jolly and lively affair (whatever else, they knew/know how to party at Bennington; every Friday night the students managed to produce a wild and woolly "Dress to Get Laid" party in one of the dorms), I witnessed a moment of truth about garbage collection. Sitting next to me at the long table was Bernard Malamud, that mostly gentle, and always eccentric, and greatly gifted man. Across the table from us was Luis, an elderly Spaniard whose last name escaped me then and still escapes me now; though I do remember that he had held high offices in the Republican government of Spain until Franco won the civil war. Later he served in the American army in World War II and then was a professor at Stanford or Berkeley or somewhere out on the coast. He had now retired and was living in Bennington and, together with his wife, teaching some Spanish there. He struck me as, outwardly and visibly, everything a Spaniard ought to be—handsome, suave, polished, knowledgeable . . .

"Luis," Malamud was saying, "tell me how things are going for you here."

"Everything goes well, thank you," Luis replied. "Everything is fine. Except for this one bad thing."

"And what might that be?"

"My house, it is swimming in garbage. There is garbage everywhere. Soon it will be completely uninhabitable. What can I do about it?"

Solid frozen silence at the table. Heavy breathing and cutlery noises. Clearly Luis might just as well have pounded on the table and shouted out a string of obscenities.

Abruptly, Malamud produced a little notebook and a ballpoint pen. Scribbled in the notebook. (I tried my best to sneak a peek, but he was protecting the notebook from the sight of others.) He ripped out the page, folded it twice to a tiny size and reached across to Luis, who deftly palmed it.

"Luis," Malamud said, "you seem to be a very nice person. And you come from another country. Call that number and tell them it was given to you by Professor Malamud and that Professor Malamud personally recommends you. Of course, I can't promise anything; but I think it may work."

Everyone brightened. All voices began talking at once. I took a good gulp of my wine, thinking: *I am only here for this year, anyway.*

Flying Elephants

Michigan, which I experienced first as a visiting writer, then later for a couple of years as a regular faculty member, was charged with life and energy. With that many thousand people all in one place, how could it not be so? And I loved the static electricity of it, the rowdy history, the global variety of people.

Like any other shiny, academic apple, it had a bitter core to taste if you bit deeply enough. But I wasn't there long enough to reach the heart of the matter.

My best-all-around anecdote from those days was my Harold Bloom story, already used as the occasion for and the title of a book of mine—*The Sorrows of Fat City*.

Once upon a time, at the University of Michigan, where I was teaching, I attended a lecture by the celebrated Harold Bloom entitled "The Sorrows of Facticity." It was long enough and knotty enough to satisfy all but the most jaded admirer of contemporary criticism at its most abstract and demanding. To my pleasant surprise, I found that I could actually follow his argument fairly well, at least until some distraction or other allowed my mind to wander. Once disengaged, however briefly, from Bloom's text and texture, I found that I could never again catch up. But it was an interesting experience, like watching a foreign movie without benefit of subtitles or dubbing. Later, at a social reception, I stood in line to shake hands with the critic. And I did so, too, mumbling the usual platitudes of appreciation, when to my dismay, and as will sometimes happen, the line simply stopped moving. And there I was, face to face with Harold Bloom and forced to make conversation, *to say something!*, until the line moved on, if ever. . . . I told him (the truth) that I sometimes suffer from slight dyslexia and so I had misread the title of his talk on the printed posters as "The Sorrows of Fat City." Bloom, a large man, flushed red and scowled with apparent anger. In a wink of time I realized that he was completely unfamiliar with the slang expression "Fat City" and that, in his own kind of wisdom, he had concluded that I was, in a smiling, casual, perfectly offhand manner, making fun of his physical appearance. "Well! Well!" he snorted. "*You* aren't exactly a model of trim and slender fitness yourself!" (All too true!) Just then the line moved on, and I have never until now had an opportunity to explain myself.

(*Good Luck to Harold Bloom, if he happens to be reading this.*)

What is left over now from then are a few poems, mostly epigrammatic, satirical, strictly vernacular. It was there, where there were more poetry readings than any other place I had been before, or have been since then, that I began to think about and put together my still-uncompleted "Lives of the Poets," a series of epigrams, only slightly insulting, about some of the more prominent poets of our era. By now, you see, the discipline of poetry, the writing of poetry in America, was altogether merged into the academic discipline. There were (and are) almost no poets alive in America who were not employed by colleges and universities. Those few who were not—people like W. S. Merwin, for example—nevertheless depend on readings at and visits to colleges and universities to earn their keep. There are also a few, a very few, with earned or inherited money. Like James Merrill. But by the time I found myself at Michigan, the overwhelming majority of poets in America were engaged in the business of higher education. The idea of a regular salary and maybe a modest pension at the end of things quickly proved itself more attractive than hard labor or independence.

To live and endure in the system, poets have had to come to terms with intellectuals. (Who, in turn, often conceive of themselves as camouflaged poets.) A lot of our poets have learned how to invoke the names and the spirit of intellectual giants, evidently hoping to be construed as deep thinkers and deep readers. If you can't beat them, join them.

The victim here, though only lightly touched (I am, after all, only kidding and, as the poem demonstrates, I mean I know the guy) is . . . oh well, for the sake of us all call him Menalcus, who was my colleague, as a fellow writer-in-residence, the first time I taught at Michigan. In interviews and suchlike public statements, he often seemed to be talking about

major players in the intellectual game, shuffling their bright names like a
gambler's deck of cards. It's nothing personal. Old Menalcus is just a
stand-in here for all the other writers who, for one reason and another,
have to take their academic colleagues seriously:

DUMBO

That Menalcus
has really and truly
read and digested
the gnarled and knotty
(not to mention Nazi)
words of Martin Heidegger
I find about
as likely as
that one day soon
all the elephants
of Ringling Brothers Circus
will flap their huge ears
and fly away
in fabulous formation.

If that ever happens, Menalcus,
don't be caught
standing underneath.

Snickering in Solitary

The glorious setting of the University of Virginia ought to make it an incongruous, if not impossible, place for the ordinary low cunning, the routine, if sly, habits of backstabbing, the lead-footed dance of petty politics, the run-of-the-mill lying, stealing, and cheating that haunt the academic life. Amidst such a beautiful preservation of its founder's vision, and, indeed, with Mr. Jefferson, himself, overseeing it all from many angles, in bronze and stone, painted on canvas, it would seem at once inappropriate and unlikely that we could go about our ways and means without being stricken by the guilt of self-aware hypocrisy. And the truth is that all of these good qualities of the surroundings do serve to mute loud voices and to reduce somewhat the rages of confrontation. So much so that it is possible to be deluded by good manners and gentility into believing that we have managed to pass beyond brutish behavior and to arrive at a more civilized level of discourse and self-discipline.

It was at Virginia that I suddenly found myself, that selfsame person who had not planned to be among the academics for long and still didn't, rewarded, or punished as the case may be, with tenure. An adventure in irony. The only change this made in my life was that now, placed at the outer edges of the inner circle, I had to go to more meetings; and sometimes my vote, if not my opinion, mattered.

So I earned tenure and learned a few things, too. By that time, for better and worse, schools all over the country were beginning to hire poets and writers and were already finding ways to evaluate and credit their publication records. Soon enough—almost overnight is more like it—writers everywhere were bucking for promotion and tenure and talking a lot about the pressures and injustice of the publish-or-perish philosophy.

I found all this to be more than a little ironic. Here I was, only biding my time, disguised and camouflaged as a conventional academic, just waiting for the chance to bail out and join the world of real writers. Meanwhile, real writers were being actively recruited for the academy and so far seemed to be at home and prospering there, not yet worse for the wear and tear of it.

Virginia has an odd shape in my experience and memory. A kind of double exposure. Because I taught there twice, first in the early sixties, then again since the middle eighties. Same place and roughly the same job with a twenty-year intermission. Most places in twentieth-century America tend to change a lot, at least outwardly and visibly, in a twenty-year period. Much of Virginia, all except for the essential Jeffersonian core—the Lawn, the Rotunda, the Pavilions, the East and West Ranges—is much changed and ever changing. In my first hitch, for example, the school was not yet coeducational and there was a coat-and-tie dress code and the football team set some kind of record by losing twenty-eight games in a row. When I got back, after those years, it seemed very different and yet the same. My wife put it best, most accurately: "It's like being in a strange country where you know what's around every corner."

The most interesting thing I discovered was that some places, and Virginia is surely one of them, are haunted, *spooked.* They remain forever inwardly and spiritually the same. The people are different, the place is much different; and jackhammers and cranes are daily at work making more changes. And yet, at heart, nothing changes much. New faces commit the same old low crimes and misdemeanors.

At Virginia I learned some hard lessons, some things about academic politics and about public relations.

I already knew a little bit about the rough-and-tumble of "real" politics, because various people in my family had run for elective office or worked in support of candidates. I had even done some manual and menial local chores for the two campaigns of Adlai Stevenson and for the 1960 campaign of JFK. Oddly enough, that 1960 campaign should have taught me some truth about academic politics. Believe it or not, in 1960 a very large number, perhaps even a majority, of academics and intellectuals were uninvolved or disengaged. Writers, also. They did not see much difference between Kennedy and Nixon. Not many of them (except a little crew from Harvard) worked in the campaign. And I have to believe that a lot of them did not vote at all. Later these same people became converts, even enthusiasts, celebrants of Camelot while it lasted.

I knew a little of this and a little of that about political things, but none of that prepared me for academic politics or, maybe more precisely, for politics within the precincts of the academy. At first I was not shocked. I was entertained, and I thought that other people out there in the world might find the anecdotes and details of academic politics to be mildly entertaining, too. But I found that people outside the academy didn't find it as amusing as I did. I remember some ruthless corporate types telling me that their corporations could not and would not tolerate the kinds of shenanigans and sneaky behavior that seemed to be typical of academe. I found myself sometimes awkwardly trying to defend the academics.

Once upon a time, I used to work, during vacations, for Samuel Goldwyn, Jr., in Hollywood. I was out there one summer, and my agent invited me to lunch with him and, as it turned out, a whole table of agents—those infamous white killer sharks in dark suits. They were swapping tales of savage betrayal and breathtaking treachery, of back-stabbing and groin kicking.

During a pause in this vicious litany, I jumped in and told them about a recent department meeting at Virginia, a routine mousetrap play, a double whammy, a laying on of hands upon some poor nerd who was hoping for a promotion. Not only did the agents listen to me attentively, they fell into what I took to be a stunned silence.

Finally one of them spoke up for the whole group. "Do you mean to sit there and tell me that people like that are allowed to teach our children?"

My Hollywood boss, Samuel Goldwyn, Jr., an alumnus of Virginia, having met and talked awhile with my Virginia boss, Fredson Bowers, later allowed to me: "That guy could run a major studio." It was intended to be a kind of a compliment.

Some of our meetings (and subsequent decisions) were simply foolish. I remember that when my friend Joseph Blotner, deep into the research and writing of his Faulkner biography, came up for promotion (and was denied and went on to honor, first at Chapel Hill and then at Michigan), the distinguished committee of professors who evaluated his scholarly achievement announced the following judicious conclusion: that Blotner would never finish his Faulkner biography; that even if he somehow did manage to finish it, it wouldn't be any good and nobody would ever publish it; that in any case William Faulkner was not a writer of any real importance, merely a minor regional novelist.

With prophets like that (some of them still with us), how can our team lose?

What we lost was Blotner, that's for sure.

Another of the same kind. There was a young man who arrived on the scene, a former army helicopter pilot, now possessing a brand new Ph.D. from a good graduate school. He asked Fredson Bowers directly, straight out, how to succeed in this place and this line of work. Publish, he was told. Above all else, publish. And he went and did that. Zeroing in on the vast and as yet barely examined Waller Barrett collection of American literature, he managed to publish a dozen or so major scholarly articles in major scholarly magazines. He even edited a couple of books based on discoveries he had made.

At the end of his three-year hitch, when he came up for renewal or rejection, what was his fate at the hands of the department? He was unceremoniously dumped out because, in the opinion of our boss, he was publishing too much. "Anybody who publishes that much has a real problem," Bowers said. "He doesn't take scholarship seriously enough." That fellow went off, none too quietly to be sure, to a life and career elsewhere. He wrote a fantasy novel, an entertaining one, about the academic life of the future, a novel whose general stance is reflected in its title—*Final Solution.* Last news I heard was that he is the president of a big state university. Which, depending on your own experience and point of view, may or may not be a happy ending. I, myself, sincerely believe that (as the outdated figure of speech goes) playing the piano in a whorehouse is a distinct cut above being an academic administrator.

Not all our committee actions were funny or led to arguably happy endings. There were nervous breakdowns and even a couple of suicides that might well be attributed (if you still happen to believe in cause and effect) to things we of the English Department, in our collective wisdom, did that we ought not to have done and things left undone when we ought to have done them. As far as I can tell, nobody ever lost any sleep over any of these things. As a society we Americans were already slowly and inexorably moving to the advanced stage where all public figures in power are considered to be blameless no matter what happens as a result of their action or inaction or to whom it happens. God help you, though, if you are out of power or simply unpopular. The basic contemporary position (and you have heard it more than once and recently enough) goes like this: "The buck and the blame stop here. But I am blameless. So let us agree to forget if not forgive."

Even so, there are some things that are hard to forget. I remember the case of a visiting professor, a very distinguished figure, who had come, under some program or other, to spend a year with our department at Virginia. During that year, his wife fell seriously ill, was diagnosed as suffering from cancer, operated on, then declared to be terminal. She had at most a few months, maybe as much as a year left to live. The question put before the department was his request to stay on with us for another year. He could not easily move his wife from the hospital and doctors in Charlottesville, and he had young children to consider. We were informed that he would gladly teach a full teaching load and teach anything at all that was assigned to him. Salary to be negotiable, but he had limited expectations.

It was clearly what used to be called a hardship case. Nobody questioned or denied that he was a very good teacher or that his scholarly and critical work was of the highest quality. The debate centered on his politics, as witnessed and evidenced by nothing that he had said or done at the university, but by a number of book reviews and journalistic pieces published in conservative magazines, including the *National Review*. It was on this account, for this reason and, as far as I could tell, for this reason only that his request was rejected.

He stayed on in town while his wife slowly died, then moved on to a good job elsewhere.

That was not the first or last example I have encountered of the common cruelty of academics exercising authority, but certainly it was an egregious one. I still don't know to this day what they may have been really thinking or feeling at the time. I suppose I could ask. Some of that same crew are still my colleagues. But mainly I am ashamed (and never mind that I spoke and voted for him) to have been in such company and to have been a part of the process.

Here I have to say that the only examples I have ever seen, in a lifetime in the academy, of punishment and censorship of and for political opinions have come from the left and have been visited on conservatives. I have heard that it was the other way around before my time and I have no reason to doubt the truth of that. However, I have only seen it one way and not the other.

Yet it would be false not to admit that there was often a great deal of laughter in the groves of academe. Though it is surely no trouble for anyone alive and sentient in our century to imagine such a place, I, myself, have never been anywhere, in fact and in flesh, where laughter was wholly absent or inappropriate. The late John Ciardi put it very nicely in "Snickering in Solitary," a poem about the Birdman of Alcatraz: "In every life sentence / some days are better than / others; even sometimes, / better than being free."

In the early days, there was a young fellow (now an old teacher somewhere or other) who arrived from Yale to teach at UVa. When he was given his schedule of classes to teach, he seemed nonplussed, very upset.

"I can't do this," he said. "I simply can't teach classes before noon."

"Oh? Well, maybe you better go have a talk with Fredson Bowers."

Which, in his innocence, he went and did. Swallowing our laughter we hung around the department office to see what Bowers, who was not easily amused by the problems of the junior faculty, would find to say to this young man.

The actual scene went something like this.

BOWERS: You wanted to see me?

YM: You have me teaching classes in the morning.

BOWERS: So?

YM: I can't do that. I can't do any teaching before noon.

BOWERS: Why not?

YM: Sir, I get drunk every night. Every morning I wake up with a horrible hangover. If I do things just right, I am more or less human by noon or a little after.

BOWERS: What do you think I should do about your problem?

YM: Give me afternoon classes. Once I am up and around, I am hell on wheels as a teacher. I'll be one of the best teachers you have here. But not in the morning.

Bowers looked at him more closely. It was, after all, still morning and the chap didn't look very well. He was pale; his eyes were red-rimmed and bloodshot; he was trembling a little but smiling.

BOWERS: Why not? Go ahead. Teach in the afternoon.

It was one of the most judicious decisions Bowers made while I was at Virginia.

There were the injudicious decisions, the dumb ones, also. In *Whistling in the Dark* I told the Shelby Foote story: how, in 1963, I managed to get Mr. Foote to come, for next to nothing, to visit the University of Virginia for a week; how Bowers had never heard of him and assured me that nobody would ever come to hear Foote lecture; how, one way and another (including the use of a marching band in the library), we attracted a huge crowd, so large and packed that Fredson Bowers, arriving at the last moment, couldn't even get in the room.

A little joke. This anecdote had a sequel. Twenty years later I found myself back on the job at Virginia and responsible for inviting a writer-in-residence for a week. Just as before. (*Everything changes and nothing changes,* as the French are always saying.)

This time the chairman was an Englishman who, among other things, must never have watched television much, certainly not any of Ken Burns's *The Civil War* on PBS. Somehow he had never heard of Shelby Foote, either; and so he vetoed my proposal, adding some pragmatic advice: "Politically, I think it would be wise to get the program established by bringing in big names for the first couple of years, before turning to those equally (or even more) deserving who are, for whatever reason, less well and widely known."

Less well and widely known? At that very moment Shelby Foote was the most famous, widely known living American writer.

But I can do better than that.

Have I ever told you about the time the distinguished critic Leslie Fiedler came to give a lecture at UVa during the middle of spring vacation?

A lazy Tuesday afternoon during the week of spring break. Nobody much around the place. Just a few of us, younger people with no place to go and no money to go there, anyway, hanging out at the department in Cabell Hall, supposed to be catching up on work, but not really working much; mostly sitting around smoking and talking trash. All of a sudden the battle-ax department secretary calls for me to come to the phone. (In those days we only had phones in the departmental office.) She figured that since I was the ranking member of the department—see how the gift of tenure had changed my life—I should deal with this phone call. A voice busily informed me that this was Leslie Fiedler, that he was calling from Lynchburg or Roanoke or somewhere, where he was lecturing this evening, and he was just checking in to be sure that everything was still set for him to lecture at Virginia on Thursday night.

Right here was where I made my first big mistake. I didn't know a thing about any scheduled visit to UVa by Fiedler for the day after tomorrow or ever. This was the first I had heard anything about that. Somebody must have known something, but not I. And whoever that somebody was, he or she was out of town on vacation. But somehow I did not want to admit to complete ignorance. So I heard myself say: "Yes, sir. We are all set and we are looking forward to your visit here." He then told me he would be coming up to Charlottesville on the train and what time the train would arrive. I said I would pick him up at the train station.

We—myself, junior instructors, aging graduate students—had a pretty good laugh about the whole thing. "How do you know it was really Fiedler?" "I don't. We won't know until he gets here, if he gets here." And gradually it dawned on us that we were going to be responsible for Fiedler. There wasn't anyone else.

Suddenly it was a challenge. Could we, somehow or other, in the big middle of spring vacation, put together some kind of an audience for an appearance/performance by Leslie Fiedler? Probably not, but why not give it a try? Nothing ventured, nothing gained.

Another big mistake.

We lined up a room for the lecture in the library. Then we started thinking about where we would find some people, warm bodies to fill the room.

I went directly to the only place I was certain there were some students still here—the football practice field. Spring practice was going on, vacation or no vacation. I went down there and managed to catch the attention of some football players who owed me a big favor. (Never mind what. Guess.) When I told them the problem, they quickly assured me that they could and would find enough students to come to Fiedler's lecture and to fill up the room in the library.

"It only looks empty," they told me. "There are plenty of creeps in the dorm rooms just studying and stuff. Got no place to go and nobody wants them. We will encourage them to come to this lecture. In fact, we will come, too, and be like your ushers. Don't worry about a thing."

I was worried, though, worried sick at that point. But what could I do but trust my faithful football players? I had no choice but to trust them and hope for the best.

Back at the department the gang was trying to make plans, to think of *something* we could do.

"Hasn't Fiedler got a new book out?"

"Beats me. Maybe so."

"What is the title? Does anybody know?"

"I think it's something about a wall."

"Maybe it's *The Great Wall of China*."

"Yeah. That sounds right."

So we mimeographed (this was well before the arrival of copying machines in our department) an announcement boldly stating that the distinguished Leslie Fiedler, author of *The Great Wall of China*, would be lecturing, in person, at the library at 8:00 P.M. Thursday night. We weren't quite sure what to do with these announcements. We could run around and post them on bulletin boards. We could send out a bunch by messenger mail to university people, who might or might not, most likely not, be in town. Regular mail would be too slow to reach anybody at home in time. Unless . . . And somebody—I wish I could remember who it was—had an idea. We could send out the announcements to people we thought might be interested by Special Delivery. Locally, Special Delivery would be delivered the same date it was mailed. Special Delivery cost an exorbitant thirty cents. The department, then or now, would never have paid for anything like that. We pooled all our resources, paper money and loose change, and discovered we had just enough money to buy two hundred Special Delivery stamps. Somebody took the money and headed off in a hurry to the post office. Meanwhile we stuffed two hundred departmental envelopes with our little mimeographed announcement and started addressing them to people we thought might want to know. After twenty or thirty names we drew a blank. Somebody with a flair for leadership and organization suggested maybe we should use the catalogue and the faculty directory to get more names and addresses. So we did that for a while. Twenty or thirty more names. By then the guy was back with all the Special Delivery stamps, about 150 of which looked to be wasted.

Then somebody else had a moment of pure inspiration. *The Great Wall of China*, see? Maybe we should send a Special Delivery to every Chinese name listed in the faculty directory. That gave us another twenty-five or so names. And now we were on a roll. We had purpose. We went through the Charlottesville phone book, seeking and finding what looked like Chinese names. Everyone we could find, until we ran out of stamps, was elected to receive a Special Delivery letter announcing the Fiedler lecture.

By then it was close to five o'clock. Somebody else grabbed all the envelopes and ran to the nearest mailbox and mailed them.

Here is a brief digression. Much later I ran into a guy who worked for the post office and had been working on that very selfsame day. It fell his duty to deliver the Special Deliveries of the day—usually half a dozen, he said—on the way home. For this service he would be given maybe an hour of overtime. The day we sent out the Fiedler announcements by Special Delivery is one that he will always remember. It was worse than you might imagine. Under the rules of the time he had to deliver Special Deliveries in person to the addressee. If nobody was home, he had to leave a little signed note—a handwritten and signed note, not a form. About half of the people were not at home. This postman didn't get home until after two o'clock in the morning.

Now it was in the hands of the gods. The next problem was how to keep Fiedler from getting on the grounds of the university and seeing that everybody was on vacation. We met the train and, sure enough, there

was Leslie Fiedler in the flesh. We greeted him warmly—all the more so
in our relief that it was the real Leslie Fiedler and not some imposter—
and shoved him in the car (we might as well have been kidnapping him,
and in a way I guess we were) and proceeded to drive him all over the
area, everywhere except the university, sight-seeing: Monticello, Ash
Lawn, the Blue Ridge Mountains, the Skyline Drive. Then we took him
somewhere for dinner, plied him with booze and food and kept talking
and talking, trying to disguise our anxiety in a shapeless fabric of words.
Because now we were really sweating it. Would anybody at all be there
for his lecture? If nobody showed up—and that seemed like a very real
possibility—what would we do next? What would we tell Fiedler?

In the course of dinner we managed, by slight indirection, to discover
that Fiedler had not written a book called *The Great Wall of China* and
had no evident interest in China or things Chinese.

By now it was getting dark and time to face the music. When we got
to the library, just about the right time, we had trouble getting into the
room. It was crowded to the last inch with people standing and sitting,
and more people were packed in the hallway outside. My gigantic football players, all dressed in dark suits and wearing dark glasses, were much
in evidence. They had searched the dormitories and the fraternity
houses high and low and had driven everyone they could find there to fill
this room. It was clear, too, that they had been running some rehearsals
before we arrived, because, just as we walked in, one of the ballplayers
made an emphatic gesture and then they were all standing and
applauding wildly with enthusiasm. A couple of ballplayers pushed and
shoved and helped us fight our way to the podium and the lectern, where
we were able to turn around and face the tumultuous crowd. I was just
about to launch into my very brief and vague introduction ("Ladies and
gentlemen, here is the speaker we have all been eagerly waiting for")
when I saw that the center of the room, the center of the audience, was
occupied by a large group, maybe fifty, of plainly Asian faces, all looking
intently, seriously, and with an appropriately inscrutable bafflement at
myself and Mr. Fiedler. I hurried through my introduction. Fiedler took
the stand and (we had forgotten to ask him what he was going to do) read
erotic poetry, written by himself, for about an hour. Followed by another

huge, foot-stamping, whistling, standing ovation. Which in turn was followed by a sudden exodus which couldn't have been any quicker if it had been a fire drill or a bomb scare.

Years later I ran into Fiedler somewhere and introduced myself, reminding him of his visit at Virginia. He told me that it was an important time for him, because it was at Virginia that he first became aware of his popularity in China.

"I don't know why," he told me, "but the Chinese love me."

A Perfect Stranger

I will sing for you sweetly, although
You pluck out my beard by the roots.

I was way down in Tuscaloosa, far from home, living alone in a two-story white frame house that they call the Chair House, assigned to visiting writers. It was set in a little patch of pine woods with a couple of other more or less similar houses. All around the patch of woods there was an enormous parking lot for the university. Truth is, though, it was a remarkably quiet place (you might as well have been in the real deep woods) except on football weekends when hundreds, maybe even thousands of trailers and motor homes and other big RVs of all kinds, flags flying, lights pulsing, horns tooting and beeping and playing the first few notes of the Alabama fight song, arrived to park in the parking lot, cranking up their generators, breaking out their grills, hibachis and barbecues, and settling in to a cheerful, smoky encampment.

Huge and looming over everything, the stadium is only a few shorts blocks away.

Nobody warned me that these folks were coming. This was a local joke, part of the initiation for whoever was living in the Chair House during the football season. I woke up early on the first Saturday morning to find the whole house shaking and a steady humming noise all around me. Woke, jumped up and went to the window and saw, in all directions, the enormous parking lot filled with throbbing vehicles.

Same thing for every home game.

During the week, though, the place was very quiet, even lonesome. This is a story of that lonesomeness.

Now, to get the full flavor of what follows, you need to understand that I hate the telephone. Did hate it, anyway. Hated answering it. Hated talking on it and to it. Hated listening to it. Hated even to watch other people talking on the telephone—smiling, frowning, making faces as if the goddamn machine could somehow transmit facial expressions and reactions and body language. Besides I grew up in the Great Depression where we learned to talk fast and loud, shouting when it was long distance. Where we had party lines to worry about. Where you dialed or cranked the operator to place a call. When her title was "Central."

So, anyway, early one morning the phone rang and rang. Finally I stumbled and staggered out of sleep to answer it.

Hello. (A woman's voice, young-sounding, soft and husky, maybe even a little urgent.) Is this a dorm?

No, it's not.

A fraternity house?

No, ma'am.

Is it somebody's office?

No. Not exactly.

Well, this is a university number, isn't it?

I guess so. It's a house that belongs to the university.

Oh, that's good.

Maybe you have the wrong number.

How could I?

Aren't you trying to reach somebody?

It's all right. You'll do just fine.

Who are you calling?

Listen, you don't have to tell me who you are, she said. That might spoil things.

What things?

Just talk to me. Talk to me.

What about?

Anything.

Like what?

Are you alone?

Yes.

What are you wearing?

Huh?

What have you got on?

My undershorts.

Jockey shorts or boxers?

Boxers.

How old are you?

I could hear her breathing. My first thought was that somebody or other in the English Department, or maybe one of my creative writing students, was pulling a joke on me. Maybe they were taping this conversation and would play it for general amusement at the next party.

How old are you? she asked again.

I'm too old for you, honey.

Note that I did not simply tell her the simple truth. Knowing that she would hang up on me. Did I want her to keep talking? I honestly don't know.

Are you over forty?

You better believe it.

Shit . . . ! Then: Are you some kind of a student?

No.

A teacher?

Sort of. I'm just a visitor. A visiting teacher.

Oh, a visitor . . . Then: Listen. Just talk to me. Please. Say anything you want to. Anything. Just talk and keep on talking for a little while. It won't be long. I'm almost there.

Almost where?

Please . . . !

Hey, thanks anyway, I said. You have a nice day.

And I hung up and then walked into the bathroom and took a good look in the mirror at the ruined stranger's face I have somehow earned and probably deserve. I shrugged and set about the business of putting myself together for the coming day.

I wondered if she might call back. Not bloody likely. If it was a real call and not a joke, then most likely she just punched out the university prefix and then the last four numbers without a thought or scheme. Chances are she wouldn't even remember what the numbers were. It would be better (for her), more fun that way. On the other hand maybe she would remember the number she had just called. If the phone rang again soon, would I answer it? And if it turned out to be the same woman, what would I say to her?

Would I apologize for hanging up on her?

After all, it wasn't such a bad thing she was asking for—just for me
to talk to her for a little while. All that was asked was that I talk about
anything at all for a little while to somebody, a perfect stranger who, for
whatever reason, felt she needed to hear a voice (evidently, but not definitely, a male voice). In a way it was flattering, even vaguely exciting to be
chosen, even if by blindest chance, as the brief answer to her need and
pleasure. She could easily have hung up on me when she learned I was
just an old guy, far beyond forty, in his boxer shorts. She clearly wasn't
happy about it. Who would be? But she had the decency not to hang up.
She had better manners than I did. That's for sure.

Not counting spouses and true lovers, who in real life, your whole
real life, who among all the people you have ever known, would even
think about calling you and asking you for nothing except the sound of
your voice to give them some kind of pleasure and satisfaction?

And what if the roles were reversed?

What if you, yourself, were in a state of desperate lonesome need and
began to punch out numbers blindly, randomly, hoping against hope to
hear the voice of a young woman who would possess the power to offer
or to deny your pleasure?

It was surely something to think about. All of it.

Scenario:

Girl calls and he answers. In an instant he realizes exactly what is
going on and then he is able to say all the right things she wants to hear,
leading her gently, deftly, inexorably to an ecstatic peak. Her final line
would be the sublime cliché: Oh, God, I never knew it could be like this!

She, having punched the numbers by chance and having experienced
remarkable fulfillment, now directly demands to know his number.

What can he do?

Does he tell her?

Scenario:

He gives her his number but not his name. She promises to call again
soon. Which she does. Over a little time, fairly soon in fact, they begin

to know each other, to feel free and open with each other. She tells him things to say that please her most. Knowing this much, he is able (if and when he wants to) to intensify, to maximize or minimize her experience. Or, anyway, so it seems.

They are soon oddly dependent on each other. The great danger, of course, as in real life, is that the drama of the situation will lose its raw edge of suspense, that it will gradually become routine for both of them.

Maybe she tells you that you have a rival, probably a younger man with a lovely voice and a highly active imagination. Who sometimes, though not always, can give her more pleasure and excitement than you can.

Soon you find that you are jealous of him whether he really exists or not. If he doesn't, well, then, you are equally, maybe even more jealous of the idea of a rival in her mind, now firmly planted in yours.

In a serious effort to compete with this real or imaginary rival you concentrate and focus on the creation of outrageous fantasies. Thus you soon develop a truly dirty mind. You look in the mirror and recognize that you are being corrupted (or, as the case may be, are corrupting yourself) and will soon enough be totally depraved and corrupt if this relationship continues.

You decide to break it off for the sake of the two of you.

We simply can't go on talking on the phone like this, you say in your signature cliché.

Scenario:

Soon you are both equally involved in the playing out of the experience. And one thing leads to another. You tell her your name, your real name. She tells you hers. Both of you agree that meeting in fact and in the flesh will probably be a bad thing. Too many variables and unknowns. Too many things can go wrong. Better to keep things just as they are.

Suppose even ideal circumstances. Suppose you did meet and she turned out to be wonderfully attractive and that she was not repulsed, turned off by your age and your appearance. Even so, it wouldn't be the same. You are only right for each other on the telephone, two bodiless, ageless voices. Reality adds nothing but trouble and complexity to the experience.

Say that you were able to meet under ideal circumstances and that you fell in love in reality. Then you began to live together. For a while you might be like any other couple, but soon you would probably lapse into your old, original ways.

You buy a battery-powered field telephone from army surplus. You can call each other from different rooms. The downside of this is that when the field telephone rings, there can be no exciting, suspenseful doubt about who may be calling. And doubt, even for a brief instant, is half the fun.

Next you buy lots of different kinds of phones—cellular phones, car phones. Both of you have your own phones with unlisted numbers known only to each other. Both of you have unlisted phones unknown to each other.

Sometimes you wake in the middle of the night, and the space next to you in your queen- or king-sized bed is empty. You tiptoe carefully in the dark following the sound of her whispering voice. She is whispering remarkable, memorable things to someone else. Man or woman? Does it matter? Isn't a voice on the phone finally androgynous? And what if no one is there listening at the other end?

Whether you elect to meet and then end up being together or not, you both have to work hard to create significant erotic diversity. Both of you practice foreign accents, impersonations of living and historical characters. And you make up voices for made up characters.

Sometimes for the joy of it, you cross over. She pretends to be you and you pretend to be her. Both of you simultaneously become other people.

After a while, you have a hard time remembering who you really are. If you really are anyone.

She won't tell you.

Scenario:

Suppose that you meet in fact and in flesh but do not take to each other. She is disgusted at first sight by what the years have done to you. And you find her unattractive, beyond repair.

Still, nobody else can give the good phone voice that she does. When voice is the sole reality, the most refined form of desire and satisfaction, then who cares about the real or imaginary body from which that voice emerges?

In fact, isn't it oddly exciting to know that a beautiful voice transcends its humble origins? Back in the old days men often fell in love with telephone operators. With the voice of Central. I can readily understand that now.

What if—just for the sake of argument—she really is a student or somebody in the English Department whose intentions are malicious and humiliating? How would you feel if all these conversations were being recorded to be played back in some public or private way? Would you feel betrayed; or would you, instead, find some added, unexpected nuance of pleasure knowing that from then on, your shared words, her voice and yours, were being captured? When she called again (if she should ever call again), would that serve to inhibit you?

Would you be angry and ashamed or strangely grateful?

Would you invent things to shock your students, your colleagues, the world?

When you go to class, across that vast parking lot and the campus, you see hundreds of young women coming and going, too. Which one is she? Is it that one or another? How can you ever know for sure?

All of which leads to another question.

Consider that, in fact, I am by craft and trade a writer. Suppose the man in this story were a writer also. How would the phone calls affect him?

Maybe he would become a full-time pornographer. Out of the habit and experience of making up erotic stories for the telephone, he could, slowly but surely, find himself unable to create any other kinds of stories except those designed for this sole and specific purpose and for this interacting audience of one.

But wait a minute. All his premises and scenarios are based on the assumption that only one young woman is involved. Maybe that isn't so. She could have a roommate. She could have more than one roommate. She could even be a member of a sorority or club, a group where the members, from time to time, use the telephone to enhance their private lives and pleasure. There could be a telephone harem out there.

Or—why not?—his first and only caller (so far) may have been a pledge in her sorority. Part of her initiation might be to call up a perfect stranger and get him to talk to her on her own terms.

Here that part of him that is a literary critic speaks to him in an inward and spiritual voice:

Forget the whole thing. Forget it. This is the kind of story that Robert Coover might write, but not you.

Robert Coover is a twit. He never thought of this one. He never even imagined anything like it.

But he could have, easily enough, says the smug critical voice. You are such a victim of factual reality. You would never have thought of it, either, if you hadn't actually answered a real phone on a real morning in Tuscaloosa. And now that's all you can think about. You ought to be ashamed of yourself and all your obvious limitations.

Fuck Robert Coover, you say out loud to the critic within you. And fuck you, too.

See what I mean? The inner voice answers.

Reality:

I discover that I automatically wake up every morning. I get up out of bed and go sit in an old armchair near the phone. I wait in vain for the phone to start ringing.

What will happen when I finish up my job here and go home to Charlottesville?

How will I explain my strange new habits to my wife of many years?

More to the point, how will she react to this whole story?

From her point of view you could justly argue that I have been uniformly unfaithful, in principle if not in fact, ever since the first phone call.

Scenario:

It turns out to have been my wife all along. She calls and cleverly disguises her voice and fools you. To the extent that she engages you in this ongoing fiction of the phone, she has to come to terms with the idea that you are sharing an intimate experience with someone else. Worse, it is somebody you don't even know. Worst of all, it is somebody she doesn't know. From her point of view (and you are only guessing, not planning to ask her) a three-way conference call might be better. During which she can at least monitor your verbal behavior. Or, anyway, add her own running commentary to all of it.

What next?

You buy an answering machine to screen your calls. You buy some pajamas and a nice bathrobe. You wait. Sooner or later someone will call.

How can the story end? Only with the end of me as a living body or a mindless one aged beyond the fringes of memory. Either way the anticipation, which is all that I have really and truly possessed since the first and only phone call, will fade and finally cease and desist even as I do.

Or will it?

There is always another possibility. I shall ask here and now, before it's too late, to be buried like Mary Baker Eddy with a telephone in my grave. At the least, then, old hypocrite reader, from time to time a drunk or a desperate person will accidentally dial or punch the number. And the phone in my grave will ring and ring.

You, reader, passing by the cemetery in the dark middle of the night, will be startled by the sound of a telephone ringing among the silent tombstones. You will hurry along to wherever you are going.

And I won't hear it, or even care one way or the other until, as my faith assures me, I will wake on Judgment Day and reach for the phone. Who will be calling me? Whose voice will I hear?

PART III

Essays

. . . and I
Lost count some time ago of my own odd mix
Of selves imagined, selves constructed,
Selves injured and healed, lost and found again.

R. H. W. DILLARD

There isn't much that needs to be said about these "Essays." I think they
may be parts of a work-in-progress, as yet too vague to have a shape.
Meanwhile, though, they can stand on their own and together. I mean
them to be celebrations of my blood kin, of those people to whom I owe
my (factual) self and my (fictional) selves. It should be clear where some
of the short stories and anecdotes come from, and, I hope, their links and
connections with the other parts of this book; and on their own, they
touch on the sources and nature of my fiction. And if things work out as
they are supposed to, I hope that we both, writer and reader, will have
come full circle, so that, in a sense, the end is also the beginning.

Hanging from the Trestle While the Train Goes By: Some Notes on Working for a Living

Blister, callous, scrape and scar, cuts and bruises . . .

All of us in our family worked with our hands, earned a living with our muscles, with more or with less skill, at one time or another. Moved up and down the imaginary social scale, feast or famine. Twice we were, with most other people we knew about, cleaned out. Wiped out of all capital assets and most of our valuable possessions by great, inexorable public events, those tectonic social, economic and political shiftings— wasted by the Civil War (we were mostly on the wrong side) and then, later, just as the South had begun to recover from that implacable devastation, ruined again by the Great Depression. Being fortune's children, not hostages, we rode on fortune's wheel, enjoying or enduring a staggering sequence of ups and downs.

All of us, then, without exception (but not including the disabled), for three full generations including my own, have often worked hard and long at menial and manual tasks, from time to time managing (by saving and sacrifice and sudden good luck) to work our way back to whatever it was that interested and engaged us most, some occupation or vocation that meant more to us than toting and fetching, chopping and hoeing and raking, shoveling gravel or horseshit. Sometimes on farms, in factories or shipyards, wherever we could find work when we needed it. Sometimes to recover took more than sweat and effort and austerity. Sometimes it took a good while, years, slowly to return and to reclaim what we might rather be doing, to be what we would rather be. Some, unlucky, never made it back, never recovered even though the whole family, a large, loose network all the way out to and including second cousins and such, a *community* in those days before we were scattered to the four winds, tried to help each other. Offered each other aid and comfort without stint or hesitation, without even stopping to think about it.

In a sense that is a typical American story of the times, our times, anyway. And, more to the point, prodigal or not, there was no shame and guilt involved. All kinds of work (except, maybe, playing games with other people's money, i.e., banking or telling/selling lies to others for personal profit) were good enough and could be honorable. Which meant, too, that we were embarrassed by and for and somewhat contemptuous of those who didn't have to work or wouldn't work, out of pride or laziness, or were halfhearted, those who worked halfheartedly and with poor workmanship. For ourselves, rich or poor, we did not feel inferior to anyone else. In the tradition of my colorful and gambling grandfather, we played the game with whatever cards were dealt to us. We took our luck as we found it.

I never heard the term "working class" applied to Americans until I went off to college and took a required course in the quasi-science of sociology. Were we working class? Sometimes.

My father became a lawyer, a famous lawyer (in the terms that our honest local fame was measured and allowed in those days, not by "image" but by continual performance) during the dark Depression days. But before that, trying to earn his education, he worked for some years as a miner in the huge copper mines of the Far West. He was a charter member of the union that later became the United Mine Workers. He had the scars to show for it, too. Polio put an end to that and, ironically, gave him the time to study law, "to read the Law," as they said then. He was, for the time and by its standards, a very successful lawyer, working as hard at it as he had in the mines. Wherever he lived he kept in the attic or somewhere a battered suitcase with rocks in it, samples of the different kinds of ore he had dug out by hand. Because he spent so much of his time and practice doing *pro bono* work for those who needed it, he was never a wealthy man. "I am the best," he told me once. "I don't need money to prove I'm the best." He became the stable center of the family.

Lord knows, the others, all of us, needed a stable center.

I had seven uncles, counting both sides of the family, and—I can see this now but did not even imagine it then—they were not at all typical. Or were they? Sometimes, typical or not, they seem to me exemplary of

America as it was then. Anyway, they were, when they were able to be so, respectively a dancer, a musician, a minor league baseball player (with dreams of the majors), a professional golfer, a cavalryman (later an army aviator), a professional guide and mountain climber, and a newspaper reporter who changed over to being a screenwriter when talking pictures arrived on the scene and suddenly somebody had to write some dialogue. He did pretty well at it. To be sure, he was a working man. Was one of the founders of the writers' union, the Screenwriters Guild. And when he died of a heart attack in New York, his body was labeled by the police as "unidentified laborer." He became very rich (by our standards) a few times. More so than any of the others except maybe my grandfather, who somehow managed to be both richer and poorer than any of us.

Made two fortunes and spent three is what they used to say about my grandfather. At the highest peak, the zenith of his luck, he was like somebody out of a novel, maybe a novel Fitzgerald would have written if he had been a Southerner. At the peak of his good fortune he lived in a genuine mansion overlooking the St. Johns River. He had a stable of trotting horses (one of which he sold to the king of Italy), a lean and lovely ninety-foot steam yacht, the *Cosette*, which was for a time the fastest yacht in the Atlantic Ocean. When he traveled, as he often did then, he took over a whole Pullman car for his family and friends. Near the end (he died in his nineties), he lived for a few years on a folding army cot in the back room of a rural post office. He was not noticeably different in either role.

It all started for him with work as a child laborer. Orphaned in and by the Civil War, he was first raised by a deaf-mute black man, formerly his father's slave, who taught him many things, including the ways and means of the deep woods and swamps of coastal South Carolina. How to live or to die there. He taught himself to read and write and how to speak the local African-American languages—Gullah and Geechie. Still a child, not yet twelve years old, he went to work full-time for a logger. They cut timber and hauled it out of the woods with mules. Loading the logs on an old sailboat, the two of them, his boss and himself, sailed the logs south and into Charleston harbor. One time his boss was knocked unconscious by the boom and the young boy had to sail the boat in all by himself. Later he became a licensed pilot for Charleston harbor. His great good fortune was that he was chosen, along with half a dozen others, to receive a scholarship to a Yankee college—Hobart College in upstate New York. The boys went together as a group, almost penniless for the whole time, wearing their shabby work clothes, sharing one good suit, for special occasions, among the six of them. He went on from there to become a lawyer, himself, a flashy player in flyblown courtrooms all over the South.

What about the others? Well, to earn the time to practice whatever it was they loved most—dancing, music, writing, sports—they proved cheerfully willing to do whatever they had to do. I guess (it seems a sure thing) they carried over the energy and dedication they needed for their arts and crafts to whatever work they found. They had all learned discipline doing what they pleased. And nobody was sentimental about any of it. I remember one uncle, he who was a sometime baseball player, who was the subject of much family amusement. He found a job at a factory. Job paid well enough. Just getting there was not half the fun. By far the best way from where he lived to where he worked was to follow along the railroad tracks. At one point of which there was a high, long trestle bridge. Try as he would to time it right, he was nevertheless frequently caught right in the middle of the trestle by a fast-moving freight train. He would hear the shrill locomotive whistle, then see the winking flash of the headlamp. He would just about have time enough to hang down from a cross tie, his feet dangling perilously in empty air as the whole train rolled overhead. He learned not to carry a lunch box. His lunch had to fit in a brown paper bag in the pocket of his overalls. Sometimes (at least until he saved up enough money to buy, first, a bike, then a beat-up secondhand car) he had to hang there, jolted and rattled, the undercarriage of the train inches above his clinging hands, for fifteen minutes or more. Everybody thought this was hilarious and he was expected to laugh, too.

Garrett, run over to the hardware store and pick up a can of polka dot paint . . . Hey, Garrett, see if you can find me a left-handed monkey wrench . . .

I have been a teacher for most of my adult life. A writer who teaches full-time. When I began, in the early 1950s at Wesleyan University, there were not very many of us writers in the academy. By the end of that decade there were many. Now there may be too many. But this is not about that. It's enough to say that I always took the teaching seriously and did my best at it, a carry-over from the work ethic and work experience. Before that I held all kinds of not especially skilled jobs. Worked on a family farm. Worked as a bartender all through college, working mostly at nightlong parties of the rich, for good wages and sometimes good tips. Worked with construction and for a house painter. Worked, for a time, as an installer of linoleum and of ceramic tile. (All good book-jacket stuff when that was all the fashion.) The highest degree of *skill* that I acquired was working as a soldier, an enlisted man in the field artillery. You had to know a number of things to do that and do it well; and even I, a born klutz, finally learned. Trouble was, except for the spirit of it, it didn't carry over into what we called "real life." There is not (yet) a lot of demand for a skilled cannoneer in civilian life. It gave me subjects and material for my real work, my writing; though, to be honest, I didn't think of it, or any of my other work experiences, that way at that time. I always wanted to write but never thought of my life as raw material. Not, at least, until I was old enough to be carrying a backpack of memories everywhere with me. On the other hand, I always considered my family to be fair game. The uncles and a lot of the cousins were more interesting than I was, anyway.

I hesitate to generalize very much on this subject. We suffer already from too much generalization and abstraction. Sweat and blood and tears are real. Pain is real. Weariness is real. Statistics, for example, are not.

Still, maybe a few observations and comments are in order. It seems as if the old freedom and flexibility I described, up and down and all around, so characteristically a part of the American experience, are vanishing if they haven't already vanished. You can get stuck (it seems) in a shit-kicking, entry-level job forever. Just in the last couple of decades, so swiftly you could hardly see it happening, we seem to have developed a real class system like the Europeans whom we ran away from in the first place. Maybe we always had a class system, but if we did, it wasn't so intimately related to money. And when I think about it, I can see this generational difference: that *my people*, even my grandfather, the great getter and spender, were never serious about *money*, just what money could do for them to set them free to do their real work. And I think they only wanted *that much*, enough to establish the freedom to do what they pleased and be what they could, and no more.

A lot of the fiction I read that deals with work seems to me sentimental, when it is not simply inauthentic and written by sensitive people who haven't had to work all that much or all that long. Some of it is at least well-meaning, but a lot of it is just phoney.

The new factor is a very old one—pure greed. Bring greed together with the socially acceptable rewards of celebrity and you have a culture in which image is everything, no matter if true or false; therefore a culture in which work and workmanship have no real honor.

Child of the Depression, I have always thought that robbing banks was better than working in one. But I had not imagined a world in which, without shame, people who earned large sums of money out of the misery of others—the great profiteers at all levels of health care, for a flagrant example—would be honored rather than scorned. I cannot conceive of or understand the greed of the CEOs of many major corporations.

I have grandchildren of my own now and I worry about the company they will have to keep.

I also worry about my country when it seems that good work (in *all* fields, high and low, even the arts) is irrelevant and ignored.

But all this is old geezer talk. My children are doing what they want to and can do—a schoolteacher, a classicist, a laborer. Justly, they have no nostalgia for what they have never seen or known.

It Hums. It Sings and Dances

"It takes a good man to get up seven times."

Billy Conn

The occasion for this piece is that I have been watching a video about Joe Louis (*Boxing's Best: Joe Louis*) sent to me by a friend and former student of mine.

1.

For a few years of my youth boxing was my life and joy. I have written a little about it, not much: an essay called "My Two One-Eyed Coaches," which appeared in *Whistling in the Dark* (1992); a poem, "Loser" (1961); a story, my first published story in a little magazine (1947), about which I remember nothing at all, not even the title.

Here is the poem.

Loser

Face like an old fighter's
    (that is, hurt)
a bad cough and the color
    of jailhouses
nothing to do with himself
    but hang around
gas stations post office and
    the railroad depot
watching arrivals & departures
    yawn like a cat.

Face like Roman stone
   (that is, brute)
chipped and broken nose
   eyes vague
crude hands quick to take
   a cigarette
but too slack to make
   a fist nowadays
Jesus loves him this I know
   who else can?

But anyway, my friend knows how much I have always admired Joe Louis. So he sent me the video.

I have time to watch this during daylight hours, when other folks are mostly working for a living, because I have been sick for about ten days or so with a nameless and rogue virus. Which had me flat on my back and now has allowed me, with some effort, some huffing and puffing, to wander about the house, weak-kneed and sore-footed, but apparently beginning to heal and mend. Healing and mending are so much slower now than once they were. My body is an old acquaintance, but not so friendly and eager to please as once upon a time.

I am about a month, less actually, away from my sixty-ninth birthday. It is the month of May, 1998.

And I have been watching this video, itself patched together from old black-and-white newsreels, fixed camera and everything set in more or less middle distance, of Joe Louis between 1935 when he knocked out a fighter named Lee Ramage and 26 October 1951 when he was knocked out in the sixth round by Rocky Marciano. Even though I saw that one at the time, first of all live on crude TV, then later in the newsreels, this is the first time I have ever seen the end of it. I walked away, unable to watch, in the last seconds before Marciano caught him cold with a left and a right and sent him through and over the ropes (a little like Dempsey and Firpo), knocked out. As far as I can tell, Buddy Baer was the only other fighter ever to knock Joe Louis through the ropes and out of the ring. That was 23 May 1941. It looked bad, but couldn't have been much—more a slip than anything else; because Louis bounced right up, climbed back in the ring and went after Baer. His legs looked just fine. That's the test, you know, the legs. In the sixth round Louis knocked Baer silly, knocked him down three times, though Baer was saved by the bell. When the bell rang for round seven Baer sat in his corner and the referee stopped the fight. The Baer people tried to claim that the final knockdown in round six had been a foul, that Louis had hit him after the bell. But there was nothing to that. Nothing at all.

In the sixth round against Marciano, Louis gets popped with a neat, quick left hook and goes down early, but doesn't seem hurt much. Louis had been knocked down any number of times in his career, early and late, but mostly it was a matter of balance, not injury. Marciano, though, was a very hard hitter, maybe the hardest puncher in my lifetime, and anytime he hit, it hurt. Moments after that first knockdown he really unloads on Louis against the ropes. I play the sequence again and again now that I'm willing to look at it. I can see Louis is suddenly out on his feet even before he falls.

Louis always said, long before and after the Marciano fight, that Max Baer (not Buddy) was the hardest hitter he ever fought. Louis beat Max Baer in four rounds, but always described it as his toughest fight. It could have gone either way. If Baer had tagged him . . .

There's a locker room exchange right after the "two ton" Tony Galento fight (9 February 1940) that is at once an example of Louis's uncomplicated integrity and the relativity of things. A reporter asks Louis: "Did that Galento man really hit you hard?" "Well," Louis answers, "he hit me hard enough to knock me down. I guess that's hard enough."

2.

I was never much of a hard hitter. Soon enough I resigned myself to the role of boxer rather than puncher. To win on points as a boxer you have to hit the other guy more than he hits you, and if he is a heavy hitter, you have to keep moving enough, in and out and around, so that he can't get set and knock you down and out. Easier said than done. You have to develop more skill than a puncher. You have to be in better shape (if you can) than the puncher, because you are going to be moving a lot more.

All of the above is not quite accurate. While I was actually fighting amateur fights, I knocked out other fighters only once or twice. Won some on technical knockouts (TKOs). But mostly had to win (or lose) on points. Later, when I wasn't really training for anything, just fooling around in the gym, sparring a few rounds with this one or that one, I suddenly began to knock people down. Without trying to. I wasn't trying to hurt or hit anybody, just sparring.

The great boxing coach (and sculptor) Joe Brown told me and showed me how that came to pass. When I had been really fighting, I had been too tight, too anxious, too eager to put more power into my punches. Now, with nothing much to lose, I was relaxed, and coordination did the trick. Pop! And down they went.

That's something you can see in the films of Joe Louis fighting. How at his best, in the prime of his great years (say 1936–1942), he was totally focused and serious and yet, at the same time, relaxed. The sequences of punches do the work, no single big hit; and the sequences are superb, quick and short and smooth—effortless. This is easier to appreciate when you can compare it with the rare times when he loses his cool and composure. In the first Jersey Joe Wolcott fight (5 December 1947), the one that went the full distance of fifteen rounds, Louis was caught a couple of times by a quick right hand over the top of his own left that knocked him down. He wasn't hurt but he got mad—as mad at himself, I guess, as anyone or anything else because it was pure and simple carelessness. And when he gets up, after the first time, you can see the muscles of his shoulders and his biceps tighten up. Because now he wants to knock out Wolcott with one big punch. The only trouble is that he can't do it with his muscles tight. Round after round he doggedly pursues Joe Wolcott. Wins the fight (you can't take the heavyweight championship while backing away), but doesn't come close to knocking Wolcott out. Had to wait until the eleventh round of the second and last Wolcott fight (25 June 1948) to put him away.

So, anyway, I was never much of a hitter, though I got better at it when I quit worrying about it and taught myself how to relax in action.

My Uncle Chester, a professional dancer with a build and body just about the same as Sugar Ray Robinson, could hit harder than any man I have ever seen (including Sugar Ray). He hit so hard that he broke bones—jaws and cheekbones—and noses with a single punch. He could do so much damage in a street fight that people thought he must have used a deadly weapon of some kind. It was all in the smooth coordination.

There is a great irony, a kind of an equalizer, about really hard hitters. They become accustomed to their power and depend on it. Then sometime, when they run into somebody who doesn't go down, who just shakes off the best shot they've got and keeps on fighting, it is profoundly unnerving. I have seen the fight and energy go out of a puncher like a leak in a balloon when he has hit his opponent with all he's got and that opponent is unfazed.

The great fighters, like Louis, didn't depend on one punch. A studied sequence of punches, requiring total concentration and coordination, did the job.

3.

There are so many things you can try to do that are doomed to failure if you try too hard.

4.

It has been many years, a long time really, since I have had a fistfight or have hit anybody in anger. Oh I have been plenty mad, murderous at heart, mad enough to shoot someone if a weapon were handy, but not ready to fight. Part of it, the inhibition, comes (I think) from knowing how much damage bare-knuckle fighting can do to your own hands. After you have been boxing for a while you don't want to hit anybody without well-taped hands and a good pair of gloves on.

I sometimes think that is the reason fighters have earned the reputation for being easygoing outside the ring. Most of them (the more or less sane ones anyway) will go to a lot of trouble to avoid a fight. What they have to do in the ring, coupled with the kind of self-discipline required to learn to fight well, will soon have burned up a lot of the energy and anger that made them fighters in the first place. They have nothing to prove, even to themselves, and everything to lose.

But there is more to it.

The last fight I had was with an editor in New York City. Sometime in the middle 1970s. Doubleday had a nice little party for me, and this guy—not my own editor, by the way—kept after me about boxing. Everybody had been drinking and it went on and on. Finally he just hit me and, almost reflexively, I hit him back. Pop! Right on the button. Very relaxed and coordinated. Down and out he went.

What I remember (to my shame) is the adrenaline rush I felt when he fell and how my feet started dancing on their own initiative. If there had been a neutral corner I would have gone to it so the counting could begin. (In some of the fights on the video I can see Joe Louis feeling that rush also. Down goes the other guy and Louis spins away and almost skips over to the neutral corner.) Even at the time I was embarrassed. But it felt so good again . . .

This is an old story with fighters.

A friend of mine, once for a while a pretty good professional heavyweight and now a bookish and bespectacled professor, a man who had had no reason to raise his hands against anybody else in years, was jumped by a couple of redneck badasses. Had to fight or run for his life. And it all came back to him. He knocked them both down and found himself dancing over their bodies for pure joy before he bent down to help them recover.

That pure joy is what it's all about, I guess. It is like no other feeling even in other kinds of violence. It may not be better (or worse), but it certainly is different. It hums. It sings and dances.

5.

A recent *New York Times Book Review* has a drawing of Norman Mailer, shown wearing a fighter's robe, with his hands in big, puffy boxing gloves. The headline: "Still On His Feet: Fifty Years After 'The Naked and the Dead,' the contender is back, unbowed, unbloodied, with 'The Time of Our Time,' a Norman Mailer anthology." It's a full-court press (to switch the metaphor) of publicity. Because there's also a picture of Mailer in the *Sunday Styles* section, kidding around, faking punches with Muhammad Ali at a Random House party for his book.

I have very mixed feelings about writers and boxing. (Which may be why, though it once mattered so much to me and, in a sense, still does, I have never written much about it.) Hemingway, Mailer, Plimpton, all those guys . . . Each, in his own way, out of his own experience, wrote well enough about it. They all had some experience and not just boxing with literary types, though not actually *fighting*, either. But who would claim that any of them wrote as well about boxing as Joyce Carol Oates or A. J. Leibling? I think of their connection to and experience of boxing as being the equivalent of, say, the relationship of our writer/ambulance drivers (Dos Passos, Hemingway, Malcolm Cowley, e. e. cummings) to combat soldiers in World War I.

(By the way, do you want to know what prominent American writer had a lot of combat time in World War I? John Crowe Ransom, that's who. Also J. P. Marquand. World War II? John Ciardi and, above all, the poet Richard Wilbur, who logged more actual combat time by far, in the 36th "Texas" Infantry Division, in Italy and France, than Norman Mailer and James Jones and all the rest put together.)

Anyway, back to boxing.

I have learned a lot of lessons from a variety of sports, lessons that stood me in good stead in "real life." But mostly sports analogies don't make good metaphors. And the more you know, from experience, the less adequate these comparisons become. The lessons of sports can finally be reduced (lifted from context) to simple and primitive statements, the distillation of earned wisdom. Like: "Nice guys finish last."

Joe Louis added a couple to the language—"I've been rich, I've been poor. Rich is better." (This is sometimes attributed to Mae West.) And the one he dropped before the second Billy Conn fight (19 June 1946): "He can run but he can't hide."

That's about as cosmic as it gets in the boxing world.

Writers, inevitably, try to get a little more suption out of it. Sometimes it works, more often it doesn't. Hemingway, that wonderful writer, completely misinterpreted and misjudged the Joe Louis–Max Baer fight, both what happened and what it meant. He called Max Baer yellow for not getting up one more time (after several knockdowns). Baer's shrugging reply is pure professionalism: "Anybody who wants to witness the execution of Max Baer has got to pay more than a hundred dollars for a ringside seat." On my video, right after the Baer fight, Louis is asked by a reporter if he thinks Jimmy Braddock (who was then world's champion) can hit harder than Max Baer. Louis gives it serious consideration before he answers: "He can't be much harder than Baer."

On 22 June 1937, Joe Louis knocked out Jimmy Braddock in the eighth round to become heavyweight champion of the world. It is one of the very few Louis fights with a one-big-punch knockout. Louis lays a long right hard on him and Braddock is out cold.

6.

I only saw Joe Louis fight, in person and in the flesh, once. It would have been late 1940s or maybe 1950 or 1951. Probably 1951. Louis had retired in 1948 after knocking out Jersey Joe Wolcott in the second fight. But he had to come back into the ring because of tax problems. Innocently enough he owed the government a whole lot of money. He tried exhibition fights, nineteen of them, to earn the money to pay off his taxes. But that wasn't enough. So he had to start fighting again. Older, slower, over-the-hill, he started down the road that led surely and implacably to the sixth round of his fight with Rocky Marciano. A couple of years after that, in 1954, Congress let Joe Louis off the hook. He was broke; he was pretty much down and out. He had done everything a man could do to pay off his taxes and the fault, the tax he owed, was technical, anyway.

That's something I have to admire about Louis—the unwhining, unflinching, undiluted honesty of the man. Climbing in the ring, fighting young fighters when, even if you win, you know you are not the athlete you were, called for enormous courage. This was in the age before endorsements and television commercials. These days run-of-the-mill jocks make more money in a year than Louis (or anybody else) made in a lifetime. And when they have "tax problems," they can negotiate, almost as equals. Their celebrity cushions them in all things.

The one Louis fight I saw was at Madison Square Garden. A car-load of us drove in from Princeton to New York and parked on the rooftop (free!) parking lot of the brand new Port Authority Terminal. After the fight and a little celebrating, we slept in the car that night.

Louis was fighting an old-timer, almost as old as he was—Lee Savold. Good, solid, workmanlike heavyweight with a pretty good record including a fair number of knockouts. It was, I think, a ten-round fight. Louis kept after him, shuffling along, jabbing, until he finally knocked him out late in the fight. From the distance of our cheap seats he looked heavy, balding, fairly slow of foot, though his hands were, as ever, quick and, at the end, deadly.

I remember the stink of the place and the huge crowd, the cigarette smoke in clouds and the echoing noise and yelling. And in the center of things the brightly lit space of the ring, seeming wide as a field, and the two big middle-aged men, alone together out there, ignoring everything else except each other. They were lonesome and beautiful.

It was from that time that I took an image, in this case of an imaginary deep-sea diver moving "lonely in zones of slow motion."

Except for the Savold fight, I saw many of the Joe Louis fights in newsreels, a few on television near the end of his career, and heard most on the radio. Some at home with the huge radio in the living room that we sat around together to listen to this or that. (We were all listening to Orson Welles that Halloween night he brought invading Martians to earth.) Most of all, though, because the family didn't like to listen to fights as much as I did, I would go outside, get into my mother's old Oldsmobile, an early '30s model which sported a car radio, turn on the engine and then the radio and hear and imagine the fight.

I remember that I heard the first Louis-Conn fight at my grandfather's house in the mountains of North Carolina. A big, drafty, high-ceilinged room with a large fireplace, a moosehead on the wall and a heavy caliber rifle over the mantelpiece.

That was a very exciting fight to listen to. Billy Conn almost won it. Would have, maybe, if he hadn't tried to slug it out with Louis. I was for Louis all the way. My grandfather was mostly for Billy Conn. Probably, now that I think back on it, because Conn was a white man. At the time, though, most people weren't thinking in those terms. It was all right for a Southern white boy to be a dedicated Joe Louis fan. There were plenty of us. We didn't think of him as a black man. He was Joe Louis.

The press (always lagging far behind the people) and even the fight announcers on the radio—"a credit to his race"—made more out of what we have come to call "the race card" than other people did. And no question, then and now, the best drawing card, the way to get a crowd, was to match a white fighter against a black fighter.

No trouble during those long years of the Depression of finding eager candidates of all races and colors and shades. When a dollar a day was a serious wage, the twenty-five or fifty dollars a young strong man could earn for a few minutes of public violence in some local arena or club was worth the effort and the risk. In those days, not surprisingly, there were dozens of good, experienced fighters in all the weight classes; and among that crowd there were some great ones. Like Joe Louis.

I now find myself thinking that the big civil rights movement in the 1960s was anticipated and prepared for. Might have come to pass earlier if the war, World War II, had not come along and interrupted, delayed and changed so much in America. Of course it can be, has been argued that the war opened the eyes, and hearts, of millions of veterans who came to see a larger world with more diversity than they had ever imagined. Maybe both things are true.

It seems to be true that even before the war, and certainly after it, there had been a change of heart by many, and gradually most, in their ways of thinking and feeling about race; that the South was ready for the changes that came; even that the changes would not have come without the readiness.

Who knows?

7.

I have written as if the thing that rendered Joe Louis most admirable was his great skill. And surely, from the point of view of a young boxer that would be the case. The skills were, we learned bit by bit, hard-earned. Louis was trained by the great trainer "Chappie" Blackburn. Who selected him because he saw him get knocked down and get up seven times in one round. Blackburn later said he could teach anyone the skills required to be a fighter. All but one. He could not teach anyone to get up somehow, time after time, after being knocked down. To be a great fighter, a champion, you had to have heart. The rest could be taught and learned.

That's what Billy Conn meant when he said: "It takes a good man to get up seven times."

Blackburn spent a long time, years, getting Louis ready and bringing him along slowly. Blackburn, himself, said that he wasn't really sure that Louis could be a champion, and a great one, until the first Schmeling fight when Schmeling knocked Louis out in the twelfth round. The thing was, the punch that rendered Louis unconscious came in the fourth round. For eight more rounds, unknown to Schmeling and to anyone else but Blackburn, Louis was "out on his feet," but still fighting, coming forward.

Put that kind of heart together with the highest kind of skill and you had a truly great fighter. Louis was probably the last really skilled heavyweight champion. I think the only people who might have had a chance to beat him in his prime were people who had come and gone before he came along—Jack Dempsey maybe, Jack Johnson probably. Nobody coming after Joe Louis had the schooling or the skill that he did. Rocky Marciano could hit harder, but, then, so could Max Baer. Maybe, just maybe, Muhammad Ali had hands as quick as Louis; but after studying this video, I doubt it. Ali was awfully quick on his feet, but Billy Conn was quicker.

But Louis had more than skill to admire. He had integrity and character, not charisma. He was only modestly colorful, never a showboat, never a showoff. In our own celebrity-ridden era, characterized by uninhibited self-promotion, it is hard to imagine that there ever were any athletes or performers who let their skills speak for themselves. One thing this video has taught me (again) is that every one of the fights was Louis's fight. That is, his opponents may have tried different styles and strategies against him; but every single fight became a variation on the same immemorial stalking dance from which only a few escaped. The fights are very clean. Not much clinching or holding on. No clumsy rough stuff with elbows and head butts. Because he was so good, Louis made his opponents look their best.

At the end of the video, his opponent and, later, longtime good friend Billy Conn has the last word: "He was a real high-class gentleman."

Locker Room Talk: Notes on the Social History of Football

The locker room. Here where we are (suddenly?) the shy, soft, nude old guys who once did swagger and pop towels and stand and sing in the rosy steam of showers, soaking our bruises away. You could do a history of American sports, the caste and class of it all, just from different kinds of locker rooms. The locker rooms I have seen lately would all serve for the model of the country club locker room in my youth. Of course, my youth was the Depression and ended with World War II. And my youth was almost entirely spent in the South. Which was uniformly poor and proud and fortunately ignorant of other places and their quality of life. We were always short of everything in our Southern locker rooms, from liniments to soap, from shoelaces to towels. Only years later in the dressing rooms (locker room was no longer really accurate) of Princeton University did I discover the luxuries of clean whites (jock and T-shirt) and towel every day.

In those Depression days Southerners played harder and hit harder and were meaner than other people. So it seemed.

Everything was in short supply. Not enough pads or jerseys or helmets even on the high school teams. Sometimes, routinely, we had to trade off stuff with somebody else to go in or to leave a game. And a team would have only two or three footballs, maybe one of those new enough to still have its shape. On a wet rainy day the slick, smooth, old footballs got wetter and wetter and heavier and heavier. Until passing one was like shotputting. Catching a pass was like catching a cannonball.

Shoes were a huge problem, seldom fit or were comfortable. They were heavy, in any case, leather, high-topped and blessed with hard, pointed cleats, "male" cleats with a screw on them that fit in a hole on the sole of the shoe or "female" cleats with the hole in the cleat and the pointed screw permanently fixed on the shoe sole. These latter worried you, at least if other people were wearing them; because if a cleat got loose and fell off you could be cut to pieces with that pointed metal screw. The cleats were bad enough. Once on the ground, knocked or fallen, you protected your hands and face (no face masks until the '50s) as best you could from cleats. When somebody else from another team went down you went in stomping those cleats.

Absence of face masks caused many injuries. Broken noses were common. Also missing teeth. In high school, the guy with the locker next to mine, name of Carnahan unless I misremember, had no teeth at all. Had an upper and lower plate he would leave in his locker. He had blocked a punt and lost every tooth in his head.

Well, so what? Carnahan was tough. What else could they do to him? Tough was what we wanted to be. You might not possess or develop much skill, but you could take plenty of punishment and pass it on, dish it out, too.

Nobody wanted to play "dirty." But what that meant, what the limits were, is hard to recall. None of it had anything to do with the rules. You broke the rules when you had a chance, and when you got caught you got a penalty. Some of the forbidden things to do we actually practiced doing.

Nobody wanted to have a reputation, singly or as a team, for being dirty. We wanted to look dirty, though. We would not send our game uniforms to the laundry, so we could look all grass-stained and muddy. If there was precious blood on your jersey, you preserved it. If by some chance you ended up with a clean uniform, you rolled in the dirt during the warm-up.

Sometimes, for no particular reason except that we had seen it in newspaper photographs, we put burnt cork below our eyes. Once when the coaches were out of the locker room, the whole team painted our whole faces black with burnt cork. Ran onto the field with Al Jolson faces and the coaches responded with screaming, stamping, hat-throwing tantrums. Coaches of that era did not like jokes or joking around. And they hated not just the sound but the very idea of singing on the bus.

The bus? It was a yellow school bus. Greyhound was a luxury for college ballplayers.

Before there were school teams there was the public park, in my case Delaney Park, where we met every day after school and all day, except for church, on the weekends, and played tackle football until it was much too dark to see anymore.

I owned the football, a good one my father had gotten for me. Contrary to the expectation and the figure of speech, owning the ball meant that I had no choice but to be there early and stay late. Day after day. Year after year.

You could learn a thing or two without really trying, without thinking about it much.

At Delaney Park I saw, and played with and against, the best, most gifted runner I have ever seen. I mention his name here and now to celebrate it, though I do not know if he is alive or dead. Name was Leroy Hoquist, and he had more moves, and more graceful ones, than any runner I have seen since then. And I have logged a lot of hours over the years watching football in the stadium or on TV. When I was playing, later, I have seen close up some pretty good ones. Have actually tackled a Heisman Trophy winner in the open field and have chased after and piled on some others, famous and unknown. But never a one who could run like Leroy Hoquist. He was all air and fire. Pure smoke when you went to grab him.

He was supposed to go to the University of Florida on a scholarship. But something happened—maybe a death in the family; some unanticipated hardship; who knows?—and he went to work for a local undertaker, driving a hearse, an ambulance, sometimes, in more recent times, a limousine. Last time I saw him he was driving a limo at a family funeral, in my family.

Watching that guy run with a football was like watching Baryshnikov at his best.

And what does all that mean? Nothing, I guess. Except that—do you see what I mean?—you didn't have to be a star to be a star. In the heart of the Depression good memory must have meant more than good publicity.

Almost everybody will remember how, in films and books and feature stories during the Vietnam War, the smart thing was to equate sports, especially the arena of contact sports, chiefly football, with war. Coaches, especially the hard noses like Woody Hayes and Vince Lombardi, for example, were always being compared to our generals—Westmoreland, Abrams and all that crew. It was a cheap shot, to be sure. But fashionable and with a certain resonance.

And there are plenty of people who have read about the persistence of sports, all kinds of games, in the dark heart and horror of World War II. More than one writer has mentioned the soccer team at Auschwitz. Not many remember how it was here at home when, within a year after Pearl Harbor, most of the able-bodied men and boys were in the service.

(Truth is, it might have been a fine time to begin to integrate sports in America. Because the services were still strictly segregated, until Harry Truman changed all that during the Korean War, not so many Blacks, *Negroes* as we would have said then, were drafted or accepted as volunteers. The Black population had the largest number of able-bodied males on the home front. If they had been allowed to play baseball and football in integrated leagues we might have had a decade or two head start towards civil rights.)

As it was things slowed down or went on hold. Philip Roth and others have written things, both factual and fancy, about wartime baseball. Nobody (yet) has written the book I want to write (and here stake a claim to) as soon as I can somehow earn a little free time to do it— college football during the war. Of course West Point and Annapolis had wonderful teams during the war years. In both cases they had the choice of anybody they wanted. If you went to and played for Army or Navy, you were officially in the service, as much so as any GI on Guadalcanal or in Italy, but far from shot and shell. Moreover, for the period of the war the distinctions between amateur and professional athletes were blurred. If you had been a pro, you could still play college ball at that time and, again, for a few years after the war. So you had incredible powerhouse teams at Army and Navy and, somehow or other, at some of the big universities like Michigan and Notre Dame, these latter being in part composed of various servicemen in programs there.

A lot of schools closed down their intercollegiate sports programs completely. Others reduced or modified their schedules. With gas rationing and all kinds of transportation problems, it became extremely difficult to travel to faraway games. Schools played games with their neighbors. Teams were made up of the very young, too young to be drafted; 4-Fs, deferred from service because of some physical disability; and, by at least 1943, included discharged veterans, usually physically disabled from wounds, though there were some Section 8 guys, men discharged for psychological reasons, usually combat fatigue.

In short, if you had a college team at all, it would be made up of kids, cripples, and crazies. Some of these people were wonderful football players. They usually got badly beaten, driven into the hard ground like tent pegs. But sometimes—it was bound to happen—they were able to give Army and Navy a good scare. And that's what I am hoping to live and write my book about. I was there. I remember a story or two from those times.

One happened early on in the war before they needed every man who could see lightning and hear thunder on active duty. Shortly after the war got going, some little school had a navy V-12 unit stationed there and enrolled as students. The physical education officer was a famous university coach who had been drafted. He got this idea. Furtively, almost secretly, he managed to get some of the top football players in the country, both amateur and professional, assigned to his V-12 unit. He got his team on Navy's schedule. He kept his team under wraps until that game, planning to beat the Naval Academy when the time came. I like to think he was planning to bet on the game. And he probably would have won the game and the bet, if any, except that somebody put two and two together, figured out the scam; and the entire V-12 unit was called up to active duty with the fleet during the week of the Navy game. By Wednesday all his anthology of stars were long gone. The coach discovered it was too late to cancel the game completely. He could forfeit or he could play. Out of perverse pride, maybe, he decided to play. He called a meeting, an assembly of the student body of this little school. He explained the situation and then offered a varsity football letter to anyone who would come out and practice Thursday and Friday afternoon (he promised the easiest practice imaginable—no hard exercise, no painful contact) and then put on a uniform and maybe play a few minutes against Navy. The coach didn't try to imitate Henry the Fifth at Agincourt, if he had ever heard of him or it; but he did say it would be an experience they could talk about for the rest of their lives. He also told them he didn't expect them to do or try anything dangerous. All they had to do was be there on the field and to try to line up in the right place at the right time. Still, he reminded the youngest among them, still available for the draft, a bum knee or a bad ankle could get you deferred as 4-F. If they wanted to try to block a tackle a little bit, at their own risk, of course, he would not discourage them . . .

I knew a guy, a very unathletic type, really, who put on the football uniform (with help from others) and actually played about two or three minutes against Navy, emerging from the experience (with the help of others, including the Navy players) not a whole lot worse off than when he went on the field. He said it was all very confusing, but probably worth it. He still sports his varsity letter sweater from time to time and is an active supporter of the football program at his school. Navy only won the game by sixty or eighty points. In many ways it was a moral victory for the coach and his once-in-a-lifetime team. The next week the school abandoned football for the duration of the war.

For my story I want something similar, but later in the war. Fall of 1944, just before the Battle of the Bulge. I want my team of cripples and crazies and kids to play Army—Blanchard and Davis and all that crowd. Couple of real ballplayers in our time, a one-armed guy and another one with a steel plate in his head. A bunch of frisky fifteen- and sixteen-year-old kids. A genius crazy, right out of Eastlake's *Castle Keep* or maybe *Catch 22*, who figures out how to confuse and contain Blanchard and Davis. With a little luck it just might work . . .

I am thinking about adding one other element—criminals. Back in the early 1940s, when I was at Sewanee Military Academy, we scrimmaged against the University of Chattanooga. They were a team, we heard and believed, entirely composed of people who had been deferred from the draft not for any physical disability, but because of criminal behavior. They were bad apples, athletes every other coach and school had long since given up on. They came to Chattanooga and were a pretty good team, even though they stole things from each other's lockers, from towels to wristwatches, and off the field acted like Visigoths with time on their hands. Surely I can find a good use in the novel for that bunch of rowdies, wouldn't you think?

After the war it was a wild and woolly scene in a very different way. All the veterans were back and a lot of them played football for fun or exercise or something. If you include everybody who put on equipment and went to practice, there were something like 189 guys on the Princeton team in those days. The oldest of them were in their middle thirties. My roommate, a former master sergeant in a tank company, had played tackle at the University of Maryland before the war. Down the hall was a guy who had played for the Baltimore Colts.

Now. You might think that the quality of football in the first few years after the war was extraordinary. In a way it was. It was more fun than that game has ever been before or since. None of these old-timers cared who won or who lost. Not really. How could they? Most of them had been in combat and survived the experience. They found it hard to get very excited by a ball game. They found that the coaches were far less terrifying or persuasive than the people who had regularly yelled at them in the army and the navy and the marines. They were not easily motivated by conventional ways and means. Nobody wanted to play badly, if only to avoid the embarrassment of hooting and jeering and horse-laughter. (There was a lot of laughing going on, on the field, *during the games,* in those days.) But none of them worried a whole lot about winning and losing, about records and statistics. They liked to bet on games, but all that tells you is that they came out of the war knowing more about the mystery of luck than any skills or tactics or strategy.

Sometimes, even on the loosey-goosey football fields of postwar America, luck, pure luck, ran like electricity for the old guys.

I have lived to see many better games and better players, but when I search memory for surprising and spectacular and wholly individual plays, I come back to those days when half the teams in America were half-bald and fairly fat and puffing and blowing like porpoises.

I remember, too, there was a very different attitude towards teamwork in those days, an attitude that drove coaches to distraction. Everybody in the service (then and later) learns to do a job within its own limits and without much regard for the jobs that other people are up to. Concentration on what you are supposed to be doing. (In that sense baseball was far better training for combat than football.) The veterans almost uniformly felt no serious sense of responsibility for anything beyond their own immediate area of action. Thus they didn't care about pleasing the crowd or the coach or what anyone on their own team or the other team might think about them. They played hard to please themselves.

Now I have season tickets at Virginia, where I teach, and go as often as I can. The game has changed greatly. Lots of new rules since I started. One small example among many: When I first started playing, substitution rules were very strict. If you were replaced, you could not return to the field during the same quarter.

Biggest single change, and fairly recent, is that you can block with your hands now. This means that size (bigger and stronger) is of utmost importance on the line. Means that size and weight on both sides have to be roughly equal. With the old ways of blocking, smaller players could cut the big ones down.

The whole game has become less complex, too. Not a lot of serious thinking involved, even by the quarterback, with coaches calling the plays from the bench. That was a fifteen-yard penalty in the old days— "coaching from the bench." So was signaling.

It has become a corporate game and basically a proletarian game. A kind of labor-intensive assembly line with interchangeable players. They don't hit as hard as we did. At their size and weight they would kill each other if they did. The result is a lot of missed blocks and tackles.

They tend to play a more sensible, rational kind of a game. Easing off, for example, when the game is clearly lost or won. I remember on our ragged and rundown fields (few of them fully level), there were seldom any game clocks until after World War II. We might know what quarter it was, but only one official, the one with the watch, really knew what time it was. A game could end suddenly and without warning.

Then afterwards in some crummy, grimy shower, lined up waiting our turn under the water, hoping the hot water would last . . .

Heroes

On October 7, 1991, there was a gathering of writers in Washington at the Folger Library, a fund-raising gala for the PEN/Faulkner awards. We were to be introduced (by Roger Mudd) in alphabetical order. And each of us was to read something on the assigned subject, "Heroes," for three to five minutes.

Heroes I, then, is what I wrote for that occasion. Heroes II was put together a few months later for a conference on Southern autobiography. Heroes II is an expanded version of the short original.

HEROES I

I grew up in a radical household. My father was an American radical, part populist, part prophet, and mostly a rare example of what, in our buttoned-up era, amid this glittering black-tie company, I would have to call a neanderthal Democrat. Wholly compassionate, but without an ounce or an inch of self-serving sentimentality, he was radical also in his complete integrity, unflagging open-mindedness, utter independence and consistent unpredictability. Most groups and parties and factions, as such (whether they were the Ku Klux Klan or the communists), were contemptible to him. Needless to say he was not a politician. However, in the early years of this waning century, he was an active member of the very new United Mine Workers.

Picture this much. A man who worked hard as a miner in the far West, then left that work battered and scarred, still physically powerful, but maimed and crippled enough to be fearsome to his enemies and embarrassing to his only son. Came south to Florida where he made himself into a lawyer and lived on to do many good works. Tried a multitude of cases with equal vigor and urgency before small-town magistrates and the august Supreme Court of the United States. Did not so much defeat as destroy the Ku Klux Klan in Florida. More than once had as much to do as anyone in electing and reelecting Claude Pepper to the Senate and was, alas for Claude, dead and gone when Smathers, the protégé, betrayed his hero and ran against him. By persuasion and perilous example, he saved a major bank and all the deposits therein when our banks were collapsing like shacks in a hurricane. In my presence he once single-handedly stopped a lynching. The intended victim was a monstrously evil white woman. He saved her life for the courts.

Devoted his time and energy to *pro bono* work. And thus his actions and admirable principles precluded many common kinds of material comfort and any serious estate for inheritance. Often put not only his own life at risk, but also all the lives of the family as well.

It was a joyous, noisy, loving household. But I have rebelled against it every day of my life. I confess that at his funeral I was ashamed of the crowd, that mob of black and white, raggedy-ass poor people who had come to pay their respects. Where were the good-looking people? The people worth knowing? And what kind of a legacy was this—to be told over and over again—"We feel the exact same way we did when President Roosevelt died"?

It has taken more than sixty years for me to earn the right to have these five minutes. I ought to be camouflaged by glittering jokes, or anyway, at least offering up an eccentric list of famous names as my heroes. But this evening I have a debt to pay if not to settle.

Once upon a time, in a hundred and one cases, my father brought all the powerful railroads of our part of the country—the ACL, the Southern and the Seaboard, the Florida East Coast—to their knees. They sent high-ranking representatives into our living room to offer him more money than he could ever earn if he would just *not* bring and try any more cases against the railroads. I was afraid he might throw them bodily out of the house—something I had seen before. But, instead, he heard them out and thanked them for their interest before he politely ushered them outside.

"That's a hell of a lot of money and would solve a whole lot of problems for me," he told them. "But great God Almighty, gentlemen, what would I do to have fun?"

Old warrior, American untitled knight in rusty, dented armor, I am finally able to salute you, sir, here and now.

Heroes II

Begin at the end with the funeral. The funeral service was at St. Luke's Cathedral, where I had first been a member of the boys' choir and then an acolyte and later a crucifer. Where the dead man, my father, had been on the vestry and more than once served as senior warden. The cathedral was packed with people. And there I was, still in my teens, dressed in the coat and tie reserved for weddings and funerals, shocked and numbed beyond grief. Grief would come later. Sometimes comes even now. At that moment I was observing. The high, shadowy cathedral was crowded with the plain faces, black and white, of plain people. Sure, there were a few of the locally famous and powerful, though in truth none so locally known or powerful as the dead man had been. But most of those whom I most admired and envied—the beautiful, the lucky, the altogether privileged—were either absent or hidden, well camouflaged among the common crowd.

Where did all these plain people come from? True to my age and my own kind of folly, I was as much embarrassed as I was grieved.

Before I begin to approach the grand and abstract theme of this conference ("Separate Parts: Diversity and Community in Southern Autobiography"—University of Central Arkansas), I must summon up some of my diverse community of ghosts out of the past, including even the pale, unreliable ghost of myself. To invoke them and to listen to them, to think and rethink, to design and revise the world they and I lived in, and, like everybody else I can imagine, from Adam to Einstein, what they, themselves, imagined to be the one and only world there was and will be.

I am talking about the South and the Great Depression, a hard time, tough enough for heroes and hard cases. But it was a time, also, when poverty and trouble, widely shared and diversely experienced, were great human equalizers. When even the lucky and the rich (and I have learned, only now, by reading about the then and there, that there really were some lucky and rich ones) were almost furtive in their inconspicuous consumption. Out of shame as much as any other motive; for shame was still an operative value in America those days. It was bad enough to have money when nobody else did, but it was especially shameful to spend it or to flaunt it or lord it over one's fellows. Even a false humility was considered better than pride, be it false or true. Shame was a powerful force, powerful enough to act as a deterrent against crime and consequent dishonor brought down on one's family, one's tribe or people, one's community which, with and in spite of all its commonplace inequities and injustices, was nevertheless a coherent community, belonging, for better and for worse, richer and poorer, to all of the families and tribes and peoples of a given place.

Belonged to us, too, I can see better and more clearly now than I ever could have then. Belonged to our family which was about as diverse and other than mainstream as can well be imagined. Now, with the world much changed and even the laws of the land, as well as its customs, changed, we are at once representative and separate, having become a regular rainbow coalition of races and tribes, with Asians and African-Americans and Native Americans, with Jews and Catholics and eastern Europeans bearing our family names, sharing and adding to (changing) a family history with its joys and griefs. No longer local or even regional, we are now scattered widely across the whole nation, coast to coast, wherever love and work and our restless spirits have taken us, the same restless spirits that brought us to this continent in the first place, as early as possibly could be.

If we seem to be more diverse now, what were we then? Already as diverse as it was possible to be, our bloodlines joining together English, Scotch-Irish, Welsh, Dutch, French, and Spanish ancestry.

Looking back, I can see what I never would have seen or said then (though surely I must have felt the truth of it), that our whole family, all that I knew or knew of, was what people nowadays choose to call crudely the "Other." We didn't act like other people or do like other people. We didn't even look much like other people. Some of us, believe it or not, were handsome and attractive people, though seldom shaped or cut according to prevailing fashions or conventional taste.

We were many.

I had five uncles and two aunts and all of their progeny on one side, four aunts and two uncles and a host of cousins on the other. My five uncles on the one side included a cavalry officer, a professional dancer, a PGA golfer, a musician, and a semipro and minor league baseball player. On the other side were a newspaper man turned Hollywood screenwriter and a wilderness and mountain climbing guide. There were some writers then and now. Two of the women were nurses who practiced their vocation in far-off and difficult places. All of the other women, at one time or another, supported themselves with jobs they took or created.

Some of us came to bad ends and some didn't. Some managed to make a little money. Some did not.

The family . . .

We were not ever a real coalition or caucus, a unified crew or gang, except in those cases where one of us, any of us, was attacked by others outside the family. Then we were like a phalanx. But on social and political issues we were and are deeply divided and, indeed, were encouraged by good and strong examples to be so. One great-grandfather, an admirable gentleman, had been a slave-master on a very large scale. Another had been a prominent abolitionist, in the same South, and was faithful to his beliefs. Though, when it came to war, he fought and was wounded for the Southern cause. Another was a Union general. There was a place for all of them in the family and its history.

My grandfather, my mother's father, was orphaned at the end of the war, then raised as a child by a deaf-mute black man, a former slave, who served as his parents until, finally, blood relatives who were willing and able to take him could be found. Growing up in the deep woods and swamp land of the Santee Delta, among black people, he learned and was fluent in the Gullah and Geechie languages until his dying day in his nineties. I have written about him elsewhere, in essays and in fiction: how he lived an adventurous life of ups and downs, earned two huge fortunes and spent three. Served as solicitor general (the title in those old days) of the state of Georgia. Ran for the office of governor of Florida and lost. I have written a poem about him called "Main Currents of American Political Thought." Here it is:

> Gone then the chipped demitasse cups
> at dawn, rich with fresh cream and coffee,
> a fire on the hearth, winter and summer,
> a silk dandy's bathrobe, the black Havana cigar.
>
> Gone the pet turkey gobbler, the dogs and geese,
> a yard full of chickens feeling the shadow of a hawk,
> the tall barn with cows and a plough horse, with corn,
> with hay spilling out of the loft, festooning the dead Pierce Arrow.
>
> Gone the chipped oak sideboards and table,
> heavy with aplenty of dented, dusty silverware.
> Gone the service pistol and the elephant rifle
> and the great bland moosehead on the wall.
>
> "Two things," you told me once, "will keep
> the democratic spirit of this country alive—
> the free public schools and the petit jury."
> Both of these things are going, too, now, Grandfather.
> You had five sons and three daughters,
> and they are all dead or dying slow and sure.
> Even the grandchildren are riddled with casualties.
> You would not believe these bitter, shiny times.
>
> What became of all our energy and swagger?
> At ninety you went out and campaigned for Adlai Stevenson
> in South Carolina. And at my age I have to force
> myself to vote, choosing among scoundrels.

But my grandfather, colorful as he was, is not the subject here. The man, my father, at the center of this tale, stood at close to six feet, give or take an inch depending on his posture. Give or take a hair, of which he had next to none, being almost as bald as a cannonball.

All of this is strictly according to memory now, all that is left to me of him. Except for a handsome gold pocket watch.

Notice that I did not claim the evidence of history. Surely history, rising above the memories and voices it is made of, is often accurate; but can likewise distort truth beyond valid recognition. *Item:* I was recently interviewed (by phone, which is the lowest form of interview) by a young journalist who is writing a book concerning a locally prominent newspaper editor of my youth. I knew the man and I also knew a good deal about him. He was a dangerously reactionary man and, more to the point in the larger sense, a thoroughly bad human being, small-minded, mean-spirited, dishonest, you name it. But early in the interview it was quite clear that the young journalist-biographer, deriving most of his facts and general information from a trove of notes and pages left behind by his deceased subject, was under the firm misapprehension that his hero was an admirable and ever prescient Southern liberal, a Hodding Carter or maybe an Atticus Finch. I did not have the heart or, indeed, the time to dissuade or disillusion him. Anyway, would he have been persuaded by any testimony and witness I might have to offer? I doubt it. Leave him to his false history . . .

My father wore identical plain dark suits and white shirts with the old-fashioned separate, starched collar. He had no personal vanity. He was at the center of the family, not merely his own, but the larger family, as well. I have written about him, also, in fact and fiction; and I will do so again. How he defeated and destroyed the Ku Klux Klan in Florida. No easy task at the time and performed at great and grave risk to the rest of us—his wife and children, his kinfolks. How he gave a large part of his time and energy and ambition (and thus my inheritance) to *pro bono* work for the poor and the oppressed—he, himself, having been familiar with both of these conditions before he became, later in his life, a lawyer.

I could tell you more. I will tell you some. How he prevented a lynching once all by himself, armed with nothing more than the power of his presence and his words, and his unique and impeccable reputation. How he saved the bank in our hometown when all the other banks were failing. How he managed to save the seat and the career of Senator Claude Pepper, by a single speech which turned around and delivered a hostile and populous county to the senator. The next time Pepper ran for the Senate my father was dead and the senator lost his seat. How he humbled some great and powerful corporations again and again in courthouses. And when they offered him a fortune, more money than he could or would ever make, if he simply agreed not to bring any more cases against them, he thanked them for the flattering offer, but allowed that there wasn't enough money in the whole world to compensate him for the loss of the deep pleasure he took (*fun* is what he called it) in, as he put it, beating the stuffing out of them in open court.

Six feet tall, then, bald, scarred, rock-faced, broad shoulders and a muscular eighteen-inch neck. He had worked as a miner (copper and lead) in the West and had the muscles to show for it. Had the wounds, also. Two fingers of his left hand cut off by a machine that could have killed him then and there. A bad left leg with a pronounced limp. A somewhat shriveled left arm from a bout with polio. None of these injuries or troubles stopped or even seriously inhibited him from doing what he wanted to do. *Item:* He taught himself how to be a very good tennis player in spite of these things, able to hold his own with the best and the brightest of local talent. It was, to be sure, awkward and unbeautiful; and I cringe now again with embarrassment to remember it. And even now I wince with shame to acknowledge that embarrassment.

I have searched my heart and my memory for any dramatic instances of the oppression of others, a popular theme for public confession these days. And I can find none, though I am compelled to admit that it is the tacit things, the things undone that ought to have been done, the inward and spiritual failures, often unremembered even if common enough, and quietly including lust, murder, hatred and the others, including undeniable pleasure in the pain and sorrow, the mortality of others, it is these things by which we all, in all our real or imaginary diversity, will be judged, no matter how mercifully we may choose to judge ourselves.

In our house and family—and in many others that I knew of—you earned yourself a whipping if you used the word nigger. It was partly a class thing, of course, a matter of blood and privilege that rednecks and crackers did not share or feel, though even they had to be careful in our presence, anyway. We were on top. We were not empowered (to use the recent buzzword). We had taken power on our own.

No one, not friend or enemy or even the majestic law itself, could do any wrong, including spoken wrong, to our people and expect to do so with impunity. Our people very much included the colored people who were part of our lives, those whom we knew. Paternalistic, to be sure. Bet your sweet ass it was. Powerful, with the power, as said, earned, not given or bestowed by anyone.

I have a memory that once, when we were traveling in another Southern state, a small-town hotel clerk caused some trouble by refusing to give a room to the Negro maid who was traveling with us. I remember how we all left the hotel in a confusion of baggage and children and pets while my father told the desk clerk that he (personally) would live to regret his unacceptable rudeness and behavior. So we moved on down the road, a couple of cars full of us, in the long Southern summer twilight, driving to the next town and the next hotel. And later that evening the owner of the first hotel caught up with us and profusely apologized. My father accepted his apology, adding, however, that of course neither he nor any member of the family or his people or his friends would ever so much as enter the front door of that place again. But at least that was the end of it.

We delighted in the diversity of our hometown, knowing no other. A child, of course, believes in no other world than the one where he finds himself. Can imagine other worlds, but not truly believe in them. We had a colony of Greek refugees who were, by default, members of our Episcopal church. We had a few Cubans and Filipinos. I remember the Filipino man who came around every year to the public schools to demonstrate the tricks that could be done with a yo-yo. I knew very little about Jews. I knew that, for some reason, they had different holidays. I used to play with a boy about my age in our neighborhood who was Jewish. But after a while, they moved to a new and better house and then I seldom saw him except at public school.

Excepting only our colored people, who had to deal directly with Jewish merchants, storekeepers, landlords, etc., and who did not always speak well of them, I never heard anyone say anything negative about Jews. Once, I do remember now—it would have to have been in 1935 or 1936, not any later—we were visiting kinfolks on Cape Cod. We all went to supper at the house of some very well-to-do people. I can remember to this day being deeply impressed by the food—things to eat that I had never yet seen or heard of appeared on the table. A few minutes into this magical feast one of our hosts said something or other derogatory about the Jews in Germany. It must have been a joke or a wisecrack, followed by the comment that whatever was happening to them, they deserved.

My father stood up and spoke to us in a quiet, firm voice.

"Excuse yourselves, children," he said. "We are leaving now."

And so we did.

Years and years later I met a journalist of some distinction, who told me that he had been present at that dinner and had witnessed that moment, and that in a curious way it helped him change his life. He said that he, too, disapproved of the opinions of those rich and prominent people, but thought that he could ignore them and continue to enjoy . . . Continue to enjoy what? Whatever there is to enjoy by biting your tongue and sealing your lips and numbing your feelings. Though he lacked the courage or the bad manners (take your pick, call it what you please) to stand up and leave himself, he never went back there again.

Self-righteous, you may well be thinking. Smug and self-righteous. Maybe so and maybe not. But please remember that this great country lawyer—and I use the word "great" advisedly; there is a record and you can look it up, yourselves—this great country lawyer, more in the mold of Huey Long than Atticus Finch or Gregory Peck, this highly successful, argumentative, opinionated litigator, simply got up and left the table with all his people. He did not choose to dignify their opinions with rational arguments or any attempt at persuasion.

To fill in the picture a little more, you need to know that he was not in the least sentimental. He was deeply compassionate. But suffering, in and of itself, did not trouble him. Pain and suffering were, unfortunately, essential and inevitable components of the human condition. But unjust suffering and gratuitous cruelty enjoyed his full and compassionate attention.

He was afraid of nobody. And I have to admit he could be a violent man. Any man or boy, white or black, who took a notion to sass him, to talk back, was risking and sometimes earned a beating. Of one kind or another. And he was perfectly capable of unleashing a tongue-lashing so intense and so sustained that you or I or anyone else might well wish for a physical beating instead. He made no allowances for himself and only a few to other people.

Now that I have been in the world and around and about for a good deal more than half a century, I have to say that if anybody was ever what your contemporary critics insist on calling the "Other," it would have to have been my father. And because he became so by choice, so were we, the family, like it or not. As a lawyer he chose to take on difficult and unpopular cases, regularly representing many poor people of all shades and colors, always including black people and their institutions. He was never called by anyone, in the lingo of the times, a "nigger lawyer," an insult reserved for seedy lawyers, both black and white, who did little or nothing for their clients and squeezed them for all they could get. He was more than competent. A charter member of the United Mine Workers, he also became a charter member of the American Law Institute and for years was the only member of that (then) august body from the state of Florida. He tried a number of cases before the Supreme Court of the United States. Even his sworn enemies, who were, from beginning to end, many and powerful, called him a great lawyer and were afraid of him.

But there was more, something that made life more than a little difficult then and that now has all but ruined my capacity to appreciate many of our contemporary heroes. A man with a great appetite and gusto for life, he gave up all of the usual comforting vices—womanizing, smoking, drinking, socializing—not out of any Puritanical moral streak (he was religious, but never a Puritan), but because he was then free to capture and to hold the moral high ground. He could do so only if no allowances ever had to be made for the symptoms of a flawed character. Enemies looked long and hard, studied to find some major or minor weakness that might be exploited against him. They found none. He made no excuses. Gave none away. And, in return, he was utterly pitiless when he deemed he had to be.

Think of that in our age. An age when gestures are not "real," but virtual, symbolic; when all kinds of serious character flaws in public figures are not serious enough to shame or shake them from their moral arrogance. He would rather have seen the world (with all of us in it) burnt to a crisp than to tell a lie—even a lie told for some good purpose. No good end ever justified bad or false means. That code, his, was imposed on all the rest of us and, of course, none of us measured up. But at least we saw some clear proof that it could be done if you were willing to pay the price.

I have no idea what my father might think, where he might come down, on the issues that seem to perplex us most these days—crime, abortion, national budgets, affirmative action, you name it. Only that it would almost certainly be radical and surprising and unpredictable and in no way reflexive. I cannot even begin to imagine what he might say on the subject of our conference ("Diversity and Community in Southern Autobiography"). I do not think he would approve of what I have done here and now. Well, then, it has not been done to win his approval.

The funeral service is over, all but the ceremony at the graveside. And we come out of the huge, shadowy, raw, echoing, still unfinished cathedral and suddenly we are standing outside in the sparkle and glitter of Florida summer sunlight. And there, packing the sidewalks and the street, are hundreds of people, the same kinds of common people who filled the church. Hats come off as the family appears, not for us at all, but in honor of the dead man who served them well for so long and took nothing away from them.

It seems that I have waited more than fifty years to join them and to doff my own hat, too; but I do so here and now.

Going to See the Elephant: Why We Write Stories

I can't speak for others, for you. . . . But that is not true. I can and do speak for others all the time. I think and feel, perceive and misperceive for others, suffer and rejoice with them and for them. And so can you. And so do you. It's our stock-in-trade. It's what we do (among other things) as storytellers. This leap of faith into the skin and bones of an imaginary creature (stranger?) is the true source of the energy we possess.

Where we begin, though, the home place and home plate of all of our stories, is not first of all with the history of the tribe or crew we were born into, but with our own personal history and our own stories. That many of these, our stories, are much the same when we finally do come to compare notes and lives across time and space, oceans and continental divides, in no way detracts from the differences between us and our stories.

I grew up in a large family of storytellers, some of them also writers. These, the writers, the professional storytellers, did not influence me much except, perhaps, in the most important way of all—as living and breathing examples, proving that it was possible (somehow) to be a storyteller by choice and career. On one side of the family was the Georgia writer Harry Stilwell Edwards, who began his writing of fiction in the Reconstruction years immediately following the Civil War and continued writing fiction, novels and stories, up through the 1920s. I never knew him, but often heard stories about him. One of these stuck to me like a sandspur: how he once won a very large prize ($10,000, which was, in those days, a large sum of money, a modest fortune) for a novel called *Sons and Fathers.* How he took the money and assembled a group of kinfolks and friends, rented a Pullman car to carry them all, took a few weeks off from his day job as postmaster, and went to New York City (then merely Manhattan) and spent it as quickly as possible. Then returned to Georgia and the post office and his writing. As a child, I knew next to nothing about writing, the craft of it or the business of it; but *being a writer*, ah, that was something else, involving, on bright occasions, long trips to remarkable places in a Pullman car.

On the other side of the family, among my father's brothers and sisters, there were two writers. One, Oliver H. P. Garrett, who had been a celebrated reporter in the years right after World War I, was a screenwriter who wrote dozens of screenplays, some of which you will have seen, good and bad and indifferent. More important, he was my godfather and sent wonderful and expensive presents all the way from far California for birthdays and at Christmastime. And once in a great while, without any warning as far as I knew, he would show up wherever we happened to be for a visit. What I remember is the cars he came in, extravagant and shiny, long and noisy and fast, and the beautiful women, wives (among several), who came with him. He wore a beret and could play a guitar and told stories of Hollywood and, more exciting to me, about the First World War, in which he had served and somehow survived.

And that was being a writer, too, in all its glamorous and mysterious details.

He had a sister, Helen Garrett, who taught school and wrote some of the best children's books I've ever read. She also tried for most of her life to write an adult novel about some years she had spent as a nurse in rural Newfoundland. That book never worked out—why I don't know. From her example I learned something I certainly didn't want to—that it is entirely possible, even for a demonstrably gifted writer, to fail at something that matters greatly.

Truth is, there were others in the family, close kin and distant cousins, who tried and failed as writers also. Often they had great gifts, but bad luck or bad judgment.

My maternal grandfather, the best storyteller, in or out of print, that I have ever encountered, once asked me what I wanted to be when I grew up. And I told him I wanted to be a writer. His response was: "Well, that's as good a way to be poor as any other." (Which time has proved to be the factual truth.) But more seriously he wondered what on earth I would ever find to *write about*. He had a point. He had lived a hard and exciting life, full of adventures and misadventures, and couldn't imagine what stories I might possibly have to tell. At the time I did not tell him what I already knew—that I had *his* story to tell, together with the stories of all the others. I had already figured out for myself that a storyteller is not, by any means, limited to his own tale, whether of triumph or woe, but can justly claim possession of all those lives he knows about or can well imagine.

And for the others? My father was a great storyteller as well as a man to whom many things happened. He read to me by the hour before I learned to read for myself. He cheerfully wrote down the stories I dictated to him before I learned to write down words on a page. The grandparents and the great-grandparents had stories to tell, too, if you were willing to sit still and listen. They had fading memories of the Civil War and earlier, and some of the stories they told had come to them much earlier from their elders and summoned up the earliest days of European settlement on this continent. Meanwhile there were other voices to hear, memories to share. For instance, in those Depression days we had a cook and she would bring her own grandmother, an ancient black woman, to sit in the kitchen while she worked. And that old woman told me many stories of her days as a slave before the war and the emancipation.

So it is for storytellers. We are given the inestimable gift of the stories of others and it becomes our bounden duty to preserve those stories and, at the right time, to tell them as truly as we can. They are not "material." They do not exist only for us. If anything, it's the other way around.

As for the deeper motivations: We all know the argument, a story in itself, that our telling of tales (in whatever form, from epic to lyric poem) comes from the wounds of childhood, that we are struggling to heal ourselves, to overcome ghosts and shadows of the past. And I guess there is some truth in that. Nobody goes through childhood and adolescence without wounds and sorrows, though surely some childhoods are happier than others. But the burden is greater than that. We find voice, we speak for and of the wounds and sorrows of the others, our people. We act as spiritual treasurers for their stories, their wealth of wounds. This duty and service sets us free (in a way) from the weight and limits of our own shabby stories. Our vocation is a kind of liberation.

We join the larger company of storytellers, living and dead. Something I always try to get across to student writers is that what they are doing and trying to do is only different in degree, not kind, from the art and craft of Homer, Virgil, Dante, Shakespeare. However briefly and weakly, we share the experience of all the great storytellers of all time. Whether we succeed or fail is not irrelevant, but neither outcome can deprive us of the privilege and honor we have enjoyed in sharing the experience of creation, of telling, with all the storytellers who ever were or will be. We can imagine stories which will take or have taken place in worlds beyond our imagining.

Years and years ago I saw a documentary film about the Pygmies, those furtive little shadows of the jungle of central Africa. They are a fascinating people who manage to survive in a hostile environment (not least hostile are other, full-sized tribes) and under the most difficult circumstances. They have a complex language, a *click* language known to very, very few people outside of their group. I once met a man who had spent years living with and among the Pygmies in what is now Uganda. He had never fully mastered their language, but he could talk and listen. So I asked him, what kinds of things do they talk about? "The usual things," he shrugged. Myself, persistent: "Anything unusual? Anything special?" "Well, yes," he said. "There is one thing." And he went on to tell me that from early childhood to old age, Pygmies were uniformly comedians. They told great jokes. They all told jokes about everything. Who knows if he, the expert, was having a joke at my expense? (For sure, he couldn't remember any Pygmy jokes to tell me.) But I like to think (until proved otherwise) that he spoke the truth, that these little people, far from the sound and fury of the rest of the world, deep in the camouflage and secrecy of a great rain forest, have come to terms with the absurdity of the human condition which, even in isolation, they fully share, by becoming a race of jokers, stand-up storytellers for whom laughter is the truly appropriate response to what the world has to offer and take away. Sometimes I allow myself to imagine that come the Apocalypse we all half-expect to come upon us anytime, the Pygmies alone will survive to begin the human race again, that our proper elegy and requiem will be a joke in a click language. We should be so lucky.

But back to the documentary. One of the things the film showed was a hunting party that managed to kill an elephant, thus bringing home enough meat to last them for a long time. The occasion called for a feast, and at the feast there was a reenactment of the hunt by the hunters. For the Pygmies, armed with little spears and blowguns, an elephant was a formidable prey. Most often the elephant wins at the expense of any number of Pygmy hunters. And this time had evidently been a close thing for the hunters. What was wonderful about the reenactment, something that confirmed the story the expert had told me, was that the hunters, now players acting themselves, introduced a good deal of comedy into the story. They earned much laughter as they played out comic fear and ineptitude. Perhaps if the hunt had been a failure, the documentary would have shown us a Pygmy tragedy (if such a thing exists). But since the hunt went well (one man had been slightly injured, as I recall, and played to laughter by exaggerating his injuries), it was an all's-well-that-ends-well comedy.

And at that moment, sharing the experience with them, thanks to the filmmaker and his technology, I could see clearly what our duty and function as storytellers may well be. We tell the story of the hunt and we judge it according to how it came to pass and we call forth tears or laughter as the case may be. That is our currency, the universal coinage of tears and laughter.

When I saw the documentary film, I suddenly remembered what the Civil War veterans told green recruits when they went into battle. They told the new and innocent soldiers that they were "going to see the elephant." Which seems as good a way as any I can think of to describe the indescribable and unimaginable. Combat, especially in that most brutal and savage of all our wars, is just beyond our capacity to imagine. It must be experienced. But, still, all these years afterwards we have reenactments on old Civil War battlefields where men dress themselves in the Confederate or Union uniforms and walk over the same terrain and fall down as if dead and wounded, having seen the elephant.

All of this, you may be justly thinking, has nothing specific to say to the eager generation of new poets and writers about how and why we are storytellers. I have been writing all my life and publishing some of that writing for more than fifty years, so I ought to have *something*, be it ever so humble, to share with my fellow writers. Well, all that can be truly said, in this kind of show-and-tell, is only a little. You are summoned to an ancient and honorable enterprise, at least as old and probably older than the caves where our ancestors (of all kinds and shapes and sizes and colors) painted animals on the walls to illustrate their stories and their rituals. Learn your craft, by any and all means, and practice it with all the art and care and magic you can master. Be worthy of your vocation which is, after all is said and done, a career of danger and daring.

So all that we have left, what we can give to each other, share with each other, are fragments. Bits and pieces of broken wisdom. Take a look at W. H. Auden's wonderful poem, an elegy for Louis MacNiece, "The Cave of Making." Read *The Horse's Mouth*, by Joyce Cary. If you can, maybe at the library, get hold of the Carfax edition where Cary writes a preface about his painter-protagonist, Gulley Jimson, and makes it clear that there is no justice, and no place or need for it, in a world of everlasting creation.

And the only thing more left to be said is that, finally, it can never be over and done with, never finished. The stories can be told, must be told again and again by each and every one of us for each generation. I have tried to say this, the same thing, in a poem called "Whistling in the Dark."

WHISTLING IN THE DARK

What has happened, my friends, is this:
we are saying the same things over and over again
because we have to, because there is no other choice.

We are singing the old songs, whistling the same tunes,
each like a small boy in the dark, in a graveyard,
maybe, whistling to reassure the rotten dead

that he, of course, is careless, indifferent, fearless.
We are saying the same things in exactly the same tone of voice
because we have to, because there is no other choice,

except, perhaps, that purity of absolute silence
to which our noisy music does aspire,
with which our music will be well rewarded

all in due time. Meantime, my friends, we must
say again and over again the same few things
(wise or foolish no matter, beauty of bounden duty)

without which the world goes wild and the silent dead
rise up to rattle us daft with their dancing bones
because they have to, because there is no other choice.

The Lost Brother: Summoning Up the Ghost of Who I Might Have Been

And Jacob said to Rebekah his mother, Behold, Esau my brother
is an hairy man and I am a smooth man. My father will
peradventure feel me, and I shall seem to him as a deceiver;
and I shall bring a curse upon me, and not a blessing.

GENESIS 27: 11–12

I.

Once upon a time.

A particular time in a specific place. The heart of the Great Depression in central Florida. My mother and some of her friends, on a spur of the moment impulse, turned off the highway, Route 17, just north of Sanford and the St. Johns River, and drove a little way into a shady village. Where most of the people, as it happens, maybe all of them were psychics and fortune-tellers of various and sundry kinds. Again acting on pure impulse, they decided to have their minds read and their fortunes told.

When my mother chose to tell about the experience later on, she always made it clear—at the expense of the narrative, to be sure—that she had no good use or explanation for the fortune-telling part of it. She sincerely believed that the future is out of bounds for human consciousness, that the future is as mysterious and ineffable to a psychic as to anyone else. She was willing and able to imagine and allow that a mere wrinkle or wince of awareness, a focused and trained sensitivity to events and to others could reasonably explain the ability of some gifted souls to find the missing item or clue, to solve a crime, for example. And that there was no great trick, no magic, in being aware of the deep and principal concerns of someone else. That some people could learn not to *read* somebody else's mind, but, rather, to be aware of what the other is thinking about and worrying over. These were possible and reasonable powers. And why should she not believe that much? Since childhood she and her two sisters had always been able, even without wishing for the ability, to know if any one of them or, indeed, of the larger family, was in sickness, trouble, danger, or any other adversity. They took this kind of kinship for granted. Things, signs and portents, came to them in dreams, concerning each other and the family; and then they acted on the information so furnished to them and very, very seldom were deceived or misled. Throughout their lives these three sisters wrote letters, made long-distance phone calls and sometimes set forth on journeys because of the things which came to them while they were dreaming.

I have to tell you not only that I do not doubt this kind of consciousness on their part, I came early on and continue to believe that it was not especially remarkable. It was something possessed by many people of my mother's generation. It did not seem remarkable to them because it was at once traditional and familiar for as far and as deep as memory could range and from all of the literature they knew of, and was likewise everywhere common in the stories of the Bible.

The place where it struck me earliest and most forcefully was, of course, at Christmastime and from that story, the story of the wise men, the Magi (Matthew 2: 10–12): "When they saw the star, they rejoiced with exceeding great joy. And when they were come into the house, they saw the young child with Mary his mother, and fell down and worshipped him; and when they had opened their treasures, they presented unto him gifts: gold and frankincense and myrrh. And being warned of God in a dream that they should not return to Herod, they departed into their own country another way. And when they were departed, behold, the Angel of the Lord appeareth to Joseph in a dream, saying, 'Arise and take the young child and his mother and flee unto Egypt' . . ."

I did not have any reason to doubt any of it. How else would God warn living people—if and when that was His purpose? And wasn't the Bible a dream-riddled, dream-haunted book? And when people swore on the Bible were they not swearing then and there by the whole of their mysterious consciousness to try, for example, to tell the whole truth and nothing but the truth? As a child, then, I concluded early on that the powers of deep feeling, of inspiration and intuition, of dreams and visions were essentially feminine powers, though they were in all of us. Concluded that since Bible days, obviously, these powers had gradually faded and weakened and even disappeared in many people. As a child I thought like a child and conceived that it was a gift that could be kept and cultivated on this side of madness and that it was most likely more a matter of concentration than anything else, not altogether unlike the capacity to discern and to hear and understand one voice amid noise and among the sounds of many other voices. And now, after a full-scale formal education and a certain amount of study and thinking about the subject, I haven't yet found any good strong reason to change my mind.

It is hard to test the truth of this nowadays in late-twentieth-century America. I am sometimes inclined to consider that these not-quite-extrasensory powers have mostly vanished with my mother's generation of Southern American women. It is too soon to tell, though. After all, she only died a little while ago at the age of ninety-three.

But then, when we left her, she was about thirty years old and with her friends, a carload of them, returning from a meeting or a social gathering somewhere, I would guess. And true to those times and poor as they were, they would nevertheless have been wearing hats and gloves, dressed for the world like the ladies they imagined themselves to be. On impulse, at a road sign, they turned off the highway, just north of the long, low bridge over the St. Johns, drove a short distance through swampy, shadowy hammock country, and came into the quiet shade and green of the little community. Stopped in front of a nice old house with an intriguing sign out front and, laughing a little, nervously, went inside.

It would cost them a few dollars apiece to have their fortunes told. And they all swore each other to secrecy lest their practical husbands should learn of this frivolous adventure, husbands from whom the least they could expect was ridicule, and maybe some sterner reaction. For these were hard times for everyone, and working people were putting in a whole day's labor for a dollar or two.

The women went inside the house, discovering with some relief that it was nicely, neatly furnished according to the fashions and tastes of those times. An old Florida house with many windows and high ceilings and ceiling fans in those days before air conditioning. They sat in the pleasant living room sipping sweet iced tea and waiting their turns as, one at a time, they went down a hallway and into a little room, more like an office than anything else, where a clean and decently dressed woman, middle-aged with a familiar country accent, wasted a few moments of small-talk, then briskly told their fortunes . . .

They would not, not in those days, have gone to a male fortune-teller, though surely there were some. Nor would they much have enjoyed the intimate experience with someone alien (Gypsy, Indian, European, for instance) to themselves. But this was clearly a good country woman, a rawboned cracker woman, sunburnt and hardhanded. If it was a contrived image and not a real one, then it was a very good one.

My mother's turn came and she followed the woman into the back room. Which was unusual only in that it was, conventionally for this purpose, dimly lit and shadowy. Sat down politely and chatted for a bit. The psychic, who was vaguely phrenological, touched my mother's dark hair and her head with light fingers. Then she told my mother a thing or two. Since my mother placed no value on and granted no credulity to the idea that a human being could see the future and report on it, the fortune-telling part went lightly and directly in one ear and out the other. All that Mother could ever remember to tell later (with a laugh) was that she was seriously warned to stay away from deep water. In her old age my mother's greatest weakness and pleasure was ocean cruises. I don't know how many cruises she took before she finally died in bed. Plenty. And nothing untoward ever happened. Unless you want to count the Cuban Revolution which brought Fidel Castro to power and found Mother and one of her young grandsons on a Caribbean cruise and ashore in Havana to bear witness to it. She thought Castro and his cronies needed a shave and a shampoo.

Not the future, then, but past and present. The fortune-teller told my mother (mind you, there were no names exchanged and none of these women had ever been there before—and the fact is that none of the other women, who were from Orlando where we had just recently moved from Kissimmee, knew more than superficial details about my mother's family or history) that the number 5 was much on my mother's mind. That she seemed to be constantly concerned and worried about five people who were close blood kin. Mother offered no encouragement of any kind, but that observation was painfully true. My mother had five brothers about whom she was justly worried for most of her life. The fortune-teller then continued by saying that there were *four* people about whom she was quite differently concerned, that they were a source of great joy and pleasure to her and seemed in image to be children, her children. Did she have four children? the fortune-teller asked.

"No," Mother said. "I have three children."

This answer puzzled the fortune-teller into a moment of frowning silence.

"Oh, well," the fortune-teller said finally, "I see what it is. You have three children alive and well. The fourth is in the spirit world. He is a beautiful boy and he is well and happy, also."

My mother said nothing. Finished the brief session and went off with the others, headed for home. Told none of the others or, for a time, anyone else about her dead son. Indeed, nobody except my father and an old family doctor, dead and gone himself, knew that there had been another boy in our family, one who died at birth or, anyway, shortly after.

Later, and I can't remember when, she told me that, besides my two sisters, I had an older brother who died coming into the world. At the time, however old I may have been (certainly I was still a child), I felt sad, but oddly relieved. I am not in any way psychic. Never have been. But I had already by then felt a presence, a presence which may have been more a matter of wishing than anything else. In our large, sprawling family— I had a total of fifteen uncles and aunts on both sides, and they had children, so large and small cousins were everywhere underfoot—I had always felt the need for a brother. Preferably an older brother who could be some protection, aid and comfort, a good companion and a very present help in trouble. And also, as eldest son, he would be serious and dedicated, thus setting me free for a life of adventure and careless indifference. For a career of danger and daring.

I think—thinking like a child—that I had wished so hard for him to be there that I had managed to make an uneasy presence out of him. And so, when I learned that he was real and was dead, I felt (still thinking and feeling childishly) that all my wishing had been valid but irrelevant; that it was now the right thing, my bounden duty, to let him be, to let him rest in peace without any wishes or hopes or demands from me. If there really was a spirit world and he was in it, then that was enough to know. Alive and he might have been freed to follow the life of danger I childishly longed for—not knowing how many dangers would come calling on me, like it or not, without any planning or premeditation on my part. I think I missed him, but now I did not need him anymore, at least not in the same way. He was and is, himself, as mysterious to me as Jacob's angel. You remember what I mean, the moment in Genesis (32:24): *And Jacob was left alone; and there wrestled a man with him until the breaking of the day....*

II.

We are, I know not how, double in ourselves, so that what we believe we disbelieve, and cannot rid ourselves of what we condemn.

MONTAIGNE, "OF GLORY"

In a sense, then, the simple fact of the dead brother became for me the foundation of many an imaginary companion. Became so for characters in short stories, novels, plays, even a couple or three films. For the voices in my poems. And, I ought to add, above and beyond the diversity of characters and voices, there was one character (in two forms, with two sides, to be sure, Huck Finn and Tom Sawyer at the same time) whom I was liberated, set free to imagine. Who soon became a kind of brother, a bad brother or, anyway, a most mischievous one, a trickster, a scurvy satirical rogue.

For his first name I took a common name in the family, owned by an uncle and several cousins—John, often called Jack. For his last name I appropriated the name that my Uncle Chester, the dancer, used in show business—Towne. John Towne. Years and years later, working on *Entered from the Sun,* I found the same name in a list of actors for one or another of the traveling companies of players at just that period, the mid 1590s, I was writing about. Just a name on a list of forgotten players, one about whom nothing seems to be known. And there was another Towne on that same list, someone I took to be a brother on the basis of no more evidence than the name. It was apt, though; for as his story has developed, Jack Towne, too, has a brother, quiet possibly a twin brother, who happens to be his opposite in many ways.

And so my dead brother, real and beautiful in the spirit world—and I see no reason to doubt that—has gradually been replaced by an outrageously adventurous and daring fictional character who has, in turn, been given a more reputable and less interesting brother, one not unlike myself, two sides of the same self. So far, of the two of them, only John Towne has come forward in cold print to speak and to act out. He, all by himself, is likewise divided in two. Do you see, here, how our lives are fragmented and parceled out like the bread and wine of some continuous communion? One form Towne takes is as a character in more or less realistic stories involving more or less credible characters around him in more or less chronological sequences of events.

Here is that Towne, for example, narrating the opening of a short story he is in called "Genius Baby":

> It is getting late now and finally the hospital is more or less quiet. I am now in the so-called lounge. Where people waiting to see patients gather during visiting hours to watch TV (soap operas and talk shows and game shows) or leaf through copies of ancient magazines. Together with some fairly recent issues of the *AMA Journal* and the *New England Journal of Medicine*. The latter two will sure enough scare the living pee out of you, quicker than the sight of a sadistic nurse coming straight towards your bed with a catheter in her hands. Not only scare you because of all the horrible diseases and conditions that you never even heard of until now, and from now on will be certain, as all the symptoms will clearly indicate, you have been suffering from all along. But also on account of the professional attitude openly displayed therein. The truth is that doctors are a whole lot worse than we ever imagined they could be or would be. The bad news that I have to report is that in spite of all the honor and respect and rewards, no matter, they are just like the rest of us—ignorant, insensitive, greedy, and ruthlessly dedicated to the advancement and enhancement of old number one.
>
> But never mind. I'm not bitter. Just wary.

(Remember that? Remember that story at the very beginning of this collection?)

He has the happy power not to grow any older than he wants to be; and so far he has not aged beyond forty even though I am well past sixty-five. In that sense, at least, he shares the timeless pleasures of the spirit world.

In his other shape and form he is somewhat more mythological, more voice, more air and fire, though the air is polluted and the fire has more smoke than flame. Here he is in the middle of a Baccalaureate address:

Where are we? Well, you probably know where you are, anyway. Sitting out there in your rented cap and gown getting ready to graduate. Real life is waiting. Like a cop behind a tree or a billboard. About fifteen minutes, on average, after you turn in your cap and gown, it's going to start to dawn on you. How you have spent a whole lot of money, yours and other people's, and, minimum, four years of precious time, to acquire a rolled up piece of paper that won't buy you a beer or a cup of coffee. F-worded again! And bear in mind that this isn't the last time you will hear from the folks here. This institution has already targeted you as a source of funds for the future. Your name is already in the computer.

How are you ever going to earn enough money to be able to afford to give them some of it? If you are rich already, then just don't worry about it. Statistics prove conclusively that, barring the Nuclear War, which will change everybody's luck and numbers significantly and looks like a more attractive prospect every day, you will most likely stay rich or end up even richer. Numbers also prove that most of you will stay pretty much the same as you are. You will never quite realize it because you will be earning more dollars. But those bucks will always be worth less and will buy less. In the end you will be very lucky if you make as much as your old man whether he went to some college or not. Unlike him, you stand a good chance of never being able to own your own house. You will, however, make out a little better, in the long run, than if you had *not* attended college. Let that truth cheer you up every spring at Tax Season.

In either form Towne is more visitor to than resident of our times and this planet. His habit is to say what he pleases—not necessarily what he thinks; for I believe that he often speaks without thinking at all. Speaks as he pleases and lets chips fall every which way without regard to the canons of good taste or the fate of the First Amendment. Given half a chance, he is quick to assert that all the Amendments were, after all, afterthoughts. "I mean," he opines, "nobody even thought of all that stuff until it was too late. We are basing our whole political and social system on footnotes and marginalia."

In both of his disguises Towne has been noticed. Here is how he was described in the *New York Times Book Review*—"a low-life crank." The *Village Voice* identified him as "an exceptionally sleazy picaro"; the *Roanoke Times* more gently described him as "an academic Gypsy and con man." And the *Chicago Tribune* allowed as how he is "a lecherous, misanthropic, failed academic." He was perhaps best described by my friend Fred Chappell in the *Greensboro News* as "a loathsome, racist, sexist, crude and gruesome creep." I certainly can't quarrel with that. Towne can, but claims to be above it all. "Look here," he says. "I can't worry about the half-baked, half-ass opinions of every minor regional writer in America. And as for the 'creep' part, well, it takes one to know one. Know what I mean?"

With a companion like that who needs cousins and kinfolk? Nevertheless, needed or not, I had plenty of them. Most of them proved to be very good at whatever they did. Some of them were admirable by most standards. None of them was legitimately famous. If they had been, surely you would have heard of them, wouldn't you?

My sisters, both women I admire and envy in many ways, both (years apart) went up North to be educated at Vassar. Which experience they survived. And they went on to do well in the world. Towne and I both went to Princeton, quit and ran away three different times, but finally made it through, graduating after six years. Proudly earned my own Ph.D. thirty-three years later. To tell the truth, I think Towne liked Princeton a lot better than I did. It's a guess. I never asked him. He would probably attend a reunion if I gave him half a chance.

In the kind of role reversal which is easy to accomplish in dreams and imagining, Towne has sometimes played a kind of Jacob to my Esau, tricking me out of my rightful inheritance and blessing. In another sense Towne has been a good and faithful companion, even if he is, like the human heart, desperately wicked and faithless to everyone and to everything except for himself and his private, primitive hungers.

Well, sometimes I have to admit, it is refreshing to spend some time with somebody who has all the wrong values and no shame for any of it.

At times we have clung together like Hansel and Gretel or the babes in the woods.

So much has changed all around me and us, even as much remains irreparably the same.

My mother, that young woman who once upon a time, her time, went to see a fortune-teller, lived on for many years, a great-grandmother, before she died, old and blind and frail.

Now she joins many others of her generation and our family in the silence of the spirit world. There also, I assume (still thinking like a child), she is reunited with her own beautiful firstborn son, my brother, that perfect stranger whose absence and presence have haunted me all the days of my life. I have wrestled with him just as Jacob wrestled with his angel all night long. "And he said, Let me go, for the day breaketh. And Jacob said, I will not let go except thou bless me."

And I have come first to imagine, then to believe that he and I will finally come together as, in the thirty-third chapter of Genesis, Jacob and Esau do: "And Esau ran to meet him and fell on his neck and kissed him and they wept."

The author of more than twenty-five books and the editor of seventeen others, including poetry, fiction, biography, criticism, essays, and dramas, GEORGE GARRETT is one of the prime movers in contemporary American letters. Best known for his Elizabethan trilogy of historical novels, Garrett has published stories in many venues over the years, including *Best American Short Stories*. He has been the recipient of a PEN/Malamud Award; Guggenheim, Ford, and National Endowment for the Arts fellowships; and an Award in Literature from the American Academy of Arts and Letters. He is Henry Hoyns Professor of Creative Writing at the University of Virginia. He has been married to his wife Susan for forty-six years. The Garretts, who make their home in Charlottesville, have three children and two grandchildren.

Cathryn Hankla

RICHARD BAUSCH is Heritage Professor of Writing at George Mason University in Virginia. The recipient of a Guggenheim Fellowship, an NEA grant, an Award in Literature from the American Academy of Arts and Letters, and a two-time winner of the National Magazine Award for fiction, he is the author of several story collections including *Spirits and Other Stories*, *The Fireman's Wife*, and *Rare and Endangered Species*. His novels include *Mr. Field's Daughter*, *Violence*, *Rebel Powers*, *Good Evening Mr. and Mrs. America, and All the Ships at Sea*, and his most recent, *In the Night Season*.

A native Texan, ALLEN WIER is writer-in-residence and professor of English at the University of Tennessee at Knoxville. The recipient of a Guggenheim Fellowship, an NEA grant, and a Dobie-Paisano Fellowship, he received in 1997 the Fellowship of Southern Writers' Robert Penn Warren Award in fiction. He is the author of three novels, *Blanco*, *Departing as Air*, and *A Place for Outlaws*, and a story collection, *Things About to Disappear*. He has just completed a new novel set in the nineteenth-century American West.